Runt Rejected

KIMBERLY SMITH

NEWMAN SPRINGS PUBLISHING
830 Park Ave, Suite 155
Meadville, PA 16335

First originally published by Newman Springs Publishing 2025

ISBN 978-1-63881-604-1 (Paperback)
ISBN 978-1-63881-605-8 (Digital)

Printed in the United States of America

To M.Q.K.,

My love letters start here. Not every day will be easy. But the hard days are easier to face because of you.

Love, K.S.

Prologue

"Stop! Please!" I scream at the top of my lungs. Breathing becomes so much harder. My ribs sored in pain. Tears prick my eyes. It will only be a matter of time before I give in completely. My face heats horribly, and my body temperature rises. I am too tired to fight anymore, but by instinct, my hands fly up to protect myself. I swear to myself that I'll get my revenge.

"That's enough. Leave your sister alone," our mother calls over to Leon, my oldest brother. He laughs and ceases his tickling torment on me.

"If you were bigger, you'd be able to fight back," he teases.

I jump to my feet and shove him with all my might. He barely moves. "I will be stronger when I turn eight!"

"When you turn eight, you are still going to be the tiniest of them all." He smiles smugly and pats my head, as if to measure my height.

"Stop teasing her," Maddock, my middle brother, says, pulling me under his arm protectively and shoving Leon away.

Leon crosses his arms and laughs. "I'm older than you, Maddock. I could take you out easily. You could never protect her."

"Age doesn't matter if the gap is so small," our father says, coming out of the house to watch the stare down between my brothers. "If Maddock has better skills in fighting, then who do you think will win?"

They both get into a fighting stance, and my father gestures for me to get out of the way by standing beside him. I rush over to his side and slip my hand in his large one. My brothers charge at each other. My father kneels beside me, his focus still on the movements of my brothers.

"See that, Kate?" my father asks. I don't answer. "Even younger and at a different skill level, Maddock still spars with everything he has. If you have the will to fight longer and harder than anyone else, then you will be the strongest." I nod.

"But I'm small. And everyone likes fighting with me because they're bigger than me."

"You'll be bigger one day too. But if you lose the fight in here"—he points to my heart—"then you will lose the fight out there too."

"All right, enough of all that fighting. The evening meal is in an hour. Maddock, since you're the messiest, you bathe first," My mother calls out to us. Maddock hangs his head, obviously annoyed that they didn't finish the spar.

"We'll finish this later." He points to Leon while walking into the house.

My father looks at me. "You too, princess. Go get your clothes ready." He kisses my forehead, and my mother walks me into the house.

"Daddy wants me to be tougher," I murmur while my mother rustles through drawers of my clothing.

"Your father wants you to be strong. He wants you to have the kind of strength that doesn't come from how tall or big you are. He wants your heart to be strong. Strong enough to not let the words of others hurt you."

"What words?"

"Throughout your life, there will always be people who don't want you to succeed. They will say mean things, but it is up to you to listen to them or prove them wrong."

"Why would people say mean things to me?" She stops rustling for a moment and looks over at me.

"Kate, you already know you are smaller than most children your age. Because you are shorter, people will quickly assume that you are weaker. You will have to fight for their respect. You can never use your size as a crutch." She reaches over and caresses my cheek. "Your heart will be the strongest of them all." She sounds proud, almost as if she can see an inevitable future.

The Beginning

How do you know you're alive? Is it your breath? The air filling your lungs through your nose, then being forced out? Rejected carbon dioxide. Or is it the confirmation of others that lets you know you have a life? I don't know anymore. I don't know if I've ever known. The majority of my life has rallied around a single event and then vanished to nothing but the confirmation that I am no longer welcomed in the place I once called home.

Born into a proud family of warriors, my life should have been simple, with the knowledge that I, too, would become a warrior. As fate would have it, though, that is not the direction that my life would go in. My parents had fought, till their claws had dulled to almost nothing, for our pack. They were known far beyond our own pack for their exceptional skills in combat. The beloved masters of war who bore three children. Two sons and a daughter. Their sons followed in their footsteps and trained hard to live up to their name. I, their daughter, had been adored by all pack members at my birth. My parents never needed for a sitter while they defended the pack's territory.

I had always wanted to fight alongside my family but was always reminded of my small physique. At the age of fourteen, I began to train on my own in secret. I believed that I trained harder than any other pack member. I trained till my body collapsed, and my legs would crumble beneath me.

Unlike the other pack members, I have not turned into my wolf yet. Because of this, I could not consume the strength of my wolf the way most did at that age. They say your wolf comes to you in your tenth year of life and shares with you their power. Their strength flows through you like liquid fire and is so painful the first time that you may lash out at those who are unlucky enough to be around you.

1

The first transformation is almost always during the height of strong emotions, whether that be happy, sad, or angry.

Now grown, I have surpassed the expected time of my transformation, and pack members began to wonder about the runt of the pack. Why had the daughter of such strong pack members not been given a wolf? It is eccentric. Soon, parents wanted their children sparring with Little Kate, simply to show how much *better* their child were compared to the masters of war. But my parents never gave it a second thought. I was their miracle baby. The doctors that delivered me did not believe I'd survive the night because I was so small. My parents, though, believed I had a gift to share.

There came a day when my stubbornness got the better of me. I had become so frustrated with all that I lacked and begged my parents to take me on patrol with them. I was so tired of waiting for this so-called gift to appear in my life. After weeks of nagging, they finally succumbed. The only condition was that I stay close to them at all times, and if they told me to run, I was to do so.

During that time, they told me of all the different enemies that could attack from different areas of our territory. They told me about humans that should never get too close to our territory and mages that had once been so strong but were long extinct. However, the ones they were most concerned about were rogues. It is one thing to be attacked by other packs or even humans who know just a bit too much. Rogues are a whole other story.

Rogues were once members of a pack that were exiled for being a danger to or endangering their pack. The real problem with rogues was that they knew almost everything about the territory they'd been exiled from. Some were trained warriors. Bad eggs that knew all the weak points of their old pack.

My parents said that on occasion, rogues were to attack. They could handle a loner wolf. Rarely, though, some rogues would pair up. That's what the pack elders feared the most because while one could be attacking from one side, it could all be a ruse to distract from the one sneaking in through the other side. A trained warrior can take ten innocent lives in a matter of minutes and then be long gone before help comes.

The following days, my parents allowed me to tag along during their patrol routines. One night, I began to stray from the usual path. I made sure I could still see my parents, but I ventured into the vast darkness of the forest. In the distance, I could hear what sounded like the moans of a weeping wolf. I looked back to see how far I was from my parents. They were still close enough to see and hear.

The whimpering leads me to a wounded pack member.

Fresh gashes ran down her ribs and across her snout. If I had a wolf, I would be able to ask the injured pack member what happened. Even without one, though, the smell of her blood stung my nose. A bitter vinegar smell that had turned my stomach. I take slow breaths and look into her eyes, trying to figure out what happened. When we are injured badly enough, it takes too much energy to transform into our original state. Afraid to injure her any more than she already is, I stand. My parents will know what to do. The thought is interrupted when I hear a loud and deep growl. My head whips around wickedly, my eyes straining to see in the darkness that surrounds. As my eyes adjust to the darkness, I see them—two yellow glowing eyes of a snarling wolf.

Rogue, I think to myself. The brand burned into his left peck that marked the completion of warrior training had dulled but is still very much visible. My heart nearly stops. I have trained so hard for the day that I might come across a rogue. Now one stands—large with carrot-colored fur—before me, and I can't move a muscle. Fear strikes deep into the depths of my soul through his moonlit eyes. He will kill me without ever feeling remorse.

I hear my mother call out for me, but I am too stunned to answer. A knot of bile clogs my throat, and my breathing shallows even further. The rogue takes a step toward me, and I am frozen where I stand. I hear footsteps behind me, and before I can muster up the courage to warn my mother, she is in full sprint at me. She jumps well over my head, in front of me, facing off with the rogue.

My father, not far behind, is about to come around behind my mother when another rogue pounces on her. With her neck in his jaw, she fights hard to get loose from his grip. I finally let out a scream as his jaws crush her throat, killing her instantly. The snapping sound of her bones makes me dizzy. Her body is limp as the rogue throws her aside. She never saw it coming. I hadn't even known there was another wolf there. If only I hadn't panicked, I may have been able to help.

My father rages and fights hard for his fallen wife, his daughter, and the wounded pack member. But now it's only him against them. I will my wolf to come out. I pray to the lunar goddess for my wolf to come out at that moment. For once I am heard, and my wolf is released fiercely. My entire body feels on fire. It feels as if I've lost complete control. I charge at the ground a polar bear hunting fish under the ice, trying desperately to shake the pain coursing through my body. With my father now slightly distracted by me, the rogues attack. My father is knocked from his feet but still very much conscious.

The two rogues snap their teeth and bite at his flesh. One locks their jaw on his ankle, slicing the skin clean off the bone. My father shrieks in pain. I hear the grinding of his bones against their sharp teeth. The snap of their canines as they attempt to bite at his other legs. But he won't go down so easily. He uses his other paws to get out of their grasp. Limping from his injured back leg, he moves for me, knowing that he will not win this fight alone, knowing that I am not trained to attack like I should. He never makes it, though. One of the rogues pounces, biting the back of his neck, the other attacks from the front. In the next moment, there is nothing but silence with a bite to the throat.

For the first time ever, I hear my wolf mourning the death of my parents. Both rogues turn their attention to me. Finally in control of my movement, I back away. Unfortunately for me, though, as I retreat, one comes from behind me and pounces, holding me down from the back of the neck.

Congratulations on turning. You must have been a late bloomer, *I can hear one of their thoughts.* So small, *he says.* You must be the runt of the pack. I must thank you. If it hadn't been for you, taking him down would have been a lot harder.

I can smell my parents' blood running onto my newborn fur from the rogue holding me. A whimper escapes my throat. "So I'll tell you what. As retribution, I'll allow you to live. But only you." *With that, he attacks the pack member in the throat, breaking her neck. Warrior howls can be heard in the distance, and the rogues quickly run off.*

When the others finally find us, I'm covered in my parents' blood, sobbing and holding my mother's head on my lap. When I'm taken back, they question me.

"I told you! There were three of them. I found the pack member, and then the three attacked us."

"Why would they leave you behind? It makes no sense."

"I don't know, but after I shifted—"

"You shifted?"

The two members look at one another. "Was this your first time shifting into your wolf?"

"I—yes, it was, but they didn't seem concerned after I—"

The same one interrupts again. "Look, Katherine, the only way to get out of this is by telling us the truth. When you shifted, did you act out from the pain? Did you—"

"Did I what?" I snap, annoyed.

"Did you kill them?" the other asks bluntly.

"No! I would never—"

"There is no way that two of the strongest pack members would be taken down so easily."

"Like I said before, I distracted them from fighting the way they would if I wasn't there."

"They kill your mother and your father. They kill a wounded pack member, but they leave you without a scratch?" the mean one asks slowly.

I look down at my blood-covered hands. I have begun to under-stand what they see. Because most shift, when they're young, they are never much of a threat. I, however, am older. I could do some real dam-age, having my first shift at such a late stage.

"I'll tell you what I think happened. Maybe there was a rogue. They got the girl alone, and your parents came to ward the rogue off. In the excitement of it all, you shifted and attacked your parents. Not wanting to harm you, they didn't fight back. Once you realized what you've done, you decided to tie up loose ends. No witnesses."

I choke on a sob. "I'm fourteen! I could never come up with some-thing so calculated so quickly!"

"Maybe it wasn't calculated. Maybe it was panic that made you kill the girl."

5

"I didn't kill anyone!" My hands grip the blanket I was given by Dr. Gene. I can't think straight. My head is pounding.

"You said the rogue left you alive. For what purpose would one do that?" the other one asks.

"He said it was a thank you for distracting my father." My voice is shaking.

"Really? Is that the best you can come up with?"

"It's the truth!"

The mean one rushes me in the chair I'm sitting on, one hand resting on the chair I'm sitting on. "I KNEW THEM! YOUR MOTHER HAD SAVED MY LIFE MORE THAN ONCE! STOP FUCKING WITH US AND ADMIT THAT YOU KILLED THEM!" His canines are drawn, and tears melt down my cheeks.

"That will be quite enough?" Alpha Stone says, calmly walking into the room. My heart is pounding viciously.

The mean one walks out furiously. The other, quietly. I look at my savior. The one who will make everyone understand the truth. Alpha Stone smiles gently at me.

"How are you feeling, Katherine?" he asks with the utmost care. I don't have the will to answer any more questions, though. I unsteadily shake my head. "I know this must be very hard for you, but I need you to be a strong little girl and tell me what happened."

I look up at him. I remember the things Emma had told me about him, that he was a gracious and gentle person.

"I heard the member whining in her wolf. When I found her, the Ome—" My eyes shift down swiftly. His hand is on my knee and moving slowly to my midthigh. I look up at him. His smile is still there but in a different light. A darker one.

"It would be much easier for everyone to understand what happened here tonight if I explain it to them. You can tell me every detail, in my office. Why don't we head there now?" He pulls me up by my elbow. A bitter taste fills my mouth.

"I can explain it to them myself," I say with a shaky voice. "We don't have to go anywhere."

He turns to me and bends so that our faces are only inches from each other. "I think you and I both know that it would go a long way for me *to…"—he curls a strand of my hair around his pale bony finger—"do you this favor."*

I immediately feel sick. I don't try to hold down the vomit that comes to my throat. Alpha backs away with a disgusted groan.

"Fucking disgusting." He howls. The two guards walk back in and looks us both over. Alpha looks at me and straightens. "Until we know what really happened, I think everyone would feel a lot better if you stayed in your current form." I am being punished, but I won't give in to him.

With the burn in my throat, I hang my head and grumble. "Yes, Alpha." Though the guards hadn't liked me and are very hostile, I feel safer with them around.

As the years progressed, I was known as a murder within the pack. My brothers had even attempted to get me to admit to the murder of our parents. They'd tell me that they might be able to forgive me, knowing it was an accident. It may have been the fact that I denied it, which frustrated them. Soon that frustration turned to anger and eventually, hatred. I never thought my own brothers could hate me and believe that I could do such a horrible thing. Without the transformation, my wolf stayed silent over the years. I had longed to turn and have her back. I longed to talk to anyone who believed me.

Since then, I had been assigned to kitchen duties. I was told that with my determination to protect our people, I'd be best helping to keep their hunger away. When I asked for bigger responsibilities, Alpha said, "Well, a clean ship makes for safe sailing."

My first thought was, *We're not fuckin' pirates. People can clean up after themselves.* I kept my mouth shut, though; everyone was already weary of me. No need to give them any more of a reason.

So here I am now. The maid. I prep, cook, and clean up after the pack in the gathering area, which is in the center of our larger community.

After my parents' death, kids began hazing me. It started small. Name-calling, silent treatment, and tripping me here or there. I couldn't really say it was their fault. The adults spoke about me being out of control and a danger to our community. An overall freak.

7

After a while, they stepped up their hazing to rock-throwing, the vandalization of my hut, and beatings.

I had stopped going to my brothers for support. Eventually, even they couldn't resist the "evidence" laid out before them. They had experienced the shift themselves. They both shifted at the height of their anger. They had both caused damage. They could only assume I had too. That my anger was directed at our parents. It was an honest assumption. An assumption they couldn't talk themselves out of. No matter how hard it gets, I promised not to hate them. At first, I could see the regret in their eyes, but after a few rounds, the regret disappeared.

Leon, my oldest brother, stood a foot taller than me at the age of twenty-four, and five years older than me. When we were younger, he'd laugh and smile at me. He looked at me like I was a blessing he had to protect. Nowadays, he looks at me with disgust and anger. I'd think of what to say to him to make him understand that I was innocent and that his hatred was misguided. It only ever aggravated him. He'd encourage others to do as they like with me because I was nothing to him. After I'd gotten my beating, he'd wait until the others left. A minute would pass, then another, and another, before he'd walk away. Sometimes to make myself feel better, I would pretend that the reason he stood there so long was because his conscience made him consider helping me. But then he'd walk away. I'd scold myself, as time passed, for thinking of such childish things.

Maddock, the younger of the two, never told others to beat on me. He never did anything. He'd watch with what almost looked like sympathy but never stepped in. He watched as if he was looking at a fly on the wall—something to be removed. His survey of me getting beaten was comparable to a dog in a hot car. Its owner knows how hot the car is, but the dog has no say. No matter how much it whines and begs to be let out, it falls on deaf ears.

Maddock is only three years older than me, and I always felt his emotional torture stemmed from the fact that I carried a few of my mother's physical features. I had her emerald eyes and, on rare occasions, her smile. When I was younger, people said I was the spitting image of her. I never saw it. My mother was an Amazon. She stood at five foot seven, with legs to spare. She had bronze skin compared to my fair skin. Her gorgeous golden-brown hair flowed down her back to her high waist, when she'd let it down. My hair didn't flow as easily and was closer to black than golden. But she was a fierce woman who always spoke her mind. I used to be too, but that was the least of my losses.

When my parents passed, the alpha didn't want any problems to occur, or so he said. He decided to move me into one of the pack's elder huts. Our homes had become more sophisticated in architecture, but we kept the huts to remind us of how far we've come. They came in handy for storage purposes. My brothers, on the other hand, were future warriors and had yet to finish their training. Alpha said it best that they stay in the packhouse. It was a beautiful large lodge-like two-story building. Its main purpose was to house the orphans of the fallen.

Though our architecture had matured, none of the buildings had kitchens within them. My kind views eating together as a sacred event to bring together our people. Either we eat together and put aside our differences of opinion, or we go hungry for the night. With my responsibilities, it was easy to get out of eating with the others. I always ate after clearing the gathering area of everyone else's trash. To avoid trouble, I began eating after everyone in the main kitchen left, and I was alone.

People who did not cook thought it beneath them to enter the kitchen. The few that did were older and thought it beneath them to stay longer than necessary after clearing the gathering area. So I was left on dish duty every day. I didn't mind, though. I like the solitude. In my hut, I was always afraid of who might be lurking just outside. After cleaning up, I'd sit there in silence. I'd close my eyes and imagine just how different my life could have been had I not ask to patrol with my parents. I had felt guilt for my parents' deaths, but not in the way everyone thought. It was my fault they were unprepared and distracted. I am the reason they are dead, but I will never admit shedding their blood. I was not at fault when it came to that.

Despite my passive attitude toward my pack that resented me, I did not lose my stubbornness or self-respect. No matter how much guilt I bore, I promised myself to never let them break me. Having everyone turn their backs on me hurt. Growing up with kids I once called friends, thrashing me against trees and boulders hurt more. So I returned the favor and turned my back on them. When I became a target, my former best friend, Emma, decided that I was not worth the target being placed on her back too. There came a day, after my brothers stopped speaking to me, that I went to our river, west of the community, to clear my head. Emma had befriended Ruby, a girl who'd hated me, for whatever reason, since birth. Ruby and a few of her skanky friends followed Emma to where I was.

I watch them approach and immediately know this is not going to be a good reunion. I sigh and stand from my spot on a boulder at the edge of the river.

"What?" I ask Emma as she stops a few feet from me.

"So I heard you were making the moves on my best friend's man."

I lift a brow and look past her, at Ruby's smirking face. Goddess, I'd love to break her nose. I shrug my shoulders. Denying it won't do anything. So I point out the obvious just to make this day worth it. "He's a fucking idiot, but he's got a body. And he doesn't seem to mind me at all."

Ruby's jaw drops. My guess is that she had not expected me to fight back. I gloat privately.

"Listen here, you fat whore. I won't allow your little home-wrecking ways to destroy my best friend's relationship." Emma snaps at me.

"My home-wrecking ways? Didn't Ruby jump his bones while he was still with his ex?"

Ruby turns crimson with anger. "I did not, you fat fuck. You're the one who doesn't know how to keep her legs closed."

I laugh dramatically. "Good comeback. Did you take that from someone else too?"

Before I know it, I have been punched hard in the jaw by Emma. Either she is a really weak puncher, or she wasn't trying to hurt me. I doubt the latter. I catch myself before falling and stand with my head held high. I tolerate a lot of crap, but this former "friend" pushed her luck a little too far this time.

I lick the blood that broke free from the corner of my mouth. "Emma Samantha Snow, you should know better than to tear the seal off an old promise. Wouldn't it be a shame if everyone found out who your first time was with?" Her eyes widen, and I could see the terror cross her face. "Or maybe it'd be more horrifying for them to know just how excited and free-willing you were to give it up to that person."

"I'll kill you," Emma mutters.

"Not if I destroy you first. That little secret could get the spotlight off me for a good little while. And what would your parents think?"

Emma storms away. Ruby spits in my face before leaving with her clique.

Emma, however, never approached me again no matter how hard Ruby urged her.

Coming back to the here and now, Ruby will get bored from time to time and come find me to torment. Just to speed up the process, I'd act fearful and ask her to leave me be because being strong just irks her and prolongs her uninvited and hostel visits. I'd rather just get the beating or trash talk over with and be done with her. No, I don't fight back. Defending myself physically will only get me into trouble. It will no longer be about me getting bullying; it'll be about how out of control I am—a danger to the pack.

The alpha and his wife, our Luna, made sure to keep me in my place. I am still one of their people, so they cannot turn their backs on me, but they sure as hell never gave me a shoulder to cry on. And their son, Gabriel, is around my brother's age. He is to become the next alpha. I pray to the Lunar Goddess that he is a true leader, unlike his pitiful father. I can't blame the people of this pack for how they treat me, if their alpha never corrects them of my innocence until proven guilty. Alpha Gabriel, son of Alpha Stone and Luna Marie. What am I to say to you about my innocence when we meet someday?

Heartbroken

Things today will be hectic. The thought travels from my head to my shaking hands. I woke early today. Preparations need to be made for the new alpha. Alpha Stone has finally decided that it is time to pass the torch. I wonder, though, will he pass the hate of me to his son? My stomach churns thinking about it.

"Watch what you're doing! You'll break the grains!" one of the other cooks yells at me. I had been so deep in thought that I haven't realized how hard I am cleaning the rice. I dip my head apologetically and drain the rice.

My head has been so far up in the clouds since I woke. Hope-filled thoughts swarm me, the idea that my life could get a hundred times better with a new alpha. Then thoughts that make my throat clog fills my head. Surely, the old alpha will have taught his son of my misfortune. At least it won't be pure hate. All alphas are raised away from their future packs. They are trained to be the best and ultimate warriors from near infancy. I still wonder how a mother can so easily give her child to another for them to raise.

After finishing my chores for the morning, I race home to clean up and dress for the ceremony. Ronny, a man-child who once proclaimed his love to me, bumps my shoulder hard as I pass. I catch myself before falling over.

"Ass," I mutter a little too loudly. And of course, instead of continuing on his way, he turns, balling up saliva in his mouth. I dip my head quickly so that the spit doesn't catch my face. He stays planted for a moment, waiting for me to respond. I don't, knowing the consequences.

Once he leaves, I take the long walk of shame back to my hut. I wash my hair twice in the shower. I towel-dry it and walk over to a small chest bedside my small bed. Opening it for the first time since my parent's death, I pull free a knee-length black dress. I carefully try it on. If for whatever reason it doesn't fit, I simply won't wear it. I repeat this to myself a dozen times as I slip it up my body, over my curves, and secure the zipper. It fits. Gorgeously so. My mother's dress fits me perfectly. Tears sting my eyes as I blink them away. I will not cry. Not today.

I search the chest for a pair of her shoes. Unfortunately, I have my father's feet. My size 8 feet won't squeeze into my mom's size-6 shoes. I roll my eyes and grab my worn and beat-up Converse that I found in one of the travelers' totes. I look at my reflection in the mirror, a pearl of a dress with Converse. My hair is now fully dried, going in every direction.

A memory peeks at the edge of my brain. *Women always tame their hair, Kate. It shows that we can take care of ourselves without trying to impress a male.* I pick up my comb and pull it through my wild waves. After a few minutes, my hair is tamed into soft waves. I step out of my home and head to the gathering area.

Everyone has already packed in, in hopes to get their first look at our new alpha. I am in the far back. I can't see over the taller members, and I don't try to. If I'm lucky, I will get through this without any drama from other members.

I make the mistake of letting my eyes wander. They stop on Ruby. She is dressed to perfection. Her dress reaches a few inches above the knee yet still long enough to make her look elegant. She's in tall heels that make her body look like an hourglass. Her hair is in perfect curls, which reaches her midback. I shake my head. No use in envying her. I won't regret wearing my mother's dress. They won't take that from me. A sudden joke comes to mind. What kind of wolf does everything she can to get the attention of an alpha and end up looking completely like a human? My mother made the dress I'm wearing today. Ruby's most definitely came from a traveler's tote. I shake my head again.

The ceremony begins, and I shake the weird jitters that I'm feeling in the pit of my stomach. As quickly as it starts, the ceremony is over, and I still haven't gotten a glance at the new alpha. I don't care much, though.

The less he knows about me, the better. The festivities of the celebration begin, and I greatly consider going back to my little hut. As I look down at my mother's dress, I don't want to stay in, cooped up after it fit me so well. I take a deep breath and decide to join in the "fun."

My hands begin to shake violently when people realize that I'm staying. I swallow, doing my very best to be brave. My mother wouldn't have backed down. Why should I?

Katherine, a majestic voice says. I spin fast, looking around. No one's there. *Calm yourself, Katherine. I am your wolf within.* I try my best not to look stunned. I have never spoken to my wolf. Should I speak out loud, or can she hear my thoughts?

I can hear your thoughts, she answers, making me choke on my own saliva.

So uh, been a while. What's been keeping you?

I can only awaken in the midst of courage after the passing of your parents. It wasn't until now that you had an act of courage. What has been keeping you?

Me! I— What about when I stood up to Emma?

That was anger not courage. There is a difference. You made a good decision today. You decided to stay with people who hate you, for yourself. You faced them. That bit of strength woke me from my slumber.

I nod to myself as I look around. *Well, I was just about to leave, to be honest. Not much fun by myself.*

Why not speak with your brothers? I take a glance at my brothers, who are happily far from me, chatting it up with some friends.

You've missed a lot.

Well, at least you're not leaving because they're making you. I smirk.

Yeah, there's that. By the way, can you hear all my thoughts or—

Just the ones you wish me to. I sigh a breath of relief. *Well now,* my wolf says bitterly.

Sorry, I'm just not used to having someone in my head. She stays silent as I turn to leave. A fresh fragrance fills my nose, and I hear her gasp loudly.

Geez, what's wrong?

Our mate is nearby. I smell him.

Oh, is that what that was? I ask nonchalantly.

Turn, go back! I roll my eyes and turn right into a hard broad chest. I stumble back a few feet and keep my eyes downcast.

"Sorry, I didn't—"

That's him! I allow my eyes to meet his and instantly recognize the alpha insignia on his shoulder. Instinctively, I bow my head. No, of all people, it had to be him.

"Alpha Gabriel. I apologize, I wasn't watching where I was going." I turn quickly to walk away, ignoring the protest of my wolf.

"Stop," he demands in a deep silky voice. I still in place. I can hear twigs and leaves break under his weight as he walks in front of me. "What is your name?"

My mouth goes dry, and my palms sweat. What would it matter if he didn't already suspect the worst? I inhale deeply. "Kate."

"Kate?" he says, waiting for me to give my last name. Out of nerves, my hands begin smoothing out the dress at my sides. There it is. Out of all the people here today, it was Alpha who I never want to speak to.

Still, it is a name that my parents gifted me with. And I won't be ashamed to say it out loud. "Katherine Barsotti," I finally say.

He lets out a deeply disappointed exhale. A scowl forms on his face. How do you think I feel? He ushers me further away from the gathering and away from prying eyes. He speaks firmly, "You will not mention this to anyone. We are not mates. And you will not show your face to me again, am I understood?"

My eyes wander away. I don't know why this hurts so much. I hadn't expected him to hold me and kiss me. I hadn't expected anything from him at all. So why does it hurt so damn much? Why do I feel like I'm losing him when he was never mine to begin with?

Before I could answer, he grabs my face hard and turns it back to him. His claws edge out, digging into my skin. "Am I understood? I won't have some weak runt by my side." My breath hitches and my eyes narrow. "I know what you did. It sickens me to know that my father allowed such a loose cannon to stay and endanger this pack." His darkened eyes pierce my soul like a sharp blade.

My breathing becomes fierce, and my pulse quickens. I push away from him, hard. He stumbles back a bit in shock but recovers quickly. "What exactly is it that you know? Stories you've heard. Whispers from people who weren't there." I square my shoulders. "You don't know a damn thing. Furthermore, you don't know a damn thing about me, *Alpha*. You only just got that title. A real alpha knows everything about his pack and everything about the people in it." I turn my back on him. "Don't worry, I won't tell a soul. I won't look at your face. I will forget ever meeting you." My voice is even and calm. I walk slowly back to my hut, leaving silence between us.

I look up at the sky as I walk. I think of our deity and how our stories tell of a beautiful goddess. A woman of grace in both beauty and strength. Yet her touch is one of love and nurture.

"Why? Why me? I do everything right! I do as I'm told! I keep my head down, and I never fight back, even when that's all I want to do. So why punish me! Was I really so terrible in my past life?" The wind drowns out the noise of my words. There is no one around to hear them, but I still look over my shoulder to be sure. Pitter-patters of raindrops hit the ground. How cliché. Of course, it would rain at a time like this.

By the time I make it back home, my anger has mellowed. I carefully take my dress off and hang it to dry. Crawling into bed, I hug my knees. The piece of wood that makes my door keeps the little chill out. Curling up into a ball is my only real warmth.

"Good riddance," I whisper out loud.

You do not have to be strong in front of me, I feel what you do, my wolf whispers back to me. I tuck my head under my blanket and let out a quiet sob. Just tonight, I'll give in to the sorrow.

A sudden jolt of pain runs through my entire body. It passes slowly, and when it's over, I hear a ringing in my ears. Perspiration dampens my forehead as I roll out from under the blanket.

What the hell was that?

Our mate has officially rejected us. It is done.

What does that mean?

He has rejected us out loud.

I cover myself again. Rejection. My heart is still beating a mile a minute, but I manage to get it under control. I lay my head on my pillow. It is done? Well, fuck him then. I hoped for the best but got the worst.

Shallow Hellos

I wake up slowly the next morning. I snooze my alarm clock twice before finally getting dressed. I run my fingers through my hair and tie it into a messy bun. Thin strands of hair come loose and rest on my neck. I pull up my jeans and put on the first shirt I grab. Ugh, I feel like shit.

Our body is drained of energy, my wolf comments.

Ya don't say.

Our mate… he will reconsider.

I—we don't need him. And he doesn't want us.

We do need him. We need his love and affection.

I walk to the gathering area, not wanting to push this conversation. I stop dead in my tracks when I see Ruby huddled against Alpha's side, his arm circling her waist. There is a tug in my chest that I choose to ignore. I continue walking with my head down till I'm in the kitchen.

Is that what we need? Circe doesn't respond.

After I finish my chores and everyone else has gone, I unwrap my plate to eat. The food makes my stomach waver a bit. I sigh, wrap it back up, and place it in the storage fridge. I collect my old jacket and make my way out. I stop when I notice that Alpha is speaking with the cooks. When they hear the door swing shut behind me, their attention shifts to me.

"She's the reason we were late on preparations, Alpha. It's her job to prep the flour and eggs in the morning. But she was late today." I look away, annoyed. I was ten minutes late! And I got my prep done on time. "But what do you expect from her? I heard she was out late last night fooling around with different males."

Gabriel's eyes fly to me. "Is that right? You were late because you can't keep your private life private? We shouldn't all have to wait to eat because of your irresponsibility of being on time."

Well, that's why there should be a delegator. Goddess forbid anyone can't cook because they're sick. I suck in a deep breath.

"Forgive me, Alpha, I won't be late again."

Anger crosses his face as I bow my head and continue on my way.

See, there is no affection to have in his eyes. Again, Circe doesn't respond. I don't even know why he's angry. I apologize and politely excuse myself. No one would think anything of it. What was I supposed to do, grovel? His little title is going to his head.

I'm about to pass by Gabriel when Ruby shoves past me, knocking me back a few steps. Ugh, she's asking for it.

"Oops! So sorry, Kate. I didn't see you." A fragrance passes by my nose. The smell is so vile I want to gag from it. Is it just me, or does Ruby smell worse than usual?

I smell him on her, my wolf says quietly. I look from Gabriel to Ruby and then back again. Gross. Of all horrible people to take, he had to choose her.

I exhale, annoyed with myself. It shouldn't bother me, but it does. I give a polite smile and respond with, "No harm done."

"Anyways." She smiles too big. "Alpha Gabriel and I are going to the gathering hall to watch a movie. Do you wanna join?" I'd rather eat dirt, quite literally. Ruby clings to Gabriel's arm as she gives her false invitation.

"Ya know I would," I start while walking backward. "But I have prior engagements." I turn and walk toward the river. Geez, if they get serious, Ruby will become Luna. Wouldn't that be something? Something horrible.

I find my spot on a large boulder at the rim of the river. "I should leave," I say out loud.

It will hurt worse than the rejection, to be so far from him, my wolf responds.

"Better than staying here, watching him make that witch Luna. Do you really wanna watch him choose another, have a bunch of babies, and live happily ever after without us? Isn't that a worse torture?"

She whines quietly. *No. I don't think I could bear it. Are you prepared to leave, though? To live on your own? There are still rogues out there.*

"No, I'm not ready. Not yet, but I will be. I'll gather things little by little, then we'll just leave."

I hear a sigh from her before the sound of rushing water fills the void. I've never even seen my wolf, and she has suddenly become my best friend, my rock, the most important person in my life. I'm deep in thought about how I would survive on my own when I hear footsteps approaching from behind. Ugh, what now?

"See, didn't I tell you this was better than sitting inside and watching a movie?"

Really? She just had to come and gloat. I ignore them the best I could until Ruby calls me out.

"Kate? Is that you? I thought you had a date or something. It's okay. I'm sure there is someone out there for you."

Oh, fuck off. Your insults are so childish, it's sad.

"I never said I was going on a date, Ruby," I say, rolling my eyes as she pulls herself and Gabriel into view.

"Oh, honey. Rolling your eyes isn't ladylike." Neither is opening your legs for every guy around, but that hasn't stopped you. I give her a polite smile. She wiggles Gabriel's hand. "Didn't I tell you it was great out here?"

He nods tensely. "But I'd like a bit more privacy."

Yes, why don't you two broadcast your affection elsewhere because there is no way you'll have privacy in this pack.

"I guess you're right, love."

Really, a pet name? You've known each other for all five minutes. Ugh, whatever. I assume them to be leaving till Ronny and Leon walk up. My chest clenches a bit at the sight of them. Stupid happy memories.

"Alpha." They both bow in unison.

Gabriel smiles widely at Leon. I guess it's a given; Leon and Gabriel were great friends before it was his time to leave for alpha training. I had never personally spent time with Alpha when I was younger. The Luna only allowed him to befriend Leon because he was already ahead in his training and because of who our parents were.

"Cut that out. What do you need?"

Leon grins. "Nothing really, but we did want to speak to you about—"

"Ugh." I sigh, standing. "Pardon me, Alpha, but isn't this place a bit too open to be discussing business at? Don't get me wrong, this place is usually void of noise, but it has become increasingly loud lately."

Leon slaps me hard. "How dare you insult our alpha? He can do whatever he damn well pleases." His voice booms in my ears. The side of my face is hot with pain. I could leave right now and never regret it. I'll leave and never look back. I'd leave no one behind. In fact, they may celebrate my departure. The only ones that would really notice would be the cooking staff when I don't show up for my shift.

"It's fine, Leon. I will meet you in my office. I have to check on things there now anyways."

Unfortunately for me, Gabriel is the only one who leaves. Ruby, Leon, and Ronny still surround me. I can do it. I can survive for a little while.

"Well, lookie here, Little Kate all alone," Ronny says distastefully. I try walking around them, but Ruby cuts me off.

"You really shouldn't be speaking to my future husband that way."

I choke on a laugh. "Your future husband? Oh, please get real, Ruby. He's just going to play between your thighs for a little while before he moves on to something tighter." Filter gone.

There you go, my wolf praises.

Ruby grabs me by the shoulders and shoves me hard. I miss my footing and slip. I fall into the water, and my head hits something hard. I try to intake air as the current pulls me. Water fills me completely, burning my lungs. I'm pulled a ways away before I somehow manage to grab on to what feels like a branch and pull myself up just enough so that my head is out of the water. I choke on the water in my lungs, and then—everything just goes dark.

Leon

Somewhere deep in the pit of my stomach, panic begins to seep. I had already punished her in front of the alpha. What need was there for Ruby to continue further? Kate hadn't resurfaced immediately after Ruby pushed her into the water. It's not like she was hurt, and she's an excellent swimmer—I taught her myself. Still, I couldn't help feeling uneasy when we left.

*****

Everyone is at the gathering area, awaiting our last meal of the day. It has already been thirty minutes late, and Alpha Gabriel is becoming impatient. He exhales loudly and stands.

"I'm going to see what's keeping them," he says before disappearing into the kitchen. I can't control my knees as they bounce rapidly under the table.

"What's up with you?" Maddock says with furrowed brows.

I will not let you forget, my wolf whispers.

I shake the nerves as Gabriel rejoins us. "So uh, what's keeping them?"

"Apparently your sister didn't come in tonight, so they are backed up."

I exhale, running my fingers through my hair. "I'm going to go look for her."

"I'm sure she's fine," Maddock says.

"Yeah, it's only water." Ruby chimes.

Both Gabriel and Maddock look at her questioningly. "What's only water?" Maddock asks.

"I told her she shouldn't speak to an alpha that way, and well, she slipped and fell into the river."

Both Maddock and Gabriel are on their feet. Maddock's eyes dart to mine. An unspoken threat passes between us.

"Let's go!" Gabriel snaps.

"Oh, love, she'll be fine, it's just a little water," Ruby says innocently.

He bends close to her face. "Like it or not, she is still a member of this pack. If you don't like it, then you are free to leave."

Her mouth hangs open as we head for the river. It takes us ten minutes to reach it from the gathering area. I squint, forcing my eyes to see without the moon's bright glow.

"Kate!" I hear Maddock shout.

He shouts her name again and again. Before I can follow in his lead, Gabriel does the same. I run ahead of them; if she didn't pull up right away, she was probably carried off. I run faster, searching as much as I can as I go. I trip over a large root sticking out of the ground. I follow where it ends in the water and see a stain of blood resting on a boulder that is only just peeking out from the river. The root seems to have grown around it.

"Kate," I whisper in horror. Where the hell is she? In full-on panic, I shift and launch myself into the direction that the scent of her blood leads. The others must have heard me because they are by me in seconds. I'm too afraid to tell them what I suspect. It has already been hours. If anyone found her there, she wouldn't be taken to the Med Center.

The scent leads to her small hut. I'm grateful to the goddess for that. I burst through the front door. It shatters to pieces on the floor. She's not in sight. The bed is neatly made, and the room is dark. Someone behind me switches on a lamp. A warm glow fills the room, but she is still missing from it. I go to the little sink next to the tub and see blood at the rim of it and splattered inside it. She was here. I turn to see Maddock pulling open drawers and shoving them closed, harsher than needed.

"She's gone." He snaps. "There's no clothes or anything personal left. She took it all and left." He looks at me with new anger. I feel it for myself as well. She's out there alone.

"Let's go then," Alpha says. We both look at him. "She couldn't have gotten far, and by the looks of it, she's injured. She is still a part of this pack." He walks out, shifts, then bolts in a direction leading to our closest territory lines. The scent of her blood grows stronger with each step. A bad feeling turns again.

Alpha finally halts and shifts back. He walks slowly, and I don't know what he sees till he kneels. A pale Kate is at his feet. A bag lays next to her. Her lips are blue. She looks—

You did this, my wolf says, *to your own sister.*

Maddock rushes past me and Alpha. He picks her up, cradling her against himself. Her body is completely limp. My breath becomes rigid.

"Is she—" Gabriel starts. He is incredibly calm but still seems concerned.

Maddock puts his head to her chest, trying to hear a beat. He exhales, relieved. "She's alive!" Maddock stands quickly with her. "She needs a doctor!"

"Give her to me. I run faster," Gabriel says. Maddock and I follow his lead to the pack doctor's home.

Your parents would never forgive you.

Gabriel

Damn it, Kate. You better keep breathing. I look down at her. She's so pale, and there's a deep gash hidden under a blood-soaked bandage on her forehead.

She's innocent. My wolf calls. *She will not have you now. Look at what you've done.*

"I know," I say under my breath. I could have saved her. I could have kept her safe beside me. Or at least I could have kept everyone else away from her. "Forgive me for not protecting you," I whisper in her ear.

We come up on the doctor's home quickly. My father had me memorize this house first. He said that if ever I was in trouble, this would be the best place to take cover in. I nearly knock down the door and rush Kate inside.

"What's happened?" the doctor says, jumping from her seat on a long sofa.

I place Kate on the sofa and strip my shirt off to cover her with it. "Hypothermia and a concussion, maybe. She fell in the river and hit her head, then walked home," I answer.

The doctor rushes over to her and checks a number of other things. "And a dislocated shoulder. Okay, pick her up and run her to the Med Center. I'll be right behind you. I just need to gather a few things."

A dislocated shoulder? I hadn't even noticed that. I fought the urge to demand that the doctor do something for her now. What was the point of coming here at all? Lifting Kate carefully, we rush to the Med Center with a couple of large blankets from the doctor. I forgot all about Leon and Maddock. They, too, look concerned, standing in the doorway.

By the time the doctors had seen her and ran multiple tests from outdated machines, I'm out of patience. No one has told us a thing about how she is doing. The tests didn't seem to be telling us a thing, and Kate still looks so pale. Even with the heating blankets.

We wait inside her room for confirmation that she was going to be okay. Finally, the doctor walks in.

"Well, Alpha, she's gone through a lot. In her state, I'm not sure how she'll recover, but I've seen others walk away from worse." We all exhale sighs of relief. "Her shoulder will take a bit more time to heal. The concussion has her in a comatose state. The hypothermia hasn't helped, but it is under control now."

"What's wrong with her shoulder? Why will it take longer to heal?" I ask.

"I assume when she pulled herself out of the water, she was running on pure adrenaline and ended up pulling herself out of the water without even realizing that her shoulder was dislocated. Many ligaments were torn. I don't know if she will be able to recover from it. We'll put a brace on her shoulder so she won't be able to move it. Not that she will be moving it in her unconscious state."

"Wait, if her shoulder doesn't heal, she'll never be able to run as a wolf," Maddock says accusingly.

The doctor nods. "It doesn't seem that she has shifted any time recently anyways. Her healing process is that of a human. It's slow and concerning. Her wolf is strong, but—" The doctor shakes her head. "But she has years of bruising and fractures that her wolf has yet to heal."

"She hasn't shifted since that night," Leon says. "The old alpha forbade it."

The doctor nods. "I remember. And that is why she will take longer to heal. I suspect that her attempt at walking away without any medical help is the reason behind her comatose state."

"I'll stay with her," Maddock says.

"Me too." Leon rushes.

"No, the fuck you won't. If it weren't for you, she would be fine right now." Maddock snaps, standing in full territorial stance.

I grit my teeth. I have no right to intervene further. I already walked away from her. Even as the thought goes through my mind,

I bear so much guilt for her injuries. I left her in the hands of people who hated her. Honestly, though, I never thought Leon would let this happen to her. No matter the anger he had for her. Looking at him now, I can see every emotion that crosses his face—anger, sadness, remorse, pain, frustration.

I look back to Kate. Her skin is white as snow, but I can see the yellows, greens, and purples of old bruises. They decorate her arms and collarbone. I shouldn't have left them with her. I noticed the bruises before but ignored them. Like my father did. It is shameful for an alpha to ignore the abuse of one of his pack members. Even if she had killed her parents during her first shift, five years of abuse and hatred for something she had no control over—it is punishment enough.

I rejected her because I let the idea of my appearance to the pack cloud my judgment. She was right, a good alpha would have done the research. I should have spoken to her normally. I should have spoken to those who'd found her that night. I judged her on unproven accusations. A mistake I promise not to make again.

"I think it would be best if you all leave for the night. You can visit her tomorrow. I will contact you if there are any changes," the doctor said.

I nod. "Let's go. There's nothing more we can do for her here."

Both look at me, and I could see the worry and guilt in their eyes. I feel it too, but I am still Alpha, and I cannot allow this to distract me from my duties. I give them both a meaningful look. Leon treads slowly toward the door. Maddock stays firmly planted.

"I'm staying. I've never been there for her before. I'm not going to leave her when she needs me the most." Maddock takes the open chair beside Kate's bed. The doctor gives me a glance, but I allow the defiance only because I know I won't persuade him to leave.

Admit that you want to stay too, my wolf says in a gruff voice.

I clear my throat, ignoring him. "We'll be off then," I say as Leon and I make our way out the door.

Once we're outside the Med Center, I hear Leon speak softly. "She'll never forgive me."

I turn to him, and for the first time since we were children before my father sent me to train, I see him in tears.

"I should have pulled her out. She didn't come up for air, but I thought she was being dramatic. Trying to get attention." He shakes his head. "It should be me in there, not her."

I had seen this behavior before, while I was training. The test of endurance. We were told to stand in the river, which was chest-high, for hours. There was a gentle current that gradually became harder to stand in. By the fifth hour, one of the trainees lost his stance and pulled on another. They both tumbled into the water. The one who lost his footing began cramping at the ankle, and in a desperate attempt to keep his head afloat, he dragged the other under. Only one of them walked out of the water that day. The guilt of what he'd done nearly finished him off.

I put my hand on my best friend's shoulder. "Then I guess you better find a way to make it up to her." The idea brought him back a bit. "She's gonna need help when she wakes up. She's gonna need you to be patient and relentless. You're her brother. I remember how happy you were when she was born. I'm sure she'll remember if you help her too."

He still looks grave but better than he had. His tears have ceased, and he looks in a state of worrisome calm.

"I'm gonna go and see if there is anything I can do to make her...home comfortable."

I nod, understanding that he needs the time to himself to do something for her. Even I have the urge to—

I stop the thought immediately. I have already rejected her. I will not give in to the guilt and apologize for my decision.

Yet you still want to be beside her tonight. I'll tell you this. If she convinces her wolf that you are not worth her time, she will never give you so much as a sideways glance. She will find a new mate, and they will live happily without ever thinking of you again.

Something about that information churned my stomach. I will be nothing to her. Well, I'm nothing to her now. She didn't even flinch when Ruby paraded me around. Ugh, Ruby. For someone so fierce, she sure knows how to talk your ear off. I thought for a moment that she would be a good distraction and a worthy female mate. She's strong and speaks her mind, but she is also materialistic and is entirely too interested in her own appearance and title. She would not be an adequate Luna, as I previously thought.

"Will uh…" I hear someone from behind me. I turn quickly to see a girl standing in the shadows. It takes someone with true skill to so easily sneak up on me. Or I'm letting Kate occupy too much of my attention. "Will Kate be okay?"

"Who are you?"

She turns her head away from me. "She looked terrible," she says softly.

I exhale. I guess she not gonna tell me her name. "She's in a coma. They don't know if she'll wake."

The girl looks down and simply walks away, a look of sadness in her eyes. Something in my gut tells me that I should have asked what she was doing there.

I head for my office in the great lodge, also known as the alpha house. Just as I'm about to pull the door open, Ruby runs up to me.

"Gabriel! I'm so sorry about everything. I shouldn't have acted the way I did. I'm sorry, love."

Annoyance, once again, blooms within me. "I have never given you permission to call me by anything other than Alpha. You will do well to remember that. Also, I do not think it would be in my best interest to continue seeing you."

Her nose scrunches as her face turns a shade of bright pink. "What about my best interests? Or does that not matter to you?"

"No, not really. The next Luna must care for the well-being of the entire pack, not just herself."

"I do care for the pack! Hell, I'm a part of the pack! Unlike that runt you pulled from the river. She should have been exiled after she tore her own parents apart! Or better yet, she should have been strung up. Yet you leave me to care for her and say I'm unworthy!"

Anger boils over. I couldn't contain it, and my wolf was ready to attack at her snide threat. I march at her, making her back up with a fearful look on her face. Good.

"You listen very closely. I am Alpha. My father obviously allowed you way too much leniency for you to think that you will *ever* be allowed to raise your voice at me. Every member of this pack is under my command and my protection. That includes Kate. If you ever give me a reason to believe that you are a threat to *my* pack, I will remember the day you admitted to attempted murder. And you better hope she wakes up because, if she doesn't, it will be you who is exiled for the death of a pack member."

I watch her eyes water with shock just as I turn away and walk into my office. The doctor says Kate had older bruises and fractures that were untreated. I wonder how much my father turned a blind eye to when it came to Kate's well-being.

Behind Closed Eyes

Darkness, I'm surrounded by it. There is an ache deep in my chest. The ache is so overwhelming that I collapse to my knees in the darkness. My hands clutch my chest as I begin heaving hard breaths. Then a light, brighter than day. I squint, forcing my eyes to adjust. No, it's not a light. A huge white wolf approaches. It has beautiful white fur and dark-green eyes.

It stops just a foot from me. Looking down at me. How pathetic I must look.

"Kate," she says. And I immediately recognize the voice. She is my wolf. "This will be the only time we meet like this."

"How—" I try asking while still holding my chest.

"You are in a coma. When Ruby pushed you, you hit your head on a rock. I will not let that happen again." She speaks, but her mouth never moves. I can hear it echo, but she stays perfectly still. Watching me, as she stands tall.

I manage to get control of myself and sit back. I hold my knees close to my chest. "What do you mean you won't let that happen? It's not your fault. I was just too…naive and stupid. I should have seen it coming."

"No, Kate. You have a blind spot."

"What do you mean?"

"When it comes to your brothers, you believe that they will never go too far. Obviously, that is not true. This time they went too far. You need to let go of the past and open your eyes to what is. Forget that Leon and Maddock were ever your brothers. If you never knew them as your brothers, and knew them for how they treated you, would you still feel comfortable around them?"

Would I feel comfortable? *"I don't know. I guess* comfortable *isn't the right word, but I suppose I would keep clear of them."*

"You must learn to recognize when it's time to cut loose the old memories of your happy family."

I stay quiet. I haven't thought of those memories since Leon first turned against me. I have no family left. I know that. Still, I will not avoid every person simply because I know they don't care for me. "I'll stay clear of Leon and Maddock and really anyone with the nerve to confront me. Apart from those people, I will live day to day till I have gathered enough supplies to leave."

"Leaving may no longer be an option."

"Why not?"

"The one who carried you here and whispered apologies to you was Gabriel. His wolf still longs for us, and because of that, he has no choice but to care for us."

Bitterness seeps from me. "I don't want Gabriel."

"Yes, you do," she continues before I can protest. "Don't fight what you feel. It is not hatred that you feel from him, it is hurt. You are hurt that he so easily dismissed you. Even if hate does control your view of him, remember that the opposite of love is not hate but indifference."

I look down at my fingers. "Will I wake up?"

"That is your choice."

"My choice?"

"Yes, if you are ready to return, then will yourself to wake."

"Will I remember this when I wake?"

"No, but you will remember what you feel, and you will think differently about each person."

"Do you think that the world is worth returning to, knowing what awaits us?"

"Yes, I'm not afraid of a fight. Neither are you. We are unwilling to step aside and unwilling to die like this. Otherwise, I would not be your wolf."

I nod, but then something occurs to me. "Do you have a name?"

Her head pulls back as if she is taken off guard by the question. "Yes, Circe."

I nod in appreciation. "I like knowing your name. I hate calling you my wolf as if I own you. We're more like soul sisters sharing the same vessel."

"Yes, I suppose we are." She pauses. "Soul sisters."

It is the last thing I hear before the darkness takes over again.

My Open Eyes

"Kate!" Someone is calling my name.

I can feel anger and betrayal deep within me. Betrayal? I was betrayed. By who? An image of Leon, and then Gabriel, flash in my mind. My family. My mate. Memories of being belittled and harassed for years reappear. Bruises, scrapes, and the sound of my own bones cracking under my skin. Hot tears that run down my cheeks. The pain of the last five years crashing down on me. The feeling of loneliness that I had ignored. All the times I told myself I'd be okay when nothing was okay. My own screams fill my ears. The sound is deafening, and then suddenly, complete silence. As if everything has been set on mute.

I try speaking, but the darkness swallows my voice. My parents appear in the darkness. The rerun of their deaths plays before me. Guilt consumes me.

"Her heart rate is spiking again." A voice echoes through the darkness, pulling me out. "Kate if you can hear me, I need you to calm down." I force my eyes open and am immediately blinded by a bright light. My eyes shift back and forth, searching for something I recognize. My vision is obscured, though, and I feel a tugging at my hand. My eyes slightly adjust to the lighting, and I see a hand gripping mine.

My eyes follow up the hand, to the arm, to the face of Maddock. His face looks pained and pale. I look back down at my hand and swipe it away. What the fuck is going on?

"Kate! It's me, Maddock. I'm so sorry. My wolf told me, but I didn't—I'm so sorry." He is speaking in jumbled apologies. I look around the room. Gene, a pack doctor, is standing on the other side of my bed. No, not my bed, a Med Center bed.

"Welcome back, Kate," she says when our eyes meet. I remember the last time I came to her. My parents were still alive. She was one of the few that never looked at me in anger or resentment. No, her eyes had always been filled with pity when looking at me. It wasn't a look I cared for, but then maybe, I looked pitiful. "Can you tell me what you remember last?"

Leon comes bursting in through the doors before I could answer. "Kate!" My heart pounds and aches at the sight of him. He ran up to me and kneels. "I'm so happy you're alive. I'm sorry for not pulling you out, I should have—"

"That's enough, she needs time to process everything. I need you both to leave the room immediately."

"She just woke up!" Maddock shouts, making me flinch at the sharpness.

"Yes, and she needs quiet, and I need to assess her mental state."

I'm no doctor, but I don't think you're supposed to say that in front of the patient. I look away when they both attempt to make eye contact.

Leon lingers as if wanting to protest but follows suit. Why are they here? They had never cared if anyone had gone too far before. They had never stopped to question if I was okay. And they had damn sure never apologized for any of it. What changed?

"Kate, I need you to tell me what you remember." Dr. Gene asks, pulling me from my thoughts.

I inhale deeply, looking at a whiteboard on the wall that says my name and the date. I've been unconscious for nearly a month. "Is that date correct?" I ask, bewildered.

Doctor Gene looks at the wall, then back at me. "Yes, Kate. You've been in a coma for twenty-three days."

I shake my head, slowly trying to deal with the fact that I slept in a bed for a month, and no one yelled at me for it. The thought makes me smirk. Still, it's unsettling; it felt like I had slept for minutes.

"I remember—" I begin, but then it occurs to me that it doesn't matter what I remember. I would be to blame somehow for provoking the situation. My smirk turns to a scowl as I look away from her eyes. "I don't remember anything."

"Are you sure?"

I nod. Dr. Gene presses her lip together in a firm line. Disappointment and pity fill her eyes. What's she expecting? I'm no coward, but when on fire, I don't reach for the gasoline? No, I would never speak of what happened. Even as I make this vow, the pain of seeing Leon stand at Ruby's side angers me. So much for family.

"Um, when can I go home?"

"Well, most of your injuries have healed, but I want to keep you for a few more days to make sure there is nothing else to worry about. You may have headaches on occasion due to the trauma, but I can give you herbs that will help with them."

I nod. "Can I eat? I'm starving."

She smiles widely and nods. "Yes, but we'll have to start you off with broths and clear foods. Your stomach needs to adjust to food as you haven't eaten in a while."

"Well, let's get adjusting. It's not every day I almost die." The morbid joke seems to take her off guard. "Sorry, you have your ways of coping, and well, I have mine."

"If it helps," she says, trying to be understanding.

Beginning Again

Maddock and Leon had returned every day till my discharge. I refused to see them. I don't want any trouble. I don't even know why they keep showing up. Shaking the annoyed thoughts, I continue combing my hair. Since I am being discharged today, I want to leave looking better than I did coming in. As I look around the room to see if there is anything I am forgetting, I notice that I have absolutely nothing to forget here. My small bag of clothing that I had planned to take—the contents of the chest of my deceased parents' belongings, and myself—all fit comfortably within a woven bag about the size of a child's backpack. Besides that, I am ready to go.

"They are here again," Dr. Gene says, waiting for me by the door.

"Can I sneak out any other way?"

She shakes her head. "I'm sorry I can't shoo them away this time. Alpha is with them." The comb slips from my hand. I bend to pick it up. What the hell is he doing here?

He's here for you, Circe says, nearly scaring me half to death.

A little warning next time, Circe!

You remember my name?

Didn't you tell me once before? She remains silent. I haven't heard from her since waking. I turn slowly to the door, Dr. Gene standing beside it. I exhale dramatically and give her a nod. She pulls the door open and walks out with me.

Standing across my room door are Maddock, Leon, and Gabriel, all three leaning against the wall. Leon approaches first.

"Kate," he whispers. His voice is filled with sorrow. His eyes have dark circles, and he seems much thinner. "I'm so sorr—"

"I heard you the first time," I say, looking up at him. It is cruel how much he looks like our father. He seems to go speechless, so I turn to leave when someone grabs my wrist. I whip my head around and see Maddock's teary-eyed face.

"Kat," he starts.

My eyes widen, and my heart clenches. I'm taken aback by the nickname that hasn't been used in years. My own eyes begin to sting, and the sense of betrayal digs deep this time.

I yank my hand back, hard. "Don't ever call me that again. That little girl died five years ago." I turn and walk off before I can see the expression on his face. Dr. Gene stays beside me till I'm out of the building. She gives me a sad smile and wishes me well.

I begin walking to my soon-to-be-ex home when I'm stopped again. This time Gabriel cuts me off. "Look, I understand that you feel hurt and betrayed by them, but they have been here every day waiting to see you. The guilt nearly destroyed Leon."

The nerve. "I'm sorry, how is this any of your business?"

He was worried, Circe says.

His jaw clenches. "They are my friends. I came to support them."

"Fine." I whip my arms out. "Support them, but there's no reason for you to speak to me."

"They just want to speak to you." Annoyance is in his voice.

I step up in his face, fully aware that I'm speaking to the pack alpha. "They had years to speak to me. They had years to apologize. I suffered alone for five years with everyone's back to me. Where were they then! Where was anyone to speak to me with understanding! To this day, not a single person has ever said to me, 'I'm sorry for your loss.' Do you want to know why? Because according to everyone in this pack, only my brothers had the right to mourn the loss of our parents. My brothers. The ones who swore to my mother and father that they'd always protect me! The ones who would give me piggyback rides and told me not to be afraid of the dark! And they are the ones who left me completely alone. You have no right to tell me how much they suffered these last few weeks. I was fourteen when I was told it was better off that I stay separate from the rest of the pack. And that was your family. Don't ever talk to me about what they went through out of guilt. It's none of your damn business!"

Before I turn away, I spot Leon and Maddock at the entrance of the Med Center. Both with destroyed looks on their faces. I'm too angry to care. I leave without another word. No one tries to stop me. I only then realize that I'm in tears. My throat feels like it's about to close up from the saliva. I wipe my face with my sleeve and force myself to stop crying.

This is neither the time nor the place. I won't submit to a false apology. I'm in pain. So I admit it. I've been in pain for a long time, though. It is nothing new to me. With time and distance, I will overcome it. I don't need them the way I once thought I did. I am determined to never need anyone again.

*****

Walking into my home makes me feel out of place. There is something different about it. Looking around, I can't tell at first, but then I notice it. Everything had been cleaned. The old grime-covered mirror above my little sink had been scrubbed clean. The small chipped-to-hell dresser beside my bed looks like it had been sanded down and the wood treated. My floor is so clean I could eat off it. Even the few pieces of laundry that I hadn't packed are neatly folded on my bed.

After the feeling of shock passes, new anger sets in. Anger is beginning to be my go-to mood lately. The thought of someone coming into my home, the only space that I have to myself, sends chills down my spine. I now feel that there is absolutely nowhere I can go where they won't reach me. I take a few steps till I'm standing in front of my bed. I slowly sit.

I can feel Circe as if she were sitting beside me. Trying to comfort me. So much. I've been through so much, and I'm not sure how to process it. A familiar fragrance passes by my nose.

"Leon cleaned it up."

I don't look to see who it is. It will take a while to forget his scent. I keep my head down. I had been so determined and optimistic on the short walk here, it changed so quickly. Just what I need, some kind of bipolar disorder. Silence fills the void for several seconds.

"I won't say I believe you're innocent, but I do believe that if you were allowed to stay...," he trails off. "My father may have let some things slip from his control when it came to your treatment in this pack."

I swallow the bile building in my throat. "I don't need your pity."

His wolf, Circe says. *I hear him.*

What?

His wolf is— she stops.

I look over at him. There is an expression on his face that I can't quite place. It's not remorse or anger. It looks almost as though he's having some kind of battle with himself. He's leaning against my doorframe.

"You need your brothers as much as they need you." The statement sounds forced. His face contorted uncomfortably.

"Don't pretend to know anything about me. Why are you even here? Are they outside waiting for me to crumble?" Even though I want to sound angry, my voice is soft with a quiver. I look back down. I feel so tired. Dr. Gene said I'd feel drowsy from the herbal tea she gave me, but this isn't what I imagined. This feels like defeat.

"Kate?" My vision blurs for a moment. "Kate!"

The feeling of exertion is overwhelming but is displaced slightly when I feel his hands on my forearms, keeping me upright.

I shove away. "I don't need your help," I say, pushing past him. "I need you to go. It may not look like much to you, but this is my home."

"What happened that day?" he asks ignoring me.

"Didn't you hear me? I said I want you out."

"And since when have you ever gotten what you wanted?"

There's a bitter taste on my tongue. Circe begins to whine in my ears. I'm not sure what's happening until I collapse into Gabriel's arms.

Him. It's him. I can feel it. I never responded to his rejection, and it's weighing on me now. Him being here. Him touching me. It's draining all my energy.

"Fine," I whisper.

"C'mon, you're just tired from the day." He lifts me and places me on the bed. He begins making his way out.

"I, Katherine Barsotti, reject—"

A Ways to Go

Before I know it, my mouth is covered. I look up at Gabriel. He has a firm grip from jawline to jawline across my face. My breathing accelerates. I don't understand what's happening.

"Don't." It's a command.

Don't? Is he serious? He rejected me, and it's depleting my energy. Returning the rejection is the only way I can get my strength back. I try pulling his hand away, but his grip only tightens to near painful.

"I'm not letting you go until you agree not to finish the rejection." My blood boils. Not reject him, after all this! He sees the anger in my eyes and continues, "Just give me some—"

I sink my canines deep into his hand, making him whip his hand away. "You must be kidding! Now I don't even have the right to return *your* rejection? How many other freedoms are you planning on taking from me?"

"I may have rushed into my rejection," he snaps, stilling me silent.

"Regret is an ugly thing, Alpha," I say, nodding. "But it changes nothing."

"It changes everything!" he yells, and I annoyingly cower at his tone. "I know what you did, and still I—" He runs his good hand through his hair. "I don't know how to fix everything. I can't fix the problems of the past. I can't send for an investigation on something that happened five years ago! I can't take the years of suffering away from you. And I can't take you as my mate."

I don't know how to feel. He almost sounds apologetic but accusing at the same time. My drowsiness and emotions really begin to make me droop, but I force myself to stay aware.

"I don't know what you're telling me. I already know this. You already rejected me. All you're doing is rubbing salt in the wound." I have to blink away tears that begin forming.

"I'm saying that if things were different—"

"But they're not different! It is what it is. I'm guilty till proven innocent. People here will always hate me. You are Alpha. I am nothing. Stop pretending that things could be different." I look away. "Just go. You have nothing more to say to me, and the rejection will continue making me weak. You can't stop me from rejecting you. And I will be damned if I allow you to keep me down while you figure out what you want on any given day. It makes no difference anyways because tomorrow, I will no longer be a member of your pack." He straightens, and his jaw ticks annoyingly fast. "I will leave, and then it won't matter at all. You, Leon, and Maddock can live happily ever after without ever having to think of—"

"I, Gabriel Black, renounce my rejection." Almost instantly, I feel ten times better. Again, I'm stunned. This is becoming a bad habit.

"What?" I ask in disbelief.

"I need time. I need to figure out a way to appease everyone. I can't just—I need to make it better before I place you beside me." His voice is almost desperate.

"You want me to wait for you?" I say, appalled. "Your rejection would have made it easier to walk away from each other."

"I can't see you with someone else." His jaw clenches. "I won't."

Tears finally fall. "Damn shame I can't reject an Alpha without him rejecting me first." I bite down on my lower lip to keep my chin from shaking. "I've never known a more selfish person. You and Ruby really deserve each other." I sniffle and wipe my tears away. "Is there anything else you need, Alpha?" I ask flatly. He stays silent. "If you don't mind, I need to rest. I have a long day tomorrow, and I will need all my strength."

"Katherine."

"Please go." I gesture to the door. He doesn't leave, and I know he's waiting on a promise. "I still need medicine from the doc. I won't leave until she says I don't need it anymore." When he turns, I lay back and face my back to the door. Why? Why did it have to be him?

He wants to start new with you, Kate.

I don't want him. He's not good for me.

The goddess believes he is.

She made a mistake.

He wants to make things more comfortable for you before he intro-duces you as his mate. You have to take that into consideration.

No, he wants the thumbs-up from a pack who has hated me for years. He wants to keep his image up. It has nothing to do with him wanting me comfortable.

He is Alpha, Kate. He cannot have separation in the pack. It will make it weak. Yes, his image is important, but you are also important to him.

Then why doesn't he believe me about my parents?

Kate, he needs proof that those rogues were there. Otherwise, every-one will scorn him for accepting you. They will not trust his judgment. You just need to give him time to find a way for you to be together.

"Stop!" I snap. "Stop defending him! I should be proven guilty before I'm punished. He has taken away any chance of me falling in love with another. I will be chained to him till he realizes that no one will ever accept me as his mate." I let out a sob and cry hard into my pillow.

I'm sorry, Kate. I'm sorry things aren't different. You don't deserve the treatment you're receiving, and this pack doesn't deserve you. But this is the reality. Together we will become stronger, and we will prove to them why they should respect us. I nod, letting my sob cease to silent tears as I let myself wish for a better future with Circe.

Sleep finally consumes me.

I wake sometime later to a tray of food on my dresser. I exam-ine it for a moment before deciding that I shouldn't eat it, especially because I can't be sure who brought it. Sighing, I grab the tray and walk it outside. Once my eyes adjust to the bright sun, I see Leon, standing about five feet from my entrance.

I look back down at the food. He probably brought it. I should definitely throw it out now. "I thought you'd be hungry." His voice is quiet. I've never seen him so feeble. I hate the part of me that feels uncomfortable with the sight of his thin sleep-deprived state. My mother would have tied him to a bed to rest and spoon-fed him if she could see him now.

"Well, I'm not." I put the tray on the ground between us. "You eat it," I say and walk back inside. I hear him call out my name, but he doesn't follow me in. I'm thankful for that. I've had too many visitors today. What could he possibly have to say to me after all this time?

His wolf is weakening, Circe says. *Soon he will not be able to turn.*

The thought grips at my chest. But why should I care? It wasn't until I nearly died that he suddenly wanted to speak to me.

I suppose I understand why you can't leave your love for him in the past.

I shouldn't care what happens to him.

And yet it bothers you that he is restless and starved.

He tortured me and allowed me to be tortured for years.

Then forget that he's out there. Pretend he doesn't exist. My brows furrow. *You can't, can you? No matter how much he put you through, you will always remember the times he tucked you into bed and told you to dream big. How can you fight those memories? Even now, you still hold them both close to your heart. If you can't forget, then you might as well try to forgive.*

We have a ways to go before I ever consider forgiveness.

Yes, we have a ways to go.

To Go or Not to Go

I had intended to go to work, like always, the following morning, but just as I got there, they said they didn't need my help and that they were managing just fine without my assistance. It was a harsh blow to my ego, but in the end, the herbal teas I had gotten made me very numb and tired. The feeling is both a blessing and a curse. I am happy that the pain from both my arms' soreness and the headaches are nearly nonexistent, but then I can't function. The smallest tasks would nearly make me collapse. Even though Dr. Gene told me to drink the tea twice a day, I couldn't bring myself to laze about all day. So I decided that I'd only take it if my pains and headaches were unbearable.

It's been three days since I came home from the Med Center. Three days of Leon bringing me every meal. Three days of staying cooped up because I know going out brings unwanted company. Three days of not having a purpose in this pack. If it's going to be like this, I shouldn't wait to leave; I should just go now. I take a peek out of my small window to see if Leon is still waiting. He's not directly out front like he's been the whole time I've been home. I take a breath and rush out before he comes back.

Where are you taking us, Kate? Circe asks.

"I can't stand being inside. I figured you'd want some air too."

She's quiet for a moment. *Yes, and it is a warm day.*

I nod as I make my way to the river. Once I can hear the rushing water, I halt for some reason. *Fear is a terrible feeling, but it can be useful at times. Don't worry, Kate. I am with you. I will not allow you to be blindsided.*

Even though her words sound accusing, they make me feel calm. I continue to walk till I reach my little spot on the boulder I was pushed from. The view overlooks the rushing water and the fish that flop out, trying to swim against the current. It's still so peaceful here, considering everything that's happened. I fold my legs against my chest and think about my next move. If I gather a variety of seeds from the farming house and tools to cut and carve wood with, I could start a new life in a few days.

Alone, Circe says. *I'm sorry, but your thoughts were transparent.*

I shake my head. "I don't mind. This is as much your choice as it is mine. I know that my decisions will affect both of us. I know it's not smart to live alone out there, but why would I stay in pack that would love nothing more than to watch me go?"

Think about it this way, if you go, it will confirm what they already suspect—that you killed your parents. The logic behind it would be, why would someone who claimed to have run into rogues choose to live away from the pack? Bile builds in my throat, forcing me to gulp.

"I don't care what they think anymore. I stopped being a member of this pack when they first accused me. No matter how much I pleaded, they never believed me. So I'm in the exact same position if I stay. At least out there, I will never have to see their condemning glances."

Someone is coming. I stiffen at her words.

"Kate."

Leon. I don't turn to look at him.

"Can we talk?" I twitch when I hear Maddock too.

"Doesn't look like I have a choice," I say, gripping my knees tighter.

"Apparently you do." A painful shock goes down my spine at the sound of Ronny's voice.

Get up, Kate. He doesn't mean you well. I stand quickly, doing my best not to look intimidated. My eyes lock with Ronny first. His expression is hard and closed off.

"Well, if that's the case." I begin my way down from my little spot. I see both Leon and Maddock's faces drop.

Kate! I react, turning quickly. No one behind me. *I smell them!* Leon and Maddock are at my sides in seconds.

"Who?" I say out loud, panicked.

She's quiet for a second, and I know she's trying to decide. *Rogues!* My heart pounds. *Shift!* Without hesitating, I let her take over.

Pain shoots through my entire body, but it isn't unbearable. Now it is my turn to sit in the passenger seat and let Circe take control. She jumps off the boulder, across the river. She runs hard, and from my state, it feels amazing. I notice Leon and Maddock on both sides of me, their wolves holding back to allow Circe to take the lead. In moments, we come across two very large wolves. Much larger than me. Circe growls forcefully, completely unafraid.

This is our land! she says dominantly. *Leave or be removed by force.*

A bitter laugh escapes one of them, the larger dark-gray one. *And who will remove us? You? A little runt?*

White fur? the other says. *It's not a very common coat, is it? It reminds me of something.*

Anger flares, and my impulse to hurt them drives Circe to pounce. She locks her jaw on the throat of the dark gray, pinning him in place. Maddock pounces on the other, but he slips form Maddock's grasp.

Stay with her! Maddock's wolf yells before chasing after the other. The state of my body begins to take its toll, but I am unwilling to release the rogue. Leon steps closer, and Circe growls, keeping a steady eye on him. Gabriel runs up, along with two others. The others hold down the rogue.

Release him, Gabriel's wolf commands. Circe does and steps back. *Turn, rogue.* The rogue doesn't comply at first. Gabriel steps closer and says lowly, *Or be put to rest.*

After a moment, the rogue turns to a raggedy-dressed man. His hair is shaggy and long. Dirt and grime cover his body. It occurs to me then that they may have crept in as men and turned once inside. It would be a stupid risk if they hadn't covered themselves in filth. They got this close because no one caught their scent up to this point.

Leon, take him to his cell, Gabriel commands.

"There is another. Maddock went after him. In that direction," Leon says after turning back. The other two pack members give me a once-over before charging in the direction Maddock and the other rogue went in. Circe releases control and shifts as well.

Gabriel looks at Leon. "Can you handle him?" Leon nods and begins walking the rogue back. Gabriel turns and faces me.

My heart is still pounding in my chest. I turned, and even though it hurt like hell, it was amazing. I was able to hold a rogue down long enough for help to arrive.

"You did good," Gabriel says, pulling me from my internal gloating.

I don't look him in the eye. "They might know something about the deaths of my parents. I wasn't going to let them get away so easily."

I walk past him and head for the river. Strange how something so beautiful nearly killed me, yet I still return to it. I hear Gabriel's footsteps behind me. He's quiet and keeps his distance. I stop, facing my boulder from the other side of the water.

"Why are you following me?" I ask, slightly annoyed by his presence.

"You woke up from a coma less than a week ago, and you manage to take down a large rogue. I need to make sure you're okay both physically and emotionally."

"I'm fine. I'm not some kind of fragile porcelain doll. I may be one of the smaller pack members, but I am by no means weak." I snap over my shoulder.

I feel him moving closer. "No, you are not."

I move away. "Stop it." I cross my arms and turn to him. "Don't you have some interrogating that you should be doing? I think talking to them is a lot more important than talking to me."

He moves toward me again, but I stay firm. "I know what you want from them, Katherine. But I don't think you should get your hopes up."

I glare at him. I have no hope to get up. I have nothing to lose, though. He sighs. "I will speak to them. Go home and rest. You're pushing your body to the limit."

"I said I'll be fine!" I take a step away and whip my arms out to show him I'm not hurt. I actually feel amazing. My headaches have gone away, and my shoulder hardly hurts at all.

He sighs, running a hand through his hair. "Okay, Kate. I'm speaking to you now as your alpha. Go home immediately."

Do not disobey Alpha's command.

*****

Sometime later, Maddock is at my door with food. He has three deep gashes just beneath his neck. He offers the food to me. I take the tray and put it on my bed. I guess it is easier to accept food from him when he looks this horrible.

"Kate, I—"

"Don't. I don't want to hear your apology again. You chose to believe whatever they told you to. Live with yourself and leave me the hell alone." I could see the anguish in his eyes.

"No." His expression hardens. "I will not leave you alone again. Hate me. Punch me if you want, but I will not leave you again. I will be here every day trying to gain your trust and forgiveness. I don't care how long it takes. And I will protect you from anyone else who tries to hurt you because that is what I promised Mom and Dad." He looks at the food on my bed. "Eat up. You're going to need your strength for the trial."

I don't say anything as he leaves.

I suppose we have no reason to leave anymore.

Gabriel

"I swear, we don't know anything," the rogue says. "If we did, we'd tell you."

This rogue has no shame to rat on his friends if it saves his skin. I am positive that he really knows nothing. I have already questioned them separately. He is a lot stronger when questioned separately. He hardly spoke with no one to watch him. Now in front of the other, he's opened up, fearful that the other will think he's already snitched.

I smirk. "Oh, would you now. Well, now I'm just disappointed in you." His eyes shift fearfully from side to side. "See, now I think I know why you were exiled."

"You don't know anything," the other says through gritted teeth.

This one, however, hadn't so much as spoken a word till now. Even after his own blood choked him only an hour ago. He's had a sneer the entire time, and I knew for a fact that he did have some information to share.

"Enlighten me, rogue. Tell what it is, I don't know." He glares at me before facing forward again. "What did you do to get exiled, hmm?" He adjusts slightly. I hit a soft spot. "How about I guess, and you tell me when I've gotten closer?" The other rogue looks from me to him fearfully. "Did you steal from those in your pack? No, that couldn't be it. You are much too burly for that to be it." I look at the other. "He's a wife-beater, isn't he?"

The silent one's head whip to me, fury in his eyes. "Uh-oh, did I hit a nerve? Maybe it was much worse than that. Kids, maybe?" He attempts to bolt toward me, but the chair he is roped to keeps him in place. I don't move a muscle.

Everything about this rogue is wrong. The way he holds his head up. The way he squints slightly when I get closer to an answer.

His obedient silence would be respectable if he were of a pack. The one beside him acts more of a rogue than he does.

I look to the weaker of the two. "What's your name?" He shudders at it and glances sideways. "Now."

"Kiron," he mumbles. Yes, alone he will spill everything now. First, I will have to get rid of the other in front of him.

My eyes, once again, study his partner. There is something about him that is throwing me off, and I can't place what it is. I have decided to kill him in order to get Kiron to talk, but the decision feels wrong.

He is not weak, my wolf says. It is the first he's spoken since the interrogation started a few hours ago. *I sense anger, but one that speaks differently from other rogues.*

How do you mean?

His anger is not chaotic. It will not burst, though he makes it seem otherwise. He has no intention of violence toward you. Strange.

Very strange. It finally occurs to me that his entire persona reminds me of Katherine. The calm anger. The strong front. I begin to wonder if the thing they have most in common is the betrayal from the ones they trusted most. The condemned fate that others put on them. I stop myself at this moment. I am reading too much into what may not be there. I turn to the only other member in the room with us.

"Separate them." He nods. I walk out of the room.

I wipe my face clean with water from the nearest restroom. Kate has been occupying too much of my mind. I am beginning to act in consideration of her and only her. I had no idea of the possessiveness that came with having a mate.

A Short Trial

The interrogation took a few hours. It became the hush-hush game. Both denied knowing anything about my parents, after all. Still, neither of them talked about why they were there or what their intentions were. They had denied any relations to any rogue packs at the moment. Of course, trespassing alone was enough to have them executed. Gabriel seemed to have a hard time judging them equally. He passed a death sentence on one of them rather quickly. The other, he was sentenced to lifelong imprisonment. Both I and the rogue were outraged. The rogue thrashed around and even gotten a good kick at one of the guards attempting to hold him down. I, on the other hand, decided not to show my anger. I would go straight to the source once the trial officially ended.

Something feels off about where I am standing. I look around and notice a lot of people staring at me. Why? I don't turn my gaze away like I normally would have. I meet their eyes daringly. If years of torment have taught me anything, it was that keeping my head down did nothing for me. It was never my fault that they felt uncomfortable with looking at me. It may have been their own guilt that made them look away. *Look at me. Look at the person you projected your anger toward. The girl you teased, spat on, kicked.* All that time of me pretending that their words did not hurt me. My name is not clear, but now they know, I am not weak. Without any really training. With injuries. With a small frame, I took down a rogue. Now they know—they had mistaken my silence for weakness. Yet I have serious doubts about the members of this pack. One takedown will not persuade them to keep their distance. In fact, it may agitate them even further. I have my doubts.

"What of Katherine?" someone yells from the crowd gathered to watch the trial.

Gabriel seems to stiffen. "What of her?"

"She broke the law," another chimes. "She was told not to shift, yet she did. Surely she's done it before without permission."

"She can't be trusted," another shouts.

What? Are you people serious! Gabriel's eyes find mine. I clench my jaw and make my way up to the front.

"What is wrong with all of you?" Leon shouts, rushing to keep me from moving forward. "She saved lives! If they would have gotten loose with our community, who's to say most of your loved ones wouldn't be dead?"

"Who's to say she didn't know they were going to be there?" one woman shouts. "How is it that she magically detected rogues where nobody else did? For all we know, she helped them in and captured them in order to gain our trust."

"And you think these rogues would agree to it, knowing that their lives would be ended?" Leon counters.

"Facts are still the same, she broke the one rule she was told not to. Well, that we have proof of." Anger swells in me like never before.

"Fine." I keep moving to the front. "What punishment will be enough for you, people? Death. Will that satisfy your bloodlust?"

"Yeah," A few people cheer.

"You people are no different from us rogues." The rogue chuckles, one of the guards keeping his knee pressed firmly into his back. "You are no more civil than we are. Someone saves your ass, and there is no thank you. No instead, you put a knife to their throat. Pathetic. This is no pack. Just a bunch of rabid dogs." All eyes were on him.

"Katherine did not break any laws." Gabriel regains the crowd's attention. "In the Med Center, I granted her the right to shift. She had many old untreated wounds. We still have not gone through the list of people who haven't been brought to justice for the abuse bestowed on a pack member. Something tells me, though, that this will be a long one. I just hope that you will be as bloodthirsty during their judgment."

Murmurs spread around the crowd. Many walk away as if there is nothing more to watch.

Leon gives me a look and walks away too. My guess is that he would be nearby. In a few minutes, there are few people lingering around the gathering area but trying not to pay attention to me.

"Hello, Kate," someone says from my right.

It is one of the women I worked in the kitchen with. I remember her sneer anytime I had offered her my help with her prep. I nod my head to return her gesture of what I assume is "goodwill." It would be stupid to let my guard down. Now, more than ever, I should be watching my back.

"Ms. Barsotti," a disgustingly familiar voice says from behind me.

I turn to and bow my head to Elder Alpha Stone. The lines on his face were much more defined than the last time I saw him. His hair too is now whiter than its original black. He had aged in these last few years. Gabriel looks nothing like him.

"Alpha," I say lowly.

"I just wanted to say that I am happy that you got justice."

Justice?

"I hope you know that it was nothing personal, keeping you from shifting. I simply had to protect my pack."

Then why not simply exile me? Why punish me by keeping me here as an outsider? I remember those disgusting glances. Everything you let happen to me was personal!

"Of course, Elder Alpha. I know that it is the alpha's job to make the most logical decisions. Obviously, the rogues back then were much too clever that they were able to slip away. So I understand why your *investigation* only led to me." The insult makes his jaw dance. "Have a good day, *Elder* Alpha." I enunciate *elder*. I turn to see Gabriel watching the encounter.

He is pleased with you.

Hmm.

"Father," Gabriel says, looking past me to the old alpha. "I don't believe that was an appropriate apology. After all, your lack of leadership was the reason she ended up isolated, mistreated, and in a coma."

"Gabriel!" Stone growls, obviously displeased to see his son as his superior.

53

"Call me Alpha," Gabriel says firmly, raising a brow.

"Very well, Alpha. I apologize, Katherine...for your suffering."

Many turn to watch the exchange. Most are stunned at what they are hearing. Even I have a hard time believing it. After he is done speaking, he storms off. Something about that encounter was bitter. A kind of sour that sits in the soul. I shake the feeling and turn away from where the older man had stormed off from.

Gabriel moves in front of me, cutting off my path. "How are you feeling?" he says, holding my gaze.

I exhale a long breath. "They never admitted to knowing anything about it."

"Leon and Maddock say they did." He crosses his arms.

"No, they didn't. Even if their newfound love for me was genuine, they would not lie to you. But if they did, it would not mean anything to anyone around here. To them, my brothers simply felt guilty and are willing to say anything to get the pack to trust me."

His brows dip. "You are innocent. Anyone"—he takes a step closer to me—"who says otherwise will answer to me. You caught him, Kate. That is enough for me to know that you could never hurt someone you love and easily lie about it for years. If I believed otherwise, I would not call you innocent."

I huff, crossing my arms and looking away. Others have nearly halted in their tracks to witness the nearness between Alpha and me. I take a step back. "Why did you let the rogue live?"

"He has information I need, but something tells me that it will take more time to pry him open. He said more in front of everyone than he said when I interrogated him."

I huff and cross my arms. He looks up for a second, then returns his eyes to mine. "I was hoping you would move into the alpha house with me." My lips part in astonishment. "But knowing your stubbornness, I didn't think you'd agree to it. So I prepared a room within the alpha house where you would be safe and have anything you need." I'm silenced by it. "If you want, I can have all your things from the hut brought to it."

"You want me to move in with you?" I try wrapping my head around it, but it still sounds completely insane.

"I need you close. You are obviously much stronger than I am to be able to deny your wolf from pursuing me. But I am not so strong. I need to know that you are okay at all times."

I smirk, annoyed. "You're kidding me, right? You really think that I trust you and the people in that house?" He looks away for a moment. "I trust this whole pack about as far as I can throw them."

"Kate," he says low, shaking his head, "I'm trying. I told you before, I cannot fix everything. I cannot fix all those years of pain because I wasn't there for them. But I am here now. At least let me try."

"You walked away without knowing me. I'm walking away because you showed me who you were that night."

"You're right, that is who I was. Do you not see who I am now?" I look away, but he tugs my chin back at him. "I will change your mind." He walks away, leaving me in a daze.

Why? Why should I give him a chance? Because he did his job? Because he believed me after calling me guilty the night he found out who I was? It still hurt. No matter how much I told myself that I didn't need him, it still hurt.

"Looking pretty cozy there with our new alpha, Kate."

I roll my eyes and turn to Ruby. "It's none of your business who I speak to, Ruby."

She shakes her head and puts both palms up innocently. "Just stating an observation. You know, I wondered why our alpha would so easily put his trust in you enough to allow you to shift. I guess it's a lot simpler than I thought."

I thought she was baiting me at first, but then I realize, she is saying this for our audience. She is planting a seed in their mind. One that they will water and grow into a vicious man-eating rumor. What could I do but watch it happen?

"You know, Ruby, I really like that perfume you use. Must be a one of a kind."

"Of course it is. It was the only one that survived the trip in a tote. And I was quick enough to grab it and hold on."

"Yeah. It's just funny, the morning of the day I went into a coma, I remember smelling that exact fragrance on our alpha. But you say there is only one, how do you think that happened?" She glares at me. "You must have gotten very *cozy* to get your scent on him."

I could hear people from around us gasp quietly. She shrugs not so innocently. "It was the day you had your accident. Maybe you don't remember things the way they really happened."

I laugh dryly. "I know, the funny thing is, I remember exactly how I ended up in that river. I recall you being there." I smirk. "Thinking about it now...yes, it's all coming back to me now. Everything that happened that day is crystal clear in my mind. Should we share it together? It is, after all, your *almost* victory."

Conversations

I hadn't been able to rid my mind of the fact that there was a rogue wolf within the community. It made my throat tight to think about it. Rogues, the savages that they are. They would kill for sport like they'd done to my parents. Their kills were pointless. The rogues gained nothing from it. If by some chance, or freak accident, he gets loose, many innocent people may die. It had already been days since he was put under the watchful eyes of two fully trained warriors. I had no doubt that the warriors could handle him, but why should they have too? He has too much view of the community. Though the warriors guarding him are cautious, he seems to be watching every person in his view. Women carrying bread, warriors who are still in training. Everything.

"Does he make you nervous?" I jump at the sound of Leon's voice. "Didn't mean to scare you."

I shift my weight away from him. I have not forgiven him yet, and I have no intention of letting my guard down around him. We are standing just inside the tree line where the rogue has ignored for the last few days.

After he realizes that I have no intention of answering him, Leon continues his one-sided conversation. "I didn't see you at the first meal. Maddock brought a tray to your hu—home, but he said you weren't there."

I roll my eyes, annoyed. Before I make the decision to ignore him, I notice that we've caught the rogue's attention. His dark eyes watch us from within his cell. His eyes burn into my skin differently than the feeling of hatred that I have felt over the years from pack members.

His gaze feels uncomfortable and sorrowful. I could not name the feeling if I had a hundred years to do so. But it tells me one thing for certain—this rogue is beyond dangerous. Every cell in my body tells me this, yet I still find myself walking up to his cell, his eyes never leaving me. I stop just outside of arm's distance of the barred door.

"You are the one who discovered us," he speaks first.

I do not respond.

"Your parents attacked our alpha and paid the price for it."

My skin warms like molten lava, but I keep my expression dull.

"I never met a wolf of such white fur, but I suspect there aren't many." He looks toward the members getting along with their everyday duties. "How did they treat you when you were the only one left alive?"

That gets the smallest twitch from my expression.

"Did they let you mourn?" His icy gray eyes shift back to me, as if he could read me easily. Or at least easier than anyone else ever has. "I know what you're thinking, girl. 'What do I know?'" He smirks and leans toward the bars. "I know that you and I, we're the same."

"She's nothing like you!" Leon snaps from behind me. I hadn't even noticed him there. I thought he stayed by the tree line.

The rogue smirks. "And who are you? Not defensive enough to be a lover. Not passive enough to be a friend. You must be kin." He chuckles dryly. "A brother perhaps. A brother who'd left you out to dry."

Leon reaches through the bars and yanks the rogue against them, the two guards ready with their spears over Leon's shoulders. "What would you know? Nothing but a second-rate warrior. A criminal outcast by his own pack for goddess knows what. What would you know about kin?"

The rogue leans lazily into Leon's hold. "I know the look of someone who's been betrayed. She wears it better than anyone. And you—you stink of guilt. So you tell me, what do I know?"

Leon shoves away from the bars and storms away. The guards too stand back at their posts. Once again, I gain his attention.

"Edgy. I must be right."

"Alpha said you'd hardly spoken. Now you won't shut up."

"I don't mind riling up a conversation for a pretty girl." He grins, almost perverted, but it seems forced.

"Hmm, tell me this one thing then."

"What does the white wolf wish to hear?"

"You spoke about betrayal as if from experience. Tell me what your crime was."

His shoulders square, and his humored expression is now stern and hard. "They say I—"

"Did you?" I ask before he can continue. His whole demeanor changes.

He studies me. "Does it matter? I am still in this cage."

"You trespassed, that is why you are imprisoned, not because of past crimes."

"Aren't I?" I wait for him to continue. "Do you think they will let me go?" My eyes shift to the guards who are surely listening to every word but never look at either of us. "I am an outcast that stepped on your land, that is my crime here. The one who was found with me was killed for it. For being an outcast in the wrong place."

I shake my head slightly. "No, you plotted to come here."

He shrugs. "Maybe we were hoping to be accepted into another pack. Then we were greeted as hostiles and tried to flee but were apprehended instead and then inevitably, killed. Seems fair, wouldn't you say?"

I think about all those who still avoid me like a disease.

"You know it. The feeling of being a rogue. Even if they allowed you to stay, you will never get that trust back. They will always see you as a troublesome criminal. Just someone to be removed." My throat gets painfully tight. Again, his features change to sympathy. "You shouldn't stay where you are unwanted. I'm sure it's not healthy."

"Are you attempting to recruit me?"

He smirks with sadness in his eyes. "I would never subject someone to the life of a rogue, but there is a difference between being cast out and leaving."

The truth I hear in his words hit me hard. They were something my father would say to me. That thought screams at me as I look at the large pitiful man in this small cell. Speaking to me not with malice but with something that sounded a lot like concern.

"You're a father, aren't you?"

He hardens like stone, shutting down completely. His closed-off facade returns, and I know this conversation is over. I take a step back and examine his features. Scars almost completely covers his chest. Some peek over his shoulders from his back. Lashings. Alphas hadn't used lashing as a method of punishment, ever. I wonder if he'd gotten them from his rogue pack. Maybe as initiation of some sort.

"What are you doing?" Gabriel asks.

"Learning," I say, sidestepping around him.

He walks beside me. I can feel his agitation. He finally takes a breath and speaks, "What did you learn?"

I swallow, keeping my eyes forward. I don't want to tell him anything yet. Not until I'm sure, at least. "Very little. He's dangerous but not the way I thought."

Gabriel stays quiet for a long moment. A part of me, the wolf part, wonders what he is thinking. Finally, he speaks again. "I agree."

I'm taken aback, and he notices. "He's like none of the rogues I've encountered. He's shut tight but not for loyalty of the rogue pack." I agree silently.

"So you're going to try to earn his trust?" I guess.

"I don't think he will ever trust anyone."

But he spoke with me.

Do not make foolish choices, Circe says. *You are transparent. Repeating today's event by speaking with the rogue would be foolish.*

But if I could get something out of him, then it will be worth it.

Consider that he is giving you just enough information to get you to return. Who's to say that he isn't also prying information from you without your knowledge?

I'd like to think I'm a bit smarter than that. Also, you are here to keep me from saying too much.

You are playing with fire. Careful not to get everyone else burned with you.

Break

I had waited a few hours for the guard standing outside the rogue's cell to take a pee break or nap or something. I want more information, but I don't want it getting back to Gabriel that I was here, just yet. People had already found it strange that I spoke to the rogue at all. Like minds and all that. The guard finally wanders off for what I'm guessing is a bathroom break.

I move quickly from my hiding spot to the cell. The rogue shoots up from his lying position.

"I was wondering when you were going to make your way here." He smirked.

"You want to cause harm to the families of this pack?" I ask.

"Straight to the point, I see."

"Yes or no?"

He looks past me, in thought. I wonder slightly if he's thinking of lying. "I want the whole fucking world to hurt."

The distant look in his eyes says so much more, though. I need to hurry with my interrogation. "No, you want one person to hurt." His eyes reconnect with mine. "The one that wronged you." He fists his hands. "You're not a rogue because you committed a crime. You pissed someone off, and they got you exiled." I'm not positive, but I know I am close.

"Assuming is a bad habit."

"Only if I'm wrong."

He straightens and shakes his head, casting a bit of doubt in my mind. "You're not like any pack member I've come across." I stay quiet. "I don't—" He pauses. "Have a need to see your people hurt."

"What were your orders here?" I ask quickly but then hear footsteps. Crap, the guard.

"We all carry our weight in any pack," he whispers.

"Even at the cost of innocent lives?" The footsteps are too close. I don't wait for a response. I rush off back to my hut.

Kate, Circe says as I near home.

What is it?

You're right. He's not a rogue by choice.

Why the change of heart?

I heard his wolf.

I stop dead. Rogues lose their wolf spirit when they commit a crime against their packs. They are still able to turn, but it is almost like they are missing a piece of their soul when they do. It makes them that much more dangerous.

What did you hear?

His wolf whispered for him to be honest with himself, even if he didn't plan on being honest with you.

Was that before or after he told me that he didn't want to hurt us?

Before. He was telling the truth. I believe you got to him with your assumptions.

I run back to the alpha house and to Gabriel's room. I knock twice. When I don't hear a response, I knock again and again till he finally opens.

He's shocked to see me at his door this late. "What is it? What's wrong?" His hands go to my arms, holding me gently and checking to see if I'm hurt. I'm clearly out of breath.

"The rogue." I huff out. He straightens immediately and shoves me into his room and tries to close me in. "No, he's still encaged. But"—I take a breath—"he's not a rogue."

Gabriel's face contorts. "Kate." He sighs. "I know you want to believe that because you spoke to him but—"

"He has a wolf," I say.

Gabriel shakes his head. "That's impossible."

"My wolf heard him!" I snap. "He was wronged and kicked out of his pack. But it wasn't because he committed a crime."

"How do you know?" I close my mouth. Gabriel stands tall, waiting for my answer.

"Because it happened to me." It's not really a lie. "I can tell because I was wronged as well."

Do not lie to our alpha, Circe reminds me.

"Stop lying to me," Gabriel says.

"I'm not—" He grabs my face in one hand and holds me against the door. My mouth is covered.

"You would not have woken me this late because of a hunch. I will ask you again, how do you know?"

He adjusts his hold so that I can speak but am still in place. "I spoke with him."

"He didn't tell you anything about that when you spoke to him yesterday."

"I spoke with him tonight." I could see the slight anger in his eyes. "I needed to know why he wasn't putting up a fight. I needed to know why they were here."

He releases me completely. "Did he tell you?" I stay quiet. "Did he tell you why they were here?"

"No, but I think—"

"No, you didn't. If you did, you would have come to me first, not sneak around behind my back." I swallow. "Am I not to be trusted, Katherine?" I can really see the anger raging inside now.

My own fuse is being lit. "I didn't want to say anything till I was sure."

"But you're not sure! You have no facts! Just blind guesses."

My eyes water in anger. "I'm sorry for wasting your time, Alpha." I turn to leave.

Why had I even come here? What was I hoping for? It was a waste of time. The more I think about it, the angrier I get. When I'm out of the house, I run. I run so hard I don't even realize that I've turned. Circe has given me full control, though.

Why do I care so damn much? Even if he didn't commit the crime, he was cast out; it doesn't mean he hasn't committed any crime since. So why am I so bothered! Before I know it, I've run out of our territory. By the time I see where I am, I am pulled to a halt by the back of my neck. Once completely stopped, I'm released. I snarl and scramble to look at my attacker. Gabriel's wolf stands proud and tall in front of me. He shifts, and I follow.

"Where are you going?" he demands.

"I need air away from this place." I gesture to the community.

"The pack or just me?" he argues.

I put my hands on my hips and huff downward. "I need space from it all. You, the pack, rogues. I don't belong here, Gabriel, and we both know it."

His demeanor changes completely, darkly. "You are not leaving the pack."

"Excuse me? You cannot keep me here by force."

"If I feel you are a danger to the pack, I can. You are angry that I didn't listen to you about a rogue, and now you are trying to leave in the dead of night. My actions would not be questioned."

I'm breathing hard. Everything hurts. My head is pulsing. My stomach feels as if it's turning over. I'm shaking with rage. Circe is speaking to me, but I can't hear a word. My vision is blurred red. I shift and snarl at him. His wolf takes action and shifts to try to hold me down. I dodge his advance and charge in the direction away from the community. Gabriel follows after me, but I lose him easily.

I run harder than I have in years. I'm angry. I'm frustrated. I stopped being a member of the pack the day I lost my parents. I'm tired of being the guest that overstayed her welcome. I'm tired of fighting for a name that is long gone. I can't live like this anymore.

I will die before I let them bind me again. I run faster. The air feels cutting. I can't tell if it is getting colder or—

STOP!

Strangers

The wind is knocked out of me. I'm lying still on the ground. My ribs ache. I open my eyes and look up to see a wolf I don't recognize, holding me down. His body is perpendicular to mine. He's not even really paying attention to me. He's simply using his weight to hold me.

The thin moon is granting us just enough light to see each other. His fur is bright red. I'm in too much pain to try getting away. My ribs hurt, but I know they're not broken. My legs feel like lead. I'm tired. I lay there for moments, panting. Both of us are in complete silence. After a minute, he pushes off me and stands there, looking at me. I don't get up; I don't think I can. I shift so that I can manage the pain in my ribs from his tackle. He turns as well. I still don't recognize him. He crosses his massive arms and stares at me unapologetically.

"It's a crime to trespass on another pack's territory without permission." Even as I say it, I find myself annoyed by the irony.

"You're a long way from your territory, princess." His flaming red hair somehow suits his response.

"Don't call me princess."

"What should I call you? Suicidal?" he asks, gesturing to the path ahead of us. When I look, I see a straight drop off the edge of Mountain View Cliff. I hadn't even noticed that I was so close. How long had I been running?

"I'm not suicidal. I didn't see it."

"Yeah, running in the dark tends to have that effect." I roll my eyes.

"Kate!" Gabriel runs up beside me. An expression of familiarity enters his face when he notices the stranger.

"Dylan," he greets the stranger with a nod. "You're early."

"I'd say I was just on time. I was about to enter your territory when I saw the little snowflake trying to fly." Gabriel looks from the cliff to me.

"I didn't see it," I say, looking away.

"Let's go. It's late," he orders us.

"No," I say, stepping away from him.

He turns to me, authoritative, and I know I'm speaking to the alpha again. "You are coming back."

The tension is thick. I have no intention of returning tonight. Alpha or not, I will not be forced back. Before the tension could get any thicker, an obnoxiously loud yawn erupts from beside us. Dylan stretches dramatically.

"Yeah, no offense, but your territory is a way off, and I'm about ready to drop. I think I'll sleep out here as well and enter in the morning."

A look passed between them, and Gabriel grabs my chin. "I will be back for you tomorrow." I nod my understanding, and he goes on his way, clearly annoyed.

"Geez. Such melodrama already," he says lazily, looking after Gabriel.

I glance at the stranger over my shoulder. "Who are you?"

He looks at me cynically. "Uh, Dylan."

"I mean, who are you to him? He wouldn't leave me here so easily. Especially with another male."

Dylan sighs as he seats himself roughly on the ground. "What can I say, I'm a trustworthy guy."

Annoyed with his lack of an answer, I look out over the cliff. I almost ran right off it. "Thank you." I don't look at him.

"It was nothing. Women naturally end up in my arms." I cross my arms and roll my eyes.

"So why are you running away?" he asks casually.

"Who says I am?" He gives me a knowing look. "I just needed space."

"From the whole pack?"

"You wouldn't understand." I shake my head.

"Yeah, you're probably right. Probably best to just keep it all inside anyways." He lies back, lacing his fingers behind his head and closing his eyes.

Since the river incident, he's the only one that hasn't tried prying for more information. A part of me knows that this is some sort of manipulation. The other part of me simply likes being asked without being forced.

"I don't belong here," I say quietly.

"Mm, me neither. Too cold all alone. I prefer a warm body next to me."

"I don't belong with the pack."

"Oh, is that what you meant?" I hear the sarcasm, but it's not as annoying as before. "Why do you think you don't belong?"

"I was accused of a crime a long time ago. People have treated me differently since."

"Did you commit the crime?" he asks bluntly.

"No, but they don't care."

"Well, apparently one of them does."

"Gabriel just wants me around because of his wolf."

"So you're his mate," he states factually.

I nod, sitting where I am across him.

"And you don't want him as your mate?"

"It's not that simple."

"It actually is. Either you want to stand beside him, or you don't." He shrugs awkwardly.

"He initially rejected me."

"And then?"

"And then?"

"Well, I'm assuming he recanted. Otherwise, why would he care if you left?"

"His wolf probably swayed him."

Dylan laughs dramatically. "Let me ask you this. Did you feel the pull from your wolf when you realize Gabriel was your mate?"

"Of course."

"But you can resist it?"

I shrug. "I guess."

"So you believe that your willpower is stronger than his?" I sit up straighter and look away. "That is what you're saying, isn't it? He can't resist the pull of his wolf, but you can."

"I'm not a possession. He can't just snap his fingers and expect me to forgive and forget."

"So it's really about pride? What is it that you expect him to do to earn your trust again?"

I never thought about it. "Since I was fourteen, I've been treated like trash or completely helpless. I just hate feeling like he's doing me a favor by accepting me simply because of my past and his title."

Dylan perches himself up on his elbows and looks at me. "So you're refusing him because you're afraid of how it will look to people who've treated you like trash. That's some reason."

"Hey, I am not insecure." I snap.

"Kinda sounds like you are." I huff, ready to end the conversation. "For some reason, the goddess felt you two belonged to each other. It doesn't matter why. It's just a fact. You two are mates. It is what it is. You don't see it as a favor because you didn't choose. He doesn't see it as a favor because he didn't choose. You both feel the magnetic pull. The only people that might see it as a favor are people who already don't like you. So who cares what they think? As far as I can tell, you're not begging him. It's the other way around."

I look down at my knees. Is it really just my insecurity holding me back? The rogues entering our land and Gabriel being overprotective put me on a spin. Maybe I overthought his want to have me beside him. I kept seeing it through my guarded vision. Not wanting him to get too close if it only meant getting hurt by him.

"Well, hearing about your sad love life is fun and all, but I'm gonna catch some sleep." He lays back again.

Circe. There is no response. *I'm sorry.* Again, silence. *Please don't ignore me.*

I swallow the growing lump in my throat. Since awakening, she has been my constant rock. I pushed her away when I should have pulled her close. I'll try talking to her in the morning, I promise myself. I lay as comfortably as I can and look up at the moon, its gentle glow almost lulling me to sleep. There is so much I need to think about, but it will have to wait till morning.

Start Again

"So this is Gabe's territory? The way he described it, I thought it'd be bigger."

I roll my eyes. Dylan has been making small talk feel like the talking about the birds and the bees with your parents. Painful and unnecessary.

"I was about to leave," Gabriel says as he approaches us.

"It's fine, I had a guide," Dylan answers.

I can see a vein on Gabriel's neck bulging. Already he's annoyed with Dylan. I smirk, thankful it's not just me. Dylan isn't actually annoying. His sarcasm is not for those in a bad mood, though.

"We woke early and walked back," I say, feeling as if I need to explain.

Gabriel nods and looks at Dylan. "I'll show you your room. Just give me a minute." Dylan nods and eyes me as he walks off into the distance somewhere. "Breakfast will be in a few minutes. You should go get a seat."

I stay planted. "I think we should talk." His expression is more serious than before. I guess I never gave us a chance to have a real conversation.

"James," he shouts to a warrior in the distance. The young man runs up. "Show my guest to his room." He gestures to Dylan.

The warrior nods and walks off. I walk in the direction Dylan and I just came from. Not fast at all; in fact, I am taking incredibly slow steps.

Gabriel stays quiet. I'm sure he is giving me the chance to talk first. Finally, I build up the nerve.

"I'm not used to this. Having people dote on me."

"I've hardly done so," he whispers.

"You've done more than you think." I stop and face him. "I don't like being forced to do or not to do things with the justification being that it's because I belong to someone."

"I got carried away last night. If you—" He looks away and swallows hard. "If you want to leave…then I will let you go."

"You will?"

His breathing becomes a bit hard like he is fighting himself. "But you have to promise me that you will be happier. Otherwise, we'll both be miserable."

I nod slowly. "Thank you." I look up at the small rays of sun that shine brightly through the leaves of the high treetops. "If I'm being honest, I don't want to be alone," I say quietly. I feel his eyes on me. I meet them. "I've never said it out loud. I miss having people who unapologetically love me. Being alone makes that impossible. It's probably why I never left all these years."

"It's funny," he says without humor, "I've never been so possessive—edging on obsessive—about anyone before you. I regret not taking you in my arms the day we met. And you avoiding me is driving me insane. I always want to know where you are and who you are with. I don't know if that's love. I don't think it is, but I can't give you to anyone else. I won't." An alpha admitting his obsession with a lowly wolf, it's unheard of. I so desperately want to hear Circe's advice, but she is still on radio silence.

"How about we start again? Without all the theatrics."

"No." His tone is flat and certain. "I made mistakes with you. I will not pretend they didn't happen. I will spend the rest of my life making it up to you, though. That is, if you accept me." He eyes me, hopeful.

"If we're not starting new, then I need time. And if I go to you with information that I think is important, don't write me off as child playing detective. The things I have learned are important, even if you don't think they are. And I am the one who has gotten him to talk."

He exhales. "I know I overreacted, but do you really believe that he is telling you this information out of goodwill? It is much more likely that he is feeding you stories because he thinks you are naive enough to believe them." I try not to feel insulted, but it doesn't work.

"Or maybe you just think that I'm too naive to be able to tell the difference between a fable and the truth."

"You have no evidence that he is telling you the truth, Kate."

"Why did you allow him to live?" I ask. "He was just as guilty as the other rogue, but you spared him. Why?"

He parts his lips but stays silent.

"It was a gut instinct, wasn't it? Something made you feel that he was somehow different."

"It was you," he says through gritted teeth.

"What?"

"I didn't kill him because something about him reminded me of you."

"Then you agree with me. Because if my suspicions are correct—and I believe they are—he is innocent of the crime he was exiled for. That is the only thing that he and I would have in common."

"Even if you're right, what am I supposed to do with that? Do you trust him enough to let him wander free in our territory?" I hesitate. "I can't risk the lives of everyone here because he *might* be innocent." I'm annoyed because I know he's right. Having this information does nothing for us or him. Gabriel cups my cheek. "Keep trying. If he talks to you, then try to find out whatever you can. About him or the other rogues. Every bit is a piece of the puzzle."

I nod. I'm a bit happy that he has trusted me to keep searching for the truth. I start to walk back when he catches my elbow. I look back at him.

"What is it?"

"Be careful. Don't let anything go to your head. I'm not saying this because you're my mate. I'd say it to any one of my warriors. Don't let anyone fool you." I see the brutal truth in his gaze. He really is concerned.

*****

After our talk, Gabriel goes to speak with Dylan. I head for the gathering area to collect my breakfast. Leon and Maddock sit with me, uncomfortably. I don't speak to them, and they don't initiate in conversation with me. My eyes drift to where the rogue sits in his cell, watching as we all eat. I could see the bowl that was given to him. I'm sure it has something inedible within it. Looking down at my half-eaten breakfast, I decide that it was too much for me to finish.

I look back to the cell and have every intention of giving my leftovers to the prisoner. Just as I am about to get up, Leon speaks.

"I'm sorry for losing my temper yesterday. I should have stayed beside you."

Maddock looks from Leon to me. He always has the perfect puppy dog eyes. "It's fine," I say indifferently. I stand, and they both rise with me. I look at them. "I don't need an escort."

"Not unless it's with me, right, princess?" I turn to see Dylan and Gabriel walking over to our table. "You're not leaving already, are you? I hadn't even gotten my food yet."

"Well, they can keep you company." I nod at Leon and Maddock.

Dylan looks at them for half a second, then back at me. "No, they have a depressing vibe about them. Like their goldfish just died."

"We eat fish," Leon says, not understanding the reference.

Dylan looks at him in disbelief for a second. "It's a good thing you're pretty." A laugh erupts from me and surprises everyone but Dylan.

"I'll be right back then."

I walk over to the cell and eye the guards. I slide the tray of food into the cell. "I ate half of it," I say to the rogue.

He scarfs it down without wasting a moment. I spy the bowl that was meant to be his breakfast. I was right; something gray and rubbery looking was inside. I wouldn't have eaten it either. I take a step back to let him eat in peace and catch the disapproving look of both guards.

When I rejoin the table, Leon and Maddock look at me, bewildered.

"Why do you care so much about the rogue?" Maddock asks.

"Because that could have been me," I say bluntly. "If anything changed back then, it could have been me in that cell or exiled." I sigh before continuing. "And for something I didn't do." I don't look at them as I say it.

"You don't think he committed the crime he was exiled for?" Leon asks.

I look at him, then the rest of them. All are waiting on my answer, though Gabriel already knows. I shrug. "Is it really so taboo to think so? Until recently, you all thought I was capable of killing my parents." I look back at the cell; the rogue is now finished and looking in our direction. "And two of you are blood-related."

"I didn't think so." Dylan has a raised hand when I look at him. "But then again, I didn't know you were accused of that." He nods with closed eyes. I smirk. His personality is really starting to grow on me. I've never met someone who could so easily make a heavy situation seem so light. Dark humor and all, I guess.

"Well, I'm hungrier than a rogue locked in a cell," Dylan says. "Show me to the food, Kate."

I smile when the others shake their heads. I cross my arms to hug myself. "This way." I point.

After Dylan and my brothers finish eating, Gabriel asks if I have taken the herbal tea that the doc prescribed. "What for? I'm fine."

"She recommended—"

"That I take it because I hadn't shifted in so long. Since then, I have shifted multiple times, and my body feels fine now."

"Mm, gotta love a strong woman," Dylan says, smiling.

"Not now, Dylan." Gabriel shoots him a look that Dylan ignores.

"No time like the present," he says, pushing past Gabriel to stand beside my seated position at the table. I almost laugh at his dismissal of Gabriel. "Gabe, how could you not tell at first sight that this girl is innocent." I lift a brow at the word *innocent*. "I mean, of what you were accused of. I won't pretend to know what you do in you free time." He winks.

I snort a laugh out, and Gabriel snaps. "Hey! She's not a—"

"Don't finish that sentence, Gabe, because I can already tell it's going to be insulting." No more insulting than your last reference to my private life.

"Like you didn't just insult her?"

"I didn't, did I?" He looks at me for support.

I raise my hands. "I want no part in this."

Dylan smiles brightly. I have never met someone so enthusiastic. "Well, how about we go for a run?"

"Uh—"

"No, she needs to take her medicine, and then rest."

"Geeze, possessive much?" Dylan says, rolling his eyes at Gabriel. "She needs them."

"I already said I feel fine," I counter.

"See, she's fine." Dylan grabs my hand and pulls me up from the bench. "Besides there's no better medicine than shifting and going for a run." I giggle.

Gabriel crosses his arms and blocks the way. "Dylan, she needs to rest."

"Gabe, she needs to shift." Dylan mocks. "If what you said is true, and she has only turned twice for five years, then you know as well as I that her wolf can heal her better than any medicine a doctor gives her." Dylan pushes past Gabriel.

I like this male, Circe says.

I smile. My heart begins pounding. *Circe! Where have you been! I've missed you.*

Now is not the best time to explain. She goes quiet again.

"Bring her back before the evening meal," Gabriel demands, holding Dylan by the bicep. Dylan gives a curt nod, and Gabriel releases him. I want to say that I'm not his possession, but I know there'd be no point. In Gabriel's mind, I belong to him. Fighting about it with him will only keep me here longer.

Dylan pulls me to the edge of our village where the river starts. "Come on, wolfie. Let's see what'cha got."

He turns into a large red-furred wolf. I turn and watch his interaction with Circe. He begins to run at a full sprint, and at first, Circe struggles to keep up. Then our second wind comes, and we dominate.

Circe leaves Dylan paces behind. We run till we reach the falls. Circe pants slowly, as if she hasn't broken a sweat. Dylan meets us seconds later and shifts. I turn as well.

"You're fast," he says with a smile.

"Circe loves to run. I should do it more often since I'm not banned from it anymore."

"Circe?"

"My wolf, her name is Circe." Something I recognize as guilt floods his eyes. It was strange seeing it on his face. What did he have to feel guilty about? "Did I say something?"

"No, it's just…Gabriel told me that you didn't get your wolf till later on in your life. I had mine for years and never had I asked his name."

I press my lips into a thin line. "Well, our wolves are our other halves. We share the same body. Isn't it only natural that we know each other's names?"

"I guess that's true." He goes quiet for a moment, and I realize that he is probably having a silent conversation with his wolf. I turn my attention back to the beautiful view of the vast forest. It is amazing how small my life's problems seem from here. The rushing water crashes off the cliff and into a smaller river, which leads to a very large lake. Beautiful.

"It's peaceful up here." Dylan breaks the silence. "It's as if every tree, every drop of water, and fallen twig is exactly where it's supposed to be. Everything has its place."

I don't respond. I think on it. *Everything has its place.* The wind blows gently and the earth's musk along with it. It's warmer today. I look at Dylan. His unruly dark-red hair is ear-length and frizzed from the run or the mist in the air. His muscles flex as his hands fall on his hips. He is an attractive guy.

"You aren't falling for me, are you?" he asks without looking.

I smile without shame. "I was just wondering…"

"Yes?"

"You're a pretty attractive guy."

"Thank you." He smiles arrogantly.

"So why wouldn't Gabriel be concerned with me being around you."

His smile fades ever so slightly and shrugs. "Haven't a clue, but ya know, if you do feel the urge to leave him in the dust." He wiggles his eyebrow up and down.

I roll my eyes. "I need to get used to these noninsults," I say, walking away.

I hear him chuckle behind me. "Come on, I'll race you to the lake."

"That's quite a run. Gabriel wants me back before the evening meal." I was never really a rule-breaker, and I care little for starting unnecessary fights.

"Come on." Dylan whines. "They thought you were a murderer for years. You deserve to break the rules every now and then."

"It's off the territory."

"Only by a bit." He turns toward me and sighs when he sees me planted where I stand. "Okay, when was the last time you did something stupid, crazy, and fun?" Never. He sees the answer in my eyes. "Well, this is child's play, and we'll be back when the food is getting served."

I sigh and nod my head. His smile breaks free, and he shifts into his wolf and begins to run. I take a look behind me. I'm suddenly more aware of my surroundings. I shift, and Circe chases after Dylan. We get to the border of the territory, and Circe stops.

Kate, I won't go unless you're okay with it too. I feel nervous, but I give her the go-ahead.

We reach the lake an hour before the last meal. We sit there in silence for a few minutes before we both agree to return. When we're back up the cliff, Gabriel's black fur catches my eye. Circe halts at his angry eyes. Dylan comes up behind me and sees Gabriel's expression as well. Both Leon and Maddock are with him.

Gabriel steps toward us, and my head and ears instinctively dips. He steps past me to Dylan. *I said before the evening meal! Where were you!*

I took her to the lake. She ran very well. Her wolf needed to stretch her legs, Dylan says, standing tall.

If I cannot trust you to bring her back when I ask—

It's not only his fault. I agreed to go, I say, trying to defend Dylan.

I DON'T CARE! Gabriel shouts, using his commanding tone. I dip my head again, and Circe let's out a small but noticeable whine. Gabriel pulls back and begins walking. *Let's go.*

When we get close to the gathering area, we all shift. Gabriel leads the way. Dylan and I follow behind Leon and Maddock. Gabriel leads us to the alpha house.

"Let's go, Kate. You need to eat," he says. Dylan gives my shoulder a reassuring squeeze, and I walk inside.

"Alpha, may I speak with you?" Dylan asks. Gabriel is already on edge but agrees.

I sit on a small bench just within the entrance of the alpha house. *I don't like the feeling of anxiety that comes with breaking the rules, Circe.*

I know, Kate. I could have said no too. I fiddle with my fingers, waiting for Gabriel to return.

I couldn't even enjoy the feeling of the lake. I was constantly thinking about how long it would take to return.

Next time we visit, it will be with Alpha's permission. She pauses. *We should speak as well.*

I'm sorry. I figure that my state of mind must have upset you.

I have guided many before you, Kate. Many with shorter tempers. I was not upset with you. I was forced out.

I gulp. *What do you mean? You were pulled away? Did the goddess change her mind about pairing you with me?*

No. The goddess has no say over who we choose. I was forced out by you. My heart rate spikes. *You were so upset. You wanted to be away from everything and everyone. Including me. You pushed me from this body. It is the first time, in all my long life, that it has happened to me. Your mind is the strongest I have ever known, and that can be dangerous.*

How—I didn't even—

Your emotions. They have strong sway over your powers.

My powers? I don't—

Every Luna has powers. Over the last three hundred years, though, none have been able to tap into theirs. I believe it is your past, which has made you so strong. Your dignity. Your willpower. It took much longer to return to you because, by natural law, you shouldn't be able to receive a wolf more than once in your lifetime. Just be cautious of this. Of your emotions. Do not let them control you.'

I'm sorry. I never want to lose you.

Nor I you.

I hear footsteps coming up behind me. Gabriel steps beside me, obviously still angry. He sighs before looking away from me.

"I won't apologize for having fun," I say softly. "I just didn't think it—"

"No, you didn't think, did you?" His favorite insult. Still, it's cutting. "You didn't think about how I would worry. Or about what would happen to you if rogues decided to attack. Do you think your parents gave their lives wanting you to put yourself in danger again?" A large lump of bile lodge in my throat. Why bring them up? "I can't allow you to shift if I can't trust you to return when promised."

I look at him, stunned. No. Not again. Please don't take that away from me again. His hard expression falters. He runs a hand through his hair and releases a frustrated grunt.

Lifting my chin, he looks me dead in the eyes. "Promise me you will return when I say, and stay within the territory when you shift." His eyes are still angry, but now I can see the concern as well. I nod. "I need to hear you say it."

"I promise." My voice is weaker than I want it to be.

He raises his head. "I want you to stay in the alpha house tonight." Before I can argue, he continues, "You can leave in the morning if you want, but tonight I need you close. I need to know you are within reach if I need to protect you."

I look around at the fading crowd. Many have already retired for the night. The few that stay to linger watch our transaction. I don't really care anymore, though. I don't need anyone's approval to speak to or love who I want. I nod my answer. He exhales, relieved.

"I will show you to your room, then I will bring you a tray of food since you missed the evening meal along with your medicine. Since it's nearly dark, grogginess shouldn't be a problem." I roll my eyes because I really don't need the herbs, but I nod nonetheless.

Lights Out

My room was very spacious. It had a queen-size bed and beige beddings. The walls were a cream color, and the personal bathroom matched. I was in awe for half a moment before Gabriel had asked how I liked it. My pride made me act as if it was no big deal. But I could live in that room and never complain a day in my life. It was twice the size of my entire hut, not including the personal bathroom. Gabriel had wished me a good night, then left. I half-expected him to hover, but I was glad he didn't.

Awaking the next morning was just as blissful as the amazing night's sleep. Even Circe was pleased with our surroundings. Dylan had talked about staying close to home the next couple of days. I figured that Gabriel must have given him a hell of a talk, not that he said. When Dylan asked to go for a run today, I denied and told him I just wanted to read by the river instead. He invited himself and tagged along. After enjoying a less-than-uncomfortable breakfast with Dylan and my brothers, we headed to the river together.

"It's been hours. Let's do something." Dylan whines for the second time since we got here.

I sigh and keep my book firmly on my lap. "It's been twenty minutes. I told you to bring a book."

"I don't have anything fun to read. And why would I want to read when we could be doing something fun and entertaining?"

"Mm, well, this is fun and entertaining to me. And you decided to come, I didn't force you." He's lying perched up with his elbows behind him, and his long legs are crossed in front of him. He turns his head to give me an annoyed look. I roll my eyes. "Here, try this." I hand him my book. "I found it in one of the containers the nomads brought."

He takes it and looks at the cover. "What's it about? Fruit at night?"

I giggle. "I just started it, but it's not half-bad. It's about a girl who is obsessed with a guy."

"Wow. She must have daddy issues."

"Well, he's kinda obsessed about her too."

"Sounds like a mental couple."

"Would you shut up?" He smiles. "Anyways, he's a vampire who goes to a normal school, and she's human. But he seems to show up whenever she's in trouble."

"Ugh, sounds like an interpretation of *Beauty and the Beast*."

"I guess it is kind of like that, except the person who would be Gaston's character is a pretty good guy."

"No such thing as a good Gaston. Bet more than anything, Gaston's character tries to make a move on her like the original Gaston."

"I guess you'll have to read it to find out, huh?"

Before he can answer, we both hear twigs snapping from behind us. I turn to see Ronny coming into view. My pulse quickens but not out of fear. Circe and I are simply on high alert now. There's just something off about him. His presence is off-putting.

"Hello, Kate." The way he says my name is almost sinister. A chill runs down my spine, and I can hear Circe growling in my ears.

He does not mean well, Kate.

I know, I respond, getting to my feet.

"What are ya guys doing out here?" His voice is low and cryptic. Dylan notices my apprehension and rises to his feet as well. He has a whole head over Ronny.

"We were just leaving actually." Dylan drapes an arm over my shoulder and ushers me to the other side of him as he guides us away.

"Don't go on my account," Ronny says, cautiously putting his hands in his pockets.

"We're not, but I just remembered that Alpha needed to speak to me."

"Well, why don't I keep Kate company while you speak to Alpha?"

"That sounds like a great idea, if only she didn't just promise to go with me."

Ronny nods unnervingly slow. "Maybe next time." We turn to leave and hear Ronny bid one last farewell. "See you around, Kate."

Once out of earshot, Dylan shudders dramatically. "Ugh, some people really can't catch a hint. Who the hell was that?"

"Ronny, he's one of Leon's friends," I say, looking down at my feet.

"And?" He moves his hand in a circular motion, urging me to continue.

"When we were younger, I'd follow him and Leon around. We'd make believe that I was a warrior princess, and they were my knights in shining armor. He told me once that he was going to marry me." Dylan smirks; I return it. "At seven years old, I thought there was no finer man to marry, except my brothers and dad. When my parents died, Ronny was the last to believe that I did anything wrong. He said he'd protect me from anyone who said otherwise." I take a small breath. "But I told him not to. I was so upset about the way things turned out for me that I snapped and told him to just fend for himself. I was upset, but honestly, I didn't want him getting pulled into the middle of it. He didn't take the rejection well. Two weeks after that, he became my biggest tormentor."

I can see Dylan shaking his head from my peripheral vision. "Man has no patience. A real man would have waited for you, especially after you had just lost your parents and had the entire world against you."

Shaking my head, I continued, "For a long time, I thought I should have accepted his protection. I would think, if only I hadn't discarded him so easily, maybe we would still be friends."

Dylan stops and turns me to face him. Both his hands find my shoulders as he dips to look me in the eyes.

"Hey, look at me. That is a toxic person with toxic intentions. You did nothing wrong. It is not your fault that he couldn't control his emotions. His actions are not your fault. He was going to snap eventually. Rejection might have just triggered it."

I know it's true, but even knowing that I triggered his rage is uncomfortable. I somehow feel like I am the cause of our friendship's demise. The thought is sickening. Dylan sighs and releases me.

"Let's go see how much trouble we'll be in if we sabotage the kitchen before the staff gets there."

His playfulness lifts my dimmed mood. "You're a bad influence." He smiles and pulls me toward the gathering area.

After the midmeal—which we didn't sabotage—Dylan and I stay seated after Gabriel had left to work on the alliance with other packs. Since he was a new alpha, he would have to prove that he is strong enough and witty enough to keep the alliances that had already been formed by his predecessor. Because of our encounter with Ronny, Dylan and I agree that it would be best to stay where we could find an easy excuse not to speak with him. What I didn't anticipate for was Ruby to approach us.

"Kate, how are you? I've been wanting to come talk to you, but it never seemed like the right time."

Dylan watches her from across the table, resting his head on his fist. "Hello, I'm Dylan."

She glances at him in what looks like repulsion but quickly plasters on a smile. "Oh yes, you're from that pack in the east. I heard you trained with Alpha. Pity you weren't chosen to be alpha of your own pack." The forced smile she plasters on while she speaks is painful to watch.

My protective instincts for my friend kick in. "This is his pack now. Alpha accepted him, so he is a member of our colony. Claiming that his loyalties should be placed elsewhere is insulting to Alpha."

Her face burns bright pink, but she bites her tongue and forces another smile. "Anyways, I was glad to hear you were okay after you slipped and fell in the river."

I nod slowly. "Yeah, I came out of it just fine. Thankfully, and I was even allowed to shift and capture a rogue who knew about my parents' deaths. Lucky me." She exhales, relieved, before I continue, "But as I recall, you were upset about something I said and pushed me into that river."

"I—" she starts, but Dylan stands, intimidating her into silence.

"That's code for you to go," he says, authorized.

She looks him up and down before looking back at me. "Well, you know you can't trust what rogues say. They may say anything to save their own skin."

I stand this time. "Why don't you say what you really came here to say."

"All right, I think you're whoring yourself out to the alpha in order to have a warm bed to sleep in. But I promise, he will never choose you to be Luna."

Bystanders and passersby halt in shock at her venomous words. I barely flinch, though. It is one of her better insults, but like a fly on the shoulder, I just swat it away.

An angry smirk plays on her lips. I swing my legs over the bench and stand in front of her. For several seconds, we stand toe to toe, and then I punch her lights out. Some bystanders look around at one another before deciding it is none of their damn business and continue on their way. Others walk up to Ruby's limp body and carry her to the Med Center, none ever making eye contact with me.

Someone must have informed Gabriel of what just happened because he came out of the alpha house and in front of me in seconds. "What happened?" he says, looking at me.

"Some girl came for a bite a bit late into the meal," Dylan answers, waving his hand toward the empty tables.

"Ruby?" Dylan shrugs. "What happened?"

"Kate gave her the bite she was looking for," Dylan gloats. He stands up and claps Gabriel's shoulder. "Be careful, Gabe, she packs a hell of a punch." He leaves with a wide grin.

Gabriel looks at me with a confused look. "I punched her. She's in the Med Center."

His expression changes to surprised. He crosses his arms, and for the first time since I've known him, I think he's speechless.

All he manages is, "Good. Don't make punching people a habit. I'm going back to work." He comes close, his lips a gentle caress on my forehead. It had been so quick of an action that he walks off before I can scold him on it. Normalcy. This is getting entirely too comfortable.

It was just a peck, Circe says.

I don't want it, I respond. *I can't stay in the alpha house tonight. He'll think that it's okay to treat me like his woman otherwise.*

I'm sure he kissed you simply because he wanted to, not because you stayed in the alpha house. Kate, if you plan to turn him down, then do so. Do not give him misguided hope. It is not fair to him, and it will only waste both of your time. Love him or leave him…permanently.

I sigh because I know she's right. Even if he had rejected me originally, he doesn't deserve me stringing him along. *I need to think about it. I'll know by tonight,* I say.

Another Betrayal

"What really happened, Dylan?" I hear Gabriel ask Dylan.

I had intended to ask about his ventures with the other alphas, or at least it would have been my excuse to speak with Gabriel to try to recognize how I feel about him. I stop short when I hear Gabriel's calm but demanding voice.

"Actually, the day started out shitty. I took her to the river because she wanted to read, and some dude named Ronny showed up."

What the hell was this? Why was Dylan giving a play-by-play of the day?

"And?" I hear Gabriel say.

"She seemed disturbed by his presence, so I made up an excuse for us to leave. She has a complicated history with him."

"Complicated how?"

"They had puppy love that seemed to become something more as they got older. When she lost her parents, her pain made her reject his affection. Now it seems—"

I burst into the room in anger. "What the fuck is this?" I look angrily at Dylan, who looks surprised by my entrance.

Gabriel stands slowly, his hand reaching in front of him. "Kate, calm dow—"

"Don't tell me to calm down! What is this! Why are you telling him everything!" I ask Dylan furiously. "I confided in you because I thought you were my friend!"

I haven't felt the betrayal of a friendship in a long time. It hurts more than I remember.

"I get it. He told you to watch me and report to him! You never gave a damn about me! Just another lie. Just a warrior following commands." Dylan looks remorseful. I bite down on my lip to not let any tears fall.

"Kate, he didn't—" Gabriel started, attempting to calm me down.

"Shut up! You put him up to this! Why? I haven't done a god-damn thing, but somehow, I'm always the one put under the scope!" My words become nearly inaudible as I choke back sobs. "Why do I always have to prove myself? I didn't do anything wrong!" I look at Dylan. "Why couldn't you just be a friend? There's always a catch with people here." My voice is low, and I can't hide the pain. I can't suck it up, and I really don't want to try.

Gabriel attempts to move around his desk to reach for me, but I turn and leave. I'm not staying here another minute. I bolt out the door.

Kate, give them a chance to explain.

I don't want to hear anything they have to say! I'm done being the outcast. Mate or not, I don't need to stay here. I don't need friends. I don't need anyone but you.

Kate, Circe's voice is soft. She attempts to change as I run through the trees. I know it's not to take control. I know she only wants me to stop and listen for a moment. But I can't. I've been hurt by everyone. I have no one who cares enough to really think about how their action might affect me.

I run and run and run. Then I find myself in front of my home. The one I lived in for the last five years. Everything happened so fast that I hadn't realized how much I missed this small hut. I walk inside and see my untouched bed. That's not surprising; the one I've been sleeping on is new. I take my shoes off and climb into bed. I curl up, and I can't lose my cool like last time. I cry myself to sleep because even though I'm angry, even though I hate that I let myself trust and ended up hurt again, I'm angrier at myself more than I am at them. Thinking about it, I shut my eyes.

I wake to the dripping sound of my old sink. I have never fig-ured out how to fix it. It is dark in the small room. I turn over to face the wall, and something near my foot stops me dead. I look down and see Leon in the darkness. I choke back a scream, but my gasp comes out loud and clear.

"I didn't mean to scare you. I just walked in." I sit up and reach for my lamp. It's not there. "No light in here other than that old lamp." I look around the small room. No one else. "I haven't told Gabriel that I found you yet. I wanted to talk to you first." His voice is very low. He may be trying his best not to scare me. A little too late for that, especially when I wake to you!

"Before you tell me that you never want to speak to me, please just listen." I stay silent, allowing him to continue. "I know I hurt you beyond repair. I'm not the person that Mom and Dad raised me to be. I know I wasn't there when you needed me. I can't take back everything that I've done to you. I wish I could, goddess knows that I wish I could." In the dim lighting, I think I see his eyes water. "I won't apologize again because I know that it can do nothing but remind you of what I've done." He takes in a deep breath. "I want you to know that I'm leaving the pack." Shock overcomes me. "I am going to hunt the rogues that killed our parents." What! "When I find them, I will bring back their heads or I won't come back at all."

I shake my head. No matter what he's done to me, I don't want him dead. And hunting these rogues will surely kill him. These rogues were seriously trained, and they will not fight honorably. "Don't be stupid. They are merciless." My words are barely audible.

"I will return when I have killed—"

I cut him off and hug him tightly. So he's won. I couldn't hold hatred against him. I tried to hate him. I wanted to hate him and Maddock more than anything. They got away with it all. As I realize this, all the sadness and feelings of betrayal come out in tears. I'm really getting sick of crying all the damn time. Without letting him go, I begin to release what I have been holding back all this time.

"You could have protected me. You could have believed in me. I don't think you ever once asked me how I was coping with the loss. You blamed me. You broke me down, and you always went for blood. Never did you ensure that I would live to see tomorrow. And if I hadn't pulled myself out of the water, I would have died when you walked away." I sniffle. "I'm tired of feeling angry or afraid of the only family I have left. So I forgive you because I will not be your excuse to leave. I hope you stay safe within the pack." I pull completely away from him. "Because contrary to what you might think, I don't want you gone, and I don't want you dead."

I see the tears fall down his cheeks, but he is silent and still. He holds my gaze until Gabriel rushes in. Leon stands and walks out. Gabriel sees my tearstained face and is about to go after him when I call to him.

"What do you want?" I ask calmer than I feel. Forgiving Leon and Maddock lifted a weight off my shoulders.

"I—why did you run from me? I was worried about where you were or if you were hurt."

"I'm fine." I look down. "I don't want you keeping tabs on me like some kind of caged pet."

"Kate, I only wanted to—" He rubs the back of his neck. "I wanted to know more about you. You never tell me anything."

"Alpha." He flinches at my formality. "I'm not your property to toy with. I really thought Dylan was my friend."

He kneels in front of me and grabs my hand. "I'm sorry. But I only told Dylan to keep you safe. He befriended you on his own. I understand your anger with me for lying to you. I just needed to keep you safe. I—"

"When you officially introduced him to me, you said we could be good for each other. What did you mean?"

"You needed someone who wasn't here for all the hatred you received. You needed someone who wasn't family and who wasn't me. I can't give you the kind of friendship you need. I never asked Dylan to befriend you, but I knew he would like you. And I hoped you'd like him too."

"And how would I be good for him?"

Gabriel looks at the door, then back at me. "He's had it rough too. Not nearly as rough as you, but let's just say he has no one else. I promise you, though, he never meant to hurt you."

I stare at him, looking for any signs of lying. I find none. Finally, I nod. "I believe you." He exhales a sigh of relief. "But I don't want to have to watch what I confide in people because I'm worried about what will get back to you."

He nods. "Fine. Will you come back to the alpha house with me?"

Please, Circe begs to me.

I nod slowly. "I will, but I don't want you coming into my room as you please. That is my personal space. Knock before barging in." He nods. "And I want a laptop." His brows raise in surprise. "I want to read online and watch movies like everyone else does."

"If I get you a laptop, you must promise me that you will not spend all your time on it. Our ancestors did not rely on technology, don't forget that."

"Do you tell everyone who has tech, that?"

"You are not everyone. You are my—you're my responsibility."

"You make me sound like such a chore."

"No. You are much harder than a chore." He smirks, and I yank my hand away. I can't help the chortle that escapes.

"Come, Dylan is waiting to speak to you outside."

I want to let go of all my anger, so before I even hear what Dylan has to say, I already know that I will forgive him.

Thank you. I know forgiveness is the hardest thing to give. We will become stronger for it, though. I promise.

I agree silently. I then think about my promise to Circe. I forgave them. Still, I didn't just receive the apology of the man; I received the apology of an alpha. Even angry, I couldn't resist him. I am his mate.

Shedding Tears

Dylan had apologized a hundred times after I forgave him the first time. Even when he asked if we could hang out today, he had apologized again for betraying my trust. Eventually, I told him that I'd start blocking him out if he apologized again. He swore he wouldn't tell any more of my secrets unless I gave him permission or if he thought I was in danger by keeping it. I agreed to those terms, and we began our friendship again.

Gabriel told me that it might be a few weeks before I get a laptop because of the distance they would have to travel to get it. I expected as much. What I didn't expect was both Leon and Maddock following Dylan and me around all day. Maddock had come each day, trying to speak to me as he promised. Once I voiced my forgiveness to him like I did Leon, they both decided they'd spend the day with Dylan and me. Uninvited and all.

"We could give them the slip if you want," Dylan whispers loudly. He's been asking me the entire time if they are making me uncomfortable.

I shake my head slightly. "No, it's fine. They don't bother me… anymore." Dylan gives me a suspicious look. I giggle. "Honest."

"Don't they have patrol or duties to get to?" Dylan asks.

Laughing, I answer, "They asked Alpha for the day off." Dylan rolls his eyes.

"So you guys up for a little run?" He calls out to Leon and Maddock.

"Sure, we could go for a run," Maddock says happily.

"Mind if I tag along?" An icy chill runs down my spine.

No, don't let him, Circe warns.

I turn to see Ronny standing a bit behind Leon. Everyone seems to sense my hesitation.

"Hey." Leon clasps Ronny's hand in respect for *friendship*, I suppose. "Sorry, but today Maddock and I have a lot of catching up to do with our little sister. Alpha asks that Dylan always stay near her, which is the only reason he's tagging along." Dylan scowls at Leon's back. "You don't mind, right?"

Ronny's expression is hard, and he remains silent for a long moment. His eyes cut to me and stay there, for what seems like minutes but really only seconds. Dylan steps in front of me, breaking the contact.

"Sorry, but we really wanted to go for a run before she has to return to the alpha house. We'll be leaving now." Dylan takes my hand, leading me away, and I can see Ronny's eyes dart to Dylan's and my hand. Something dark forms in his eyes.

Caution around him would be wise. I can only do so much if you allow yourself to be around people like him.

Do you know what he wants?

No, I can't hear his wolf, but everything about him is wrong. Before I can question her further, Dylan catches my attention.

"Cain doesn't like him. Thinks he means to cause harm," he says.

"Cain?" I ask.

"I followed your lead and asked my wolf his name." I smile. Cain.

I am here, Luna. I balk at the male voice in my head. Losing my footing, I slip.

Dylan takes a hold of my elbow to keep me upright. "Kate, are you all right?" he asks, panicked.

I stare at him and then straighten. "I'm fine. Just a little light-headed, I guess." Leon and Maddock are at my sides too, all three still wearing concern on their faces. "Really, I'm okay."

We start walking again, and I stay silent, listening for that voice again. *Don't be frightened, Kate. Cain heard you call his name. He was only responding.*

Responding? How can he hear me?

Those who are loyal to Alpha, their wolves already see you as Luna. Therefore, you have the Luna's connection to her pack. You can hear them so that if they are ever in trouble, you can find them, even in long distances.

I have the thought of them hearing my thoughts again, but I dismiss it, reminding myself that they can only hear me if I want them to.

So in other words, knowing their names—

A true Luna will know all the names of her pack's wolves. There hasn't been a warrior who has asked their wolves names in centuries. You were the first in a very long time.

Sadness envelopes me at the thought that in hundreds of years, not a single person ever asked to know their wolf's name. The one who gives them such strength and does their best to help keep them alive. With that thought comes another question.

Circe, when I die, what happens to you?

She is very quiet before she answers. *When you pass to the next life...I will find another whose traits are compatible to my own.*

That makes sense, but at the same time, it seems kind of sad. They grow these relationships with us, and then we die. Then they must start all over again.

You never...you'll never move on? What about heaven or an afterlife?

Do not feel sadness, Kate. I am here to keep you strong and safe.

"What about you?" I say out loud. Dylan and the boys look at me, confused.

What about all of you? Don't you want to go to an afterlife? Don't you want to live a life all your own? My heart breaks knowing that they are eternally imprisoned. I am both angry and saddened. We take their sacrifice for granted.

Dylan, Leon, and Maddock fall to their knees, all three clutching their heads, groaning in pain. I fall to my knees too, try helping them up, and calling out their names, but they can't seem to hear me. Panic makes my hands shake violently.

"What can I do!" I shout at them.

I try pulling Leon's hands from his head so that he will look at me. It works, but what I see in his eyes scares me to the very core. His eyes are completely black. I freeze, and in the moment, he swings for me. His hand slices through the air, missing me completely. Then it goes back to his head. A second passes when Gabriel runs up.

He shifts as he gets to me. "Kate, are you all right? What's wrong?"

"What? What do you mean?" I have tears in my eyes, and I'm sure my expression is panicked further than he has ever seen.

"My wolf, he said you were in pain. I came as fast as I could." He looks down at the boys. "What's wrong with them?" He places a hand on Maddock's back, and in a quick move, he dodges as Maddock lunges for him. He looks at me. "Did they hurt you?"

I shake my head quietly. "No, I just…I just—I can't explain it," I continue crying, and Gabriel's face becomes pained.

Kate, calm down. You are very powerful. You are reflecting your emotions on the entire pack.

What! I'm not doing—

Just calm down. Collect yourself. Close your eyes and breathe.

I do as she says. Finally, I hear their groaning stop. I open my eyes to see the three of them rise from the ground. I look around, apologetic.

"I'm sorry," I say, sniffling.

All of them look at me with a frightened expression. I tremble to think that they are afraid me. "I didn't mean t—" I can't get the words out. I'm too emotional. Gabriel clasps my shoulders.

"Kate, look at me. Stop crying."

I do my best, but the tears just won't stop falling. I want to sob loudly and hysterically.

"I can't, it hurts."

"What hurts, Kate? Tell me where. I'll make it better." He pauses. I can tell his wolf is speaking to him. "Baby, look at me. What you're feeling is the pack. It's all their wolves. You are taking on over generations of sadness from them."

Even as he says these words, he seems to understand it only just then. Instead of trying to calm me further, he lifts me into his arms and carries me back to the alpha house. As we walk through the community, many of them stare as if they're seeing a ghost. They bow their heads as they catch my eyes. I'm still blubbering like crazy.

Once we are in the alpha house, Gabriel takes me straight to the room that I'd stayed in before. He sits on the bed with me in his arms. "Let it all out, Kate. Cry as much as you want. I'll stay beside you."

I sob hard into his chest at his words. I cry for literal hours. Exhaustion relieves me of the headache that comes with crying. I fall into a powerful deep sleep. This time, though, the darkness is very much welcomed.

*****

"Is she going to be okay?"

"I said get out. I don't want anyone waking her."

I hear voices as if they're a part of a dream. They're not, though. I know they're not. One is Gabriel's, that much I can tell. The others blend together, but all are worried about me.

"She's our sister, we're worried about her too." I'm almost positive that voice is Leon's.

"I understand that she's forgiven you, but she is in my care right now. I am responsible for her. And right now, she needs rest." My eyes feel too swollen to open, but I am fully awake now. Groggy but awake.

"And who put you in charge of taking care of her?" Maddock asks angrily.

"What happened to her? She was fine one moment, then she just started crying. That was just before we all got a splitting head—" Leon's interrupted.

"Get the fuck out." Dylan! That's Dylan. "If Alpha says to leave, then leave."

"She is our family. Our repons—"

"Get out! I won't say it again." Silence fills the space. I hear footsteps retreating without another word. Then a gentle kiss is laid on my forehead.

I clear my throat and adjust in his arms. "Kate? Are you awake?" I nod, unable to properly answer. "Did we wake you?" I shake my head. "How are you feeling?"

"Sleepy." My voice is gravelly. "Thirsty."

"I'll go get you some water." He moves to get up, laying me on my pillow. A few moments later, he's back with a cup of water. I push up onto my elbows and drink it greedily.

"My eyes hurt too much to open," I explain.

"It's okay, Kate. They're swollen from the crying."

"How long have I been asleep?"

"A full day."

"I must look terrible." I hear him laugh loosely.

"You look beautiful."

"If I could only roll my eyes."

"You probably could, but I wouldn't see it."

"No point in doing it then."

He laughs again. "Your brothers were just here. They're worried."

"I heard." I try to sit up completely, but he gently pushes me back down. "I want to sit up." Even as I say this, my mind spins, making me feel as though I'm falling while sitting still.

"I know, Kate. But I want you to lie down. That is an order." I feel his command in my bones, though his voice is very gentle.

Do not disobey, Kate. I give in and lie back down.

"What happened? I felt like I had no control of myself."

Gabriel caresses my cheek. A part of me wants to pull away, but the other part of me has already accepted that I'm his mate. "It is the power of the Luna. My wolf says—"

"What is your wolf's name?" I cut him off.

He's caught off guard for a moment. "Arrio."

Arrio. I open my eyes slowly, letting them adjust to the dim lighting.

Yes, Luna, Arrio answers gently.

Pleased to meet you.

Thank you. I am pleased to meet you as well. You have already made a great Luna to your pack.

"I'm not Luna." I voice out loud.

Gabriel looks away. "No, not until you accept me as your mate."

I don't contradict him because I haven't accepted him out loud just yet. And now, with my eyes crusted shut, was not a pretty way to do it. "How can I have these powers if I'm not Luna?"

"You are my mate. I have accepted you in my heart. So you are the Luna in mind. When—if you accept, you will be Luna in spirit and soul as well." Gabriel waits a moment to let me process. "You have nearly accepted, Kate. You felt pain for your wolf and then for the wolves of the pack. You didn't choose to feel this way. You simply couldn't help but feel sorry for them. It is a sign of a good Luna."

"But I saw everyone in pain."

"Yes." He takes my hand in his. "Because you felt their sadness so deeply you took it on yourself. It was pulled out of them like a bad drug. You suffered through their sadness for a full twenty-four hours. Even in your sleep, you cried hard." He bends and kisses my forehead in awe. "Forgive me for ever doubting that you wouldn't be enough."

I ignore the last part. I have already forgiven him, and even though I haven't said so, I know he knows.

I think back to Leon and his eyes. How he swung at me. "This makes no sense. If I can take on their suffering, then why were they in such blinding pain? Leon's eyes turned completely black. Maddock charged at you. That is not normal behavior."

Gabriel nods. "They were a bit off. It was because you separated them for a few seconds." He sees that I don't understand what he means. "You separated them from their wolves. It was only seconds, but it was like a part of the soul was being ripped out. They could only feel pain and rage at that moment."

"I still don't understand. How could I separate them?"

"Think about it this way. Say our wolves are a gem tied to our soul. Over time, they get dirty with anger, pain, and sadness. You ripped the gem out, which is not painful for the gem but painful for the souls. You ripped it out, cleansed it, and then put it back. It made every wolf in our pack stronger. It was momentary agony for a beneficial outcome.

"So everyone is okay?" I ask.

He nods. "They are better than okay. I've heard some saying that it felt like a weight they didn't know they'd been carrying had been lifted off their shoulders."

"So I have the power to reap them of their sorrows. How poetic."

"Don't get the wrong idea, Kate. Doing this can make your body very weak."

He is right. The less you allow your pack to feel pain, the more damage it does to your body and overall...me. That stops my thoughts dead. I would never want to intentionally harm Circe.

"I wouldn't do that to you, Circe. Not if it meant you'd become weaker." Gabriel looks at me. Again, in awe.

"I never bothered to ask Arrio for his name."

"No one seems to. To be honest, I don't remember asking Circe. It must have been before the coma. But now it seems knowing their names is a big part of knowing them. I can speak with your wolf if I know his name, and you'd never know."

Gabriel adjusts, uncomfortable. I can't help but laugh. My ribs begin to hurt from how hard I laugh. "I'm not going invade your privacy, Gabriel. What I mean is, if something were to happen to you, and I'm nowhere near, I can call out to Arrio."

He nods slowly. "I see." Still, he looks at me skeptically.

A gentle knock takes our attention. "Come in," I answer.

Dylan steps in. "I heard laughter, and we all know Gabe has no sense of humor." I smile. "Are you okay?"

"Yes, Dylan. Ya know, you're trying too hard not to look worried." He smirks and shrugs. "Turns out that accepting someone as your mate in silence is the same as accepting them out loud."

I look at Gabriel. He has a hard look. Almost like he doesn't want to get his hopes up. When he sees that I'm not backing down, he breathes fast and smiles at me.

Dylan grips Gabriel's shoulder and smiles. "I thought you didn't have a chance in hell, man. Congratulations." Gabriel rolls his eyes, annoyed. "So you're really choosing to become Luna?"

Gabriel squeezes my hand. "Of course she is. She is my mate." Dylan doesn't look the least bit surprised by the news despite his comment.

"She's your what?" I hear Leon say from somewhere behind Dylan. Both Leon and Maddock come rushing in.

"Obviously they are mates. No one else could see her innocence except her mate." Dylan jabs at Leon and Maddock.

"That's not true," Gabriel says darkly. We all look at him. "I rejected her because of the rumors. I honestly never believed he would say it out loud. "And I will spend my life making it up to her." His eyes hold mine.

Kate, brace. Before I can question Circe's interruption, a deafening screech fills my ears. I cup them, but it does no good. I feel Gabriel pull me to him. He holds me tightly. I see him yell something to Dylan and the boys as they begin to panic. The noise makes my ears bleed. Gabriel's hand comes to cover my ears too, but it still does no good. After the longest two minutes of my life, it stops.

I'm sweating from head to toe. "No one raises their voice," Gabriel whispers to them. "Go get me Dr. Gene." Maddock nods and is out the door in a second. "Leon, find something to cover her ears with."

Let me, Kate. I can heal you much quicker. It will be painful to turn, but the pain will only last a moment, and then it will fade.

"Circe can heal me. I need to turn." The vibration from my own vocal cords sends pain through my skull.

Gabriel's grip doesn't loosen. "No, Kate. You're not strong enough."

I reach for a pen that's on the nightstand and write on my hand. *Please.* He sighs and then picks me up and walks me outside. Everyone stops to stare. He gently puts me on the ground, and I release my body to Circe.

Pain shoots through my entire body. It is excruciating but not as bad as the noise. And just as Circe promised, it was gone as fast as it came. Everyone's eyes were on me. They all look at me as though I were a new moon. Circe releases my body, and Gabriel comes to stand beside me. We spot Dr. Gene coming through the crowd, but before she reaches us, everyone bows their heads.

Luna. I hear many voices say in unison.

The noise was the last phase of becoming Luna. It was the sound of their hearts and souls tying to yours. They all know now. They will feel it when you are around, the way you feel it whenever Alpha is around. You are their Luna. And you will be the best of Luna's there has ever been.

Gabriel's arm wraps around my waist as if he, too, could hear Circe.

My gaze roams to those bowing before me. I stop at the rogue in the back, who is not bowing but simply watching. When our eyes meet, he inclines his head slightly. Almost as a sign of respect but not wanting to show it. I give him a knowing look.

A surge of power makes my heart flutter. Luna. I am Luna.

Paranoia

I'm completely drenched in sweat and blood. Tears are spilling out like a waterfall. I look down at the infant in my arms. I wasn't fast enough. I couldn't save her. Gabriel is feet from us, lifeless. Circe was pulled from me. I can't feel her warmth anymore. Oh goddess, she must be dead. I wasn't strong enough, and everyone is dead because of me. It's all my fault. I lay the small limp body in my arms on the ground and pray to the goddess.

"Please take me instead. Bring them back," I whisper through sobs.

"There's no bringing them back. But we'll take you too." Looking up, I see a rogue. He's all brute muscle and rage. "After today, it will be as if none of you ever existed."

"Kate! Kate, it's just a dream. Wake up." I bolt up and see Gabriel's concerned expression. I'm panting as if I just ran ten miles. Gabriel yanks off his shirt and uses it to rub away the moisture from my skin. "It's okay. You're safe now." He sits on my bed and pulls me onto his lap. I blink and see all those lifeless bodies everywhere. I begin to shake. They were merciless. They left no one alive. Gabriel tucks my head under his chin and rubs my back. "I'm here, Kate. No one's going to hurt you."

A few minutes later, I've calmed down. Maddock knocks on my doorframe since Gabriel left it open.

"Yes?" I answer lowly. The dream seemed so real.

"Hey, Kate. Alpha. Sorry, I didn't mean to—" I realize what he must think seeing me on Gabriel's lap.

"It's fine," Gabriel says, annoyed. "She was having a bad dream."

Maddock steps in. "Are you okay?" he asks.

"Yes."

He nods thoughtfully and then excuses himself. "When you are both ready, the first meal is prepared." We nod as he makes his exit.

I try climbing out of Gabriel's lap, but he holds me in place. "Tell me about it." His concern is still intact. I tell him all the gory details of it, and his concern seems to fade a bit. "Don't worry, my mate. I will never let that happen."

He may not have a choice. Circe intrudes.

"I think it's a warning."

He shakes his head. "I have well-trained guards all around the perimeter. Two guards on the rogue that is here. They must think by now that we eliminated two of theirs. They are a cowardly sort. They won't attempt trespassing again."

"My parents were good warriors too, but they were still killed, and the rogues still got away."

He inhales deeply. "I know this is personal for you, Kate. But there is simply no way—"

"What were the others doing in here? They risked coming in through the most populated area. What were they doing there? We should send out a search party and see if they left any—" Gabriel puts a finger on my lips.

"Calm down. It was a dream. I won't let any of that happen here."

I smack his hand away in anger. "Please don't treat me like a child. I was just asking that we take a second look. What harm could it do? Rather safe than sorry, right?"

His gentle eyes harden. I can tell he does not like to be ordered around. Well, I don't like to be patronized. "Kate." His voice is slightly agitated.

"What harm can it do?" I repeat.

"When the travelers return, I will send men out."

"That could be weeks. It could be too late by then."

"Kate, I'm not going to take guards off patrol because you had a bad dream." Anger hits me hard. I push off his lap.

"I need you to go." I point to my door.

"Kate."

"I need to get dressed."

He shakes his head and slides off the bed. He stops in front of me. I don't make eye contact. He exhales and walks out.

After dressing, I walk out, completely ignoring anything Gabriel has to say to me. Dylan and Maddock have been waiting for us and notices my silent treatment immediately. The three of us sit to eat at the gathering area. Maddock tells me that Leon is on patrol and took his meal earlier. Gabriel is sitting, frustrated, next to me. The tension at the table becomes too unbearable for Dylan.

"So I'm just about done. What about you, Luna?"

Hearing people call me Luna feels strange to me. I had accepted the title yesterday, and Gabriel had agreed to let me keep my room. He said that he would wait for me to be comfortable enough with him before sharing a bed. And at that moment, I thought him too good to be true. I was right.

"Yes, I'm done. I feel like a run. Let's go." I bid Maddock good-bye and then walk off, not waiting for Dylan.

He does catch up quickly, though. "Are you okay?"

"I'm fine." I'm very curt at the moment, and Dylan seems to know not to push the topic. We walk for a while before I stop. "I'm sorry, it's not your fault. I'm just upset. I just had a vivid dream about rogues attacking the community. It felt like a warning, but when I asked Gabriel to send men out to where we found the other rogues, he said no."

Dylan's brows rose. "He said no?"

"Well, he said he didn't want to take men off patrol because I had a bad dream."

Dylan nods. "I see why you're ignoring him."

"He ignored me first."

Dylan shoves his hands into his pockets. "So what are you going to do about it, *Luna*."

I grin. "Let's go." I shift and run, heading for the spot where we found the rogues.

We get there and find Ruby leaning against a boulder. Circe releases me, and I walk up to her. Her face pales guiltily. Likely due to my new title. She has dark bruising under her eyes and a white piece of med tape on the bridge of her nose.

"Ruby," I greet her coldly. She dips her head in respect. "What are you doing here?"

"I-I was just hanging out. Since my nose was broken the other day, I try to stay away from watchful eyes."

"I have some business here. If you don't mind, I need the privacy." Dylan runs up behind me. He shifts and stands behind me in support.

Ruby looks at Dylan and smirks. "Of course you do." I roll my eyes and shake my head. Whatever rumors she starts will be nothing new to me.

Once she is completely out of sight, I look around. There's nothing here.

"What should we be looking for?" Dylan asks me.

"I don't know, anything. Anything out of the ordinary." I pick up a long stick and begin poking around. I poke at the brush on the ground and the vines that have grown over boulders. I look nearly everywhere but come up empty.

"Find anything?" Dylan asks, walking back to me. I shake my head. He's about ten feet from me when he slips and falls hard. "Fuck!" he shouts in pain. I rush over.

"Come on, I'll help you up."

"No, don't. My leg's stuck." I look down at his legs, but one is buried in the ground.

"What the hell is that?"

"I don't know, but could you get some help. I think my ankle's broken." I nod and rush off. Circe takes over, and we call over the first two people we see. Two male members. They follow us back to Dylan.

I turn once Dylan comes into sight. "Dylan, I brought help."

"It's about time," he whines. His head then snaps up to one of the guys I brought. They hold each other's gaze for a moment before they both look down at his trapped leg. Damn, I hope they don't have problems with each other.

Either way, the two members each grab one of Dylan's arms and pull him up. Once he's on solid ground, I look to see what he stepped into. I poke it with another stick and notice that it is not earth. A hollow bang echoes as I poke it with my stick.

"It's a trapdoor," I yell at Dylan somewhere behind me.

"It worked," he yells back. I stand and walk back to Dylan who is lying flat on the ground. The two members are standing nearby.

"Thank you for helping us," I tell them.

"Of course, Luna. It is our pleasure." I don't remember ever coming across these two in the past, but then this community is larger than my circle of bullies.

"What are your names?"

"I'm Oria, and this is Taylor." I shake their hands and thank them again.

"Dylan, thank them for rescuing your leg."

"Thank you. I saw my life flash before my eyes. I don't know what I would have done if you guys hadn't come." I roll my eyes at his sarcastic melodramatics. I go back to the door and pull it open. It opens up to a large tunnel. I take a steep step in.

"Kate!" Dylan yells, making me jump. "Don't. We'll call Alpha. Don't do anything stupid."

He is right, Kate. This will lead nowhere good.

I step back out and close the door.

Arrio, I'm where the rogues were found. Please bring Gabriel to me.

In a few short minutes, Arrio is running up. He turns, and I can see the anger on Gabriel's face.

"Why? Why couldn't you listen! Why did you *have* to come back?"

"I needed to be sure!" I yell at him.

"You put yourself and Dylan in danger! There is a reason there is no one around here anymore!"

"I was right, though! Look." I pull up the trapdoor. Gabriel looks down at it. Something passes in his eyes that I don't recognize.

"Go back to the house and stay there. You two"—he gestures to our lifesavers—"take him to the Med Center." They nod and pick Dylan up. They walk back, but I stay planted. Gabriel takes a step into the tunnel. "Go back, Kate," he demands.

Let us go, Kate. I don't move.

"No, I want to see where it leads."

Gabriel looks at me and steps back out of the tunnel. He closes the trapdoor and walks to me. "Let's go." He pulls me by my elbow.

"No. I practically begged you to have someone look into this! Begged! And you thought I was being paranoid. Is it paranoia if I'm right!" He doesn't respond. "If I had waited for you to move on this, we might have all been killed." My blood runs cold. "As horrible as these people were to me, I would never wish death upon them. You should have list—"

Gabriel pulls me to him and kisses me hard. I try fighting against him but am locked in his embrace. When he finally breaks the kiss, my lips are numb, and I'm out of breath.

"I'm sorry," is all he says. "Please, go home. I'll be there once I get men up here."

Unable to refuse, I turn out of his hold and make my way back to the alpha house. I stop when just outside it, I realize the answers are right in front of me.

I rush over to the rogue in the cell. He looks me up and down. "Luna," he says lowly.

"I found the tunnel," I say flatly.

He looks away, almost bored. "Then I guess the conversation is over."

"What was it for? What were the rogues planning? When were they planning to invade?"

"I'm not sure I know what you're talking about, *Luna*," he says almost mockingly.

I step close enough for him to be able to reach me. Both guards turn so that they may be ready to strike should he try anything. I know better, though. If he were to strike, I'd be dead before they could do anything. I grab one of the bars and kneel so that I am face-to-face with him. He looks a bit surprised as I stare him straight in the eye.

"Would you give up if it were your children's lives at risk?"

His jaw clenches. I could see that I've made him out perfectly. I could see that he plans to tell me nothing. I stand and begin walking away.

"Luna." He calls when I'm feet from the cell. I turn to look at him. He looks as if he wants to say something but is fighting himself from doing so. Finally, he says in a small voice, "Don't go down there."

Descending (Gabriel)

After Kate went home, I had scolded myself for ignoring her after she pleaded for me to listen to her. She had really been frightened by her dream, and I believed it had clouded her judgment. I scolded her and humiliated her. Even if it was in private, I should not have simply written it off. She was genuinely concerned for the pack. And my refusal to satisfy her fears will haunt me.

Maddock and a few other members returned to the trapdoor with me. I told them to prepare for anything, even leaving me behind if it came to that. I pray to the goddess that it does not. I have every intention to return to Kate and tell her that she does not need to fear anything from this place.

"I'll go first, Maddock, you will follow—"

"No, Alpha. I'm sorry, but I should go first. I am an unmated male. You have Kate to return to." I look at him and slightly shake my head. I know they had a rough time together, but I know Kate still loves her brothers. She would hate herself for not being able to reconnect with him, if something were to go wrong.

"Maddock—"

"No, Alpha. She needs you a lot more than she needs me."

"She needs us both." He's not moved. I exhale and nod. "I'll follow you in, but if I tell you to retreat, then you must leave." My eyes go from him to my other warriors.

They all nod their understanding. I gesture for Maddock to go in. We descend deep into a tomb-like tunnel. After the ground becomes leveled, the tunnel is pitch-black. All my senses are on high alert. Arrio is continuously growling. *I will return, Kate.* I make my silent promise and continue close behind Maddock.

Unbearable

I race to the tunnel after the rogue's warning. I need to make sure nothing happens to them. Circe runs as fast as she can. We run up to two warriors at the entrance.

"Move aside. We need to get them out."

"I'm sorry, Luna. Alpha made us swear not to let anyone else in. That includes you, I'm afraid." I curse out loud. Damn him!

I take a breath and close my eyes. I have only practiced this along with Gabriel. I have no idea if it will work with so many around.

Arrio. I call. I'm immediately frustrated when I don't hear a response.

Calm. Try again. There are many members with him in a small space. Try again. See him in your mind.

I take a breath. *Arrio.*

I hear you, Luna. I have no time to celebrate.

Everyone needs to exit the tunnels, now! *The rogue here told me not to go in. I'm guessing that there is something dangerous down there. It may have been a trap!*

A few aggravating seconds pass before he responds. *Thank you, Luna. We are already at the end of the tunnel. It leads to their territory. We will be back soon. Alpha demands that you return home. We will see you there.*

Ugh! What if the rogues are waiting? I need to stop them. I plan to shove past the warriors when two others come up behind me and an arm each. "Our apologies, Luna. Alpha's orders. You are to come back to the alpha house with us." Infuriating man! I nod, though, and walk with them.

"I want to visit my friend in the medical center." They look at each other. "I promise not to go back to the tunnels."

"If you do, we will make sure that you make it all the way to the alpha house next time." I nod and walk to the medical center.

I sit patiently beside Dylan, waiting for Gabriel and Maddock to return. My belly is in knots at the thought of anything happening to them. Every time I close my eyes, I see their deaths, and my chest aches horribly for it. I could have just destroyed it and told Gabriel about it later. Instead, I had to rub it in his face. His perfectly sculpted face.

"What's your deal? You seem pissed," he asks.

"Fucking Gabriel!"

"If I had a coin for every time I heard that." I shoot him a deadly look, and he puts his hand up in defense. "I'm kidding, don't hit me again. What happened?"

"I went to talk to the rogue here when I left the tunnel. He told me not to go in."

"So?"

"When I told Gabriel's wolf, he ordered two warriors to escort me back."

"I'm not hearing a problem."

"Seriously! He ignored my warning! What if they are waiting on the other side? What if it was a trap?"

He shrugs. "What if your rogue friend is lying? What if they find nothing on the other side? What if you're jumping to conclusions?" I want to yell at him, but he gives me a look. I know he's only trying to make a point. "I'm sure Gabriel factored in your warning. At this point, you have to believe in him and trust that he knows what he's doing."

I exhale, frustrated. "I just hate that I'm just sitting here doing nothing."

"You're keeping me company." He laughs when I give him an annoyed look.

"Just calm down, all right. Gabriel is very smart in warfare. Has he told you how we met?"

"Alpha training."

"He argued with the elders every chance he got. He would tell them that their methods were dated and that rogues and rival packs have probably figured out their defense and offense strategies.

Whenever we were given missions to complete, Gabriel would always do the mission his way. It would always get us in trouble with the elders, but he was always the first to finish with the highest markings." I feel a sense of pride in my chest. "He broke every rule they set for him. Sound familiar?" I smirk. "Have faith in him, Kate."

I nod and sit quietly. I think about how he kissed me again. He was angry, but not at me. It was painful and still beautiful.

"Geez, Kate! That's the fifth time you touched your lips! What happened after I was carried off?"

I pull my fingers from my lips. I couldn't stop thinking about it. I had never been kissed on the lips, but I doubted it felt that good from just anyone. His lips were impossibly soft even though his kiss was hard. A chill shoots down my spine. I want to kiss him again.

"Sorry. Nothing really happened. We talked it out, and then I came back."

He snorts. "Bullshit. You were fuming a second ago, and then suddenly, you're all red-faced and calm? Nah, I don't believe you. What happened, did he give you a smooch?" I blush and look away again. "It's about time you put out, Kate. He is your mate, after all." I punch his arm hard, making him rub it. "What are you so shy about? Most members already think you guys are sleeping together."

"We've only kissed for the first time today!" My whole body has goose bumps of embarrassment at my confession.

Dylan smirks. "My point is that it's nothing to be embarrassed about."

"Easy for you to say. I bet you've kissed tons of girls. This was my first kiss." This time Dylan looks away. Guilt immediately fills me in his silence. "Hey, I was just kidding. I don't think you're a womanizer or anything."

He shakes his head. "It's not that."

For the first time since I've met him, he looks unhappy. Gone is his happy-go-lucky facade. "Dylan, you can talk to me." I grab his hand and hope I'm not pushing too much.

He studies me for a moment. "Swear you'll never tell anyone." Worry fills me. Is he in trouble? "It could bring shame down on my family." I straighten my back and nod. "I really need to hear you say it."

"I swear."

With a sigh, he rubs his face. "I found my mate."

I break into a smile. "That's great!"

"Hang on." My smile falters a bit. "It was one of the members that brought me here."

My head is in waves. "The members...they were both m—" I gasp. "Dylan!" I whisper-shout. "Why didn't you tell me before!"

He shakes his head. "I can never be with him. It will ruin my family. My sister will be ridiculed for being Alpha."

"Dylan, it's not that big of a deal. Humans have mostly accepted that people love who they love."

"But we're not humans, Kate." His voice is stern. "Humans also have innocence until proven guilty, but it did not reach here." My chest clenches at the blow. "I'm sorry. I shouldn't have said that. I'm just—I wish I wasn't the son of an alpha."

"Dylan, this is your pack now. These are the people who will support you here, especially with you being good friends with their Luna and Alpha. I understand that you want to protect your family, but I think that if your sister was chosen to be Alpha, then she can take care of herself."

"I can't put her through that shame. She's always covered for me in the past."

"She knows?" He nods. "If she loves you enough to do that for you, then I think she would want you to be happy." A knock at the door interrupts us. Leon walks in.

"Sorry, I went to the alpha house, but no one was there. Someone said you guys were here. What happened?"

I look at Dylan, who is trying hard to keep up his facade. "Dylan slipped and fell. Now he's acting like the world is ending."

Leon nods awkwardly. "Sounds like him."

I go for small talk to give Dylan some time. "Maddock said you were on patrol."

"Yeah, I just switched off."

"Anything out there?"

"Not as far as the eye can see."

"Whose eyes are we talking about? Yours or ours? Because you seem a bit nearsighted," Dylan mocks. I exhale, relieved.

Leon gives him a death stare. "Well, you seem fine."

"Thanks, I've been told that before. Usually by females, though. But don't worry, I respect your life choices." The irony.

We spend the rest of the day there waiting for Gabriel and Maddock to return. Since we were in the Med Center, I decided to pay Dr. Gene a visit. After a full physical exam, she okayed me to begin my training. When I returned to Dylan's room, it was already late in the day. I paced, trying not to let my mind wander about what could be keeping them. Leon and Dylan talked to me the entire time, trying to get my mind away from the unknown. The waiting was unbearable, but they made it easier on me. Night fell, and Dylan told me to return to the alpha house. He wouldn't take no for an answer. Leon walked me to the alpha house and said he'd come by in the morning so we could go to the Med Center together. I agreed and made my way inside.

Two hours later, I'm still lying awake in bed. The fear and loneliness begin to hit me hard now that I'm alone. The darkness invades, unwelcome.

Don't worry, Kate. He is resilient and will not return without your brother. Circe's words do little to calm me, but I'm grateful for her effort.

I toss and turn, trying to sleep but can't seem to. I sit up and hug my knees. This is driving me insane. Then my doorknob begins to turn. Relief settles over me when I see a male figure in the doorway.

"I couldn't sleep, I thought maybe something happened to you guys." Circe growls loudly in my ears.

Kate, that's not Gabriel! Run! Fear fills me. I have nowhere to go; he's blocking the doorway. *The window! Go NOW!* Just as I rush for the window, the male grabs me and throws me onto the bed. I fight back hard. Then a hand locks down both of my wrists above my head.

"Let me go!" I scream, hoping someone will hear me.

"You were always mine," the male says. His voice is all too familiar. Ronny.

"Ronny? What the hell are you doing? Get off me!"

"You should have let me protect you! Instead, you let someone you knew for five fucking minutes hold and kiss you!"

"Ronny, please get off me. Let's talk about this, okay?"

"Quiet! I believed you and stayed beside you when everyone else turned their backs on you, and you turned me away!"

"I didn't want you becoming an outcast like I was," I plead. "I'm sorry I hurt you. Please let me go."

"Hurt me? You're sorry you hurt me? You tore out my fucking heart! I loved you more than anything!" His hand slides down my waist to my thighs. I squirm in panic. "Now you stay here with him. Well, I know you haven't given it to him. I'll take it for myself." He cups my sex. The blood drains from my face.

"Ronny! Stop! Please!"

His head dips, and his tongue runs along the crook of my neck. I shake violently at the contact. Tears run down my cheeks, and then the worst comes. His hand slips between my panties, and he enters a finger inside. I scream loudly.

Gabriel. My tears crash onto the bed when Ronny flips me over. He's too heavy for me to wiggle out from under him. Moments later, he is thrown across the room. I turn quickly to see the rogue standing over him. His rage-filled eyes are on Ronny. He lands punch after punch on Ronny's face. Leon then rushes in and takes in the scene. He pulls me out of the room and takes me to Gabriel's. The door closes as he leaves me there. I'm still sobbing and frozen in place. I crumble to the floor and cry in my hands.

Unbroken

I had fallen asleep, weeping on the floor. Sitting up, I realize that I am no longer on the floor but on the bed instead. The sun stings my swollen eyes. I flinch, and I rub them. Looking down, I notice that my wrists are nearly black with redness around the edges. The events of last night come flooding back to me. Ronny. On top of me. A shiver runs down my spine.

"How are you feeling?" I squeal loudly and nearly fall off the bed. My heart is pounding hard in my chest. I look to my left and find a very angry Gabriel.

"Gabriel." My hand is on my chest, trying to calm my rapid heart rate. "I didn't—"

"How are you feeling?" he repeats, standing. He strides to me with a dark look in his eyes.

"I'm—" He sits at the edge of the bed and uncovers me. "What are you—" Before I can finish my question, he pulls me to him and cradles me against his hard broad chest.

I don't try to pull away or move. I let him hold me. I think—I think we both need it. His grip on me tightens as his head dips in the crook of my neck and hugs me hard. I feel my emotions begin to stir again. It takes everything I have not to cry again. He leans into my hand when I put it gently on his cheek. When his head comes up again, I can see everything. His rage. His worry. His pain and his self-loathing. It saddens me. I gently rest my forehead against his and close my eyes.

When I open them and pull away, I make sure he's looking at me. "I'm okay. The rogue got there in time." A growl-like noise erupts from his throat as his emotions give way. "Stop it. I'm thankful to him. What happened to him anyways?"

"He's being held in a room here. I have two guards watching him."

"He saved me. We should show him a bit more gratitude than that."

"He is still a rogue."

"How did he escape the cell?"

"There was only one guard with him when he escaped. I had the other come along with me. He knocked the one out and used the keys to unlock it. Leon watched him run toward the alpha house and went after him." I look down. He saved me, and I had only given him half my food each meal.

"If I had been here—" Gabriel stops and grits his teeth together.

"You're here now when I need you."

"I should have had guards outside the house."

"You couldn't have known what was going to happen. I should have told you about my history with Ronny and his recent interest in me. I just never thought he'd do anything like this. I'm sorry."

"Don't!" He snaps, making me jump. "Don't ever apologize for this. None of this is your fault." I nod slowly.

"I know we made a deal that I'd stay in my room...but can I sleep here tonight?" His lips quirk. It's subtle, but I catch it. He leans his head back against mine.

"Did you think I would let you sleep anywhere else?" I smile and shake my head. He stands with me in his arms and takes us to the chair that I assume he'd been sitting on all night.

"When will he be tried?" I ask, breaking the silence.

Gabriel exhales and plants gentle kisses on my forehead. "He won't be." His kisses move from my forehead to my neck. A jolt makes me block his access.

"No. He—I need to shower." His eyes search mine before he loosens his grip on me. I stand and make my way to the bedroom door.

"My shower is in there." He points to the only other door in the room.

"I need to get clothes for after." His eyes roam up and down my body before they return to my eyes. His brows furrow like he's forgotten something. He runs a hand through his hair and stands.

"I'll have someone bring your things up here. Go take your shower."

"I don't want someone I don't know looking through my things."

"Fine, I'll go get your things." He tries to move past me.

I block the doorway. "I definitely don't want *you* looking through my things."

"Kate!" he snaps. He sighs when I recoil. "I don't want you in that room," he says calmly.

"Okay" is all I can say in response.

I begin walking to his bathroom again when he says, "A doctor will be coming in a short while." I turn.

"Is it Dr. Gene?" He shakes his head. "I like Dr. Gene."

"Dr. Gene left last night. One of our allied packs needs a healer that specializes in torn ligaments."

"What is this doctor going to check?"

"He's just going to do a physical. He's going to make sure that—"

"I had a physical yesterday. Dr. Gene did it. I asked her to so that I could start training."

"That was before—"

"Gabriel, I'm fine. Well, I'm not physically hurt, with the exception of my wrists. If you want to help me, then please don't act as if he broke me." Gabriel's expression is thoughtful. He gives me a pitiful look, and my stomach turns. I don't like that look. I don't want to see it on him.

I turn my back to him and go for my shower. Maybe I'm not okay, but I'm definitely not broken. Even as I think this, though, five years of torment never prepared me for that.

Ronny had all that rage and anguish wrapped up inside him. He kept it in check until now. Until I chose Gabriel. I turn on the water and strip out of my clothes. His shower is a lot smaller than I originally thought it would be. Space for only an alpha, but of course being that I'm much smaller, it towers over me. I step into the shower, not waiting for the water to cool. The heat bites my skin, turning it crimson. Being under the water suddenly brings back the memory of last night. The darkness. His wretched scent. The pain in my arms as I try pulling out of his grasp, his hands roaming my body.

My knees weaken, and I hunch in the shower. I place my hand over my mouth so Gabriel won't hear my whimpers. Maybe I'm not okay. The thought lingers.

After I finally step out of the shower and wrap myself in a towel, I slowly open the door and peek my head out. Gabriel is sitting at the edge of the bed. His head snaps up when he sees me.

I clear the bile from my throat. "My clothes?"

He hands me neatly folded clothing. "They're new, but I'm told they'll fit just the same."

"What happened to my clothes?" I ask, taking the clothing from him while still shielding myself with the door.

"Your clothing was ruined. I asked one of the females to get you some from one of the vendors. She said that those would fit." I wonder for a brief moment how my clothes were ruined but decided to change before asking.

Once out of the bathroom, I step out, barefoot, in a black slim dress. It goes down to my mid-thigh and shapes my waist. Everything about it is wrong. Besides the fact that I would never wear something so revealing, I want to be as far away from showing my skin. I look through Gabriel's dresser and find dark-gray sweats and a matching hoodie. Both still have tags on them. He's never worn them. They must be from the traveler's totes. I strip off the extra skin that passes as a dress and slip into his sweats.

I'm completely dressed when I look down at the discarded dress. I wonder if things had been different. If I would be the kind of girl that would wear that. I can't see that possibility. Gabriel walks back in and halts when he sees me.

"Did it not fit?"

I shake my head. "It's not something I'd feel comfortable wearing." I hand it back to him. When he takes it and holds it up, I realize he had no idea.

His face is in shock, but he recovers rather quickly. "I wouldn't have let you walk out in this anyways." Gabriel throws the dress on the bed, forgotten. His eyes move to the oversized clothing I'm wearing. He kneels in front of me and moves my hand that's holding up the sweats. "Here, let my tighten the drawstring."

"I already did. This is as far as it goes."

He smirks but doesn't respond. He begins rolling the waistline down. Slowly the sweats get tight enough to stay up. He then cuffs them at my ankles and the sleeves on the hoodie. I feel like a child but saying so would make me seem like one even more.

"Why do these still have tags on these? I also saw some other clothes with tags," I ask when he finishes the sleeves.

"I'm not used to them." I wait for him to continue. "Alphas are trained as if we were still in the Stone Age. No technology. No mass-produced clothing." He smirks to himself. "No processed foods. In fact, everything we have, wear, or eat, we have to catch or make ourselves. I was never the best at sewing or making my own clothing, but they were still more comfortable than anything in that drawer."

"Hmm."

He looks at me. "What is it?"

"I was going to say that it must have been hard, but I guess it wouldn't be too hard surviving without things you never had."

He nods "You can't miss something you never had."

"Exactly," I say more to myself than him. Then something occurs to me. "But Alpha Stone wears normal clothing." I point out.

"My father has forgotten his training. He has become accustomed to everything being done for him." He stands and pulls me on his lap as he sits on the bed. A spot that is slowly becoming familiar to me. "I hope to never become so dependent on others."

"Do you think I'm too dependent?"

"No," he says as I start to resist his hold. He doesn't loosen his grip, though. "You are the most independent one in the entire pack."

"Apart from you, of course," I tease.

"Including me."

"What do you depend on then?"

A gentle smile touches his lips. "My pack. My training. You."

A knock at the door disturbs us. "Alpha, I have your meals."

I give Gabriel a look. "We're not eating with everyone else?"

He moves me off his lap as he collects the two plates of food. He places one in front of me. "I know it may sound overbearing, but I don't want you leaving this room today."

"Why not?"

"Please don't fight me on this, Kate. It's just one day. Please stay here. I need to know that you are safe here." He looks desperate.

Looking down, I say, "I promised to visit Dylan today."

"He will understand. I will speak to him." Some part of me, some part deep down, was glad. I don't think I am up for the crowd of people questioning what happened or doting on me as if I'm broken.

"Fine. I'll stay here." He sighs, relieved.

We eat our meals, and he begins to tell me about the work he has to do with the pack that Dylan's sister runs. I notice that each topic is carefully chosen. He is being cautious about what subjects may upset me. I appreciate it and choose not to tell him that there is no need for it. Instead, I listen to everything he tells me.

"Gabriel." He looks at me.

"I want to speak to the rogue." His whole body goes rigid.

"No." There is no room for conversation.

"Then I guess I won't be staying in this room for very long." The look in his eyes change from uncomfortable to angry.

"You are not going to speak to him. This is not up for discussion."

"Why do you feel the need to control me?" It comes out of nowhere, but I don't regret it.

"I'm trying to keep you safe."

"From the man who saved me from being raped. Makes sense."

"Do you honestly believe that he escaped his cell just to save you? Do you know what his intentions are? Do you know why he trespassed yet?" I go quiet. "I don't know why he did what he did, but I'm not going to make him a part of the pack for one good deed."

"Is that all it was to you? Just a decent act?" My voice is calm. "Goddess knows what Ronny planned to do with me after the fact." Gabriel's fists clench. I realize I'm not going to win this unless I appeal to his better nature. "Look, I don't want to fight about this. I'm not saying we should trust him, but I want to thank him. I don't know what his true intentions were, but maybe I could figure it out. You can have a guard there too."

He sighs and runs a hand through his hair. "Five minutes. If he even flinches, I will rip him apart."

"If you're there, he won't speak to me."

He pushes out of his sitting position hard. "Fuck." I wait for his real response. "One guard isn't enough."

"Then cuff him, but more than one guard will make him clam up."

"Five minutes," he says, looking at me.

I agree and silently celebrate my victory.

Caged Bird

The day had passed slowly. After we made our agreement, Gabriel went back to work, not before repeatedly asking if I would be okay alone for a few hours. I nearly had to force him out before he finally left. I spent the day reading what little Gabriel had to offer in his sad three-book collection. I did anything to keep myself busy so that I wouldn't have to think too much about the night before. Before long, I began going through his drawers because I was left unsupervised.

Midmeal rolled around, and no one had brought me a plate of food. I wasn't exactly hungry but staying in the room with nearly nothing to do was pushing me to the edge of insanity. I needed to be out of his room if even for just a moment.

The door creaks as I open it. *The noisy hinge needs to get oiled,* I think to myself. I poke my head out of the room. No one around. Of course not, they're all eating. I tiptoe down the hall till I get to the staircase. I do my best to stay quiet in case Gabriel had decided to stay in too. I make it all the way downstairs, clenching my teeth at every floorboard that squeaks. I start for the entrance door and then stop. Why the hell am I sneaking around if I'm about to go out and let everyone know that I'm out of his room? I doubt he told anyone else, but still. As I'm pondering this, the doorknob turns.

My heart pounds in my ears, and I race into the nearest room, which is mine. I close the door quietly behind me and put my ear to it. Footsteps move slowly past my door and fade as they ascend upstairs. I decide it's not Gabriel's because the tread sounds much too soft. I exhale when I no longer hear the footsteps, and turn my back to the door.

"Really smooth, Kate," I scold myself.

Mm-hm. I hear Circe hum-laugh.

I roll my eyes. For midday, the room is rather dark. Then I notice that my windows have been blocked off. I reach for my light switch and gasp when the bright bulb illuminates the room. Blood is everywhere. On the bed, against the wall, even on my dresser. A large bloodstain is beside the bed. I'm in such shock that I don't hear my name being called or the door hitting my back when someone enters. My whole body is shaking violently. I can't handle this. My psyche is at its juncture. My eyes are open, but I can't see a thing. A drop of cold sweat runs down my spine under the sweatshirt.

Hands are wrapped tightly around my biceps and shaking me. I can't see who it is or hear what they are saying. Before I know it, I've fallen unconscious.

"You said you would stay put," I hear Gabriel whisper. I don't know how long I was out, but the dark sky outside would suggest at least a few hours. I'm facing the window from the bed. Gabriel is sitting in front of it. His head is resting in his hands and his elbows on his knees. He hasn't noticed that I'm awake.

"Gabriel," I call out.

His head shoots up at the sound of his name. "Kate." His voice is in disbelief. I try sitting up, and he rushes to my side to help me.

"What happened?"

"You—what do you last remember?"

I think back. I remember everything. I remember the room. The blood. And something else. Grief. I felt sorrow. The feeling returns. I know now why he did not want me leaving the room. I know why he hadn't wanted me to collect my own things. My chest aches.

"I remember it all. And then nothing." He's watching me carefully.

"Kate, I—"

"You killed him, didn't you? Not the rogue. You killed Ronny." My statement takes him by surprise.

"I couldn't hold back when they told me what he'd done. How they heard you scream. You have no idea how useless I felt knowing that a stranger protected you better than I could. I couldn't get to you fast enough. You mean everything to me."

I do my best to contain my anger. I try to understand his point of view, but it does nothing for my conscience. "Please don't use me as an excuse for killing him."

"I'm not. I killed him because I couldn't stop myself. I lost control. But listen to me when I say this, Kate, I would have killed him anyways. I would have tried him guilty and sentenced him to death."

"He needed help, Gabriel! He was sick, but that was no reason to kill him!"

His expression turned cold. "You're defending him. The scum that tried raping you. You are choosing him over me?"

"Don't twist my words! I'm saying that he didn't deserve to die."

Gabriel stands abruptly but leans into my face. "He deserved every drop of his blood that was spilled. My only regret was that he stopped breathing before I was done with him."

This is not the Gabriel I know. He pulls away from me and heads for the door. "You will stay here till I feel confident that you will obey."

Obey? I'm not a fucking pet!

I feel Circe caving in under the stress. I feel her hesitation to fight against Gabriel when I rush to the door. He closes it behind him. I tug hard on it, but it's locked. I bang on it hard.

"Gabriel, let me out!" I kick the door. "Please, don't lock me in here!" Tears. Again. But it's not sadness I feel, it's rage. Both feelings that I'm very much familiar with. He thinks he can just lock me away. Well, he's got another thing coming.

I rummage through all his drawers again, looking for anything I can use to bust the lock on the other side. I find a screwdriver, and the first thought that comes to mind is ripping off the doorknob. I get to work on it, and once the knob is off, I can unlock the door through the hole. I swing the door open, hard, and hit someone on the other side. Two guards. Of course.

"Luna," one of them says, surprised. "Please get back inside. It's not in your best interest to disobey him right now."

I'm not listening, I simply continue my way down the stairs. I pass many confused and concerned faces on the way. I go straight for the entrance door when I'm pulled back.

Gabriel, my body screams.

I turn to him and try yanking out of his grasp. His eyes are dark and cold. "Let me go," I say evenly.

"You're trying my patience, Kate."

"The feeling is mutual." His grip tightens to near painful. I'm so wrapped up in my anger that my next words are carried out by anger and panic. "I, Kate Barsotti, reject—" Gabriel's eyes grow wide, and he releases me quickly. His hand flies to my mouth.

"Don't," he warns.

I attempt to shake his hand away and glower at him. How can someone make me feel so safe yet so trapped? "Let me go."

"Never." He throws me over his shoulder, but he doesn't take me back to the room. Instead, he walks outside. I struggle under his arm, but it is futile. He walks a great length before placing me down. We're in front of a small house. "Go in," he orders. Every bit of me wants to rebel.

I hate being ordered around by him, but I do as he says. I open the front door and step inside. It's pitch-dark. I search around for a light switch and find one just as I nearly trip. And then I see it. Every wall is covered with creepy writing and pictures of me, from the time that my parents were killed till now. Pictures of me by the river. Pictures of me unconscious by the riverbed. He was there. Pictures of me with Dylan and some with Gabriel. All the pictures had the male's face scratched out in them.

"This is Ronny's home. He wasn't just sick, Kate. He was obsessed." Gabriel is only a foot behind me. Besides the pictures, the place is a mess. There isn't a clear place to step. What happened to him?

"He was my friend," I whisper.

"Maybe once. I'm truly sorry about the way you found out, but I need you to understand that I will never regret it. Nor will I ever play with your safety. I will eliminate any and all threats to you and ask questions later. I will never allow what happened to you to ever happen again."

I turn, shaking my head. "And was locking me in a room part of keeping me safe? You already killed him! How much safer can I be!"

Finally, I see it. His remorse. My alpha has returned. "I don't want you caged like a bird, but you promised me that you'd stay put. It was only one day. But instead of staying, you—"

"I left," I finish for him. "Yes, I left the room to go downstairs. I had no intention of ever entering my room again."

"Then why did you!"

"Because!" I scream. "I had nearly been raped, Gabriel! I couldn't stay in a room isolated with only my thoughts. I can tell you now that it's really fucked up here." I tap my temple. "I needed to be around people who would distract me." I swallow the lump in my throat. No more crying. "I heard the doorknob turn, and I raced into the first room I saw. It just so happened to be mine. I wasn't sure if you wanted to keep people from me or me from people, so I hid." My voice is calm and level.

He's not as angry, and I can see that he is trying his best to understand what I'm saying. "I'm sorry. I didn't know it affected you that way."

"That's because you didn't ask." I exhale, frustrated. "But the truth is, I didn't know either. When you asked me to stay in the room, I was relieved. I thought facing everyone would make things hard, but being alone is much worse."

He pulls me into his large arms. "I will never leave you alone." I return his hug. "Are you hungry?" he asks blatantly.

I wipe my dripping nose with the back of my sleeve. "No, this place makes me too uneasy to eat."

"Well, you have to eat something. I will have them send something small when we get back."

On our walk back, Gabriel holds my hand the entire time. He tells me that he's spoken with one of the training officers and that I'm to start the day after tomorrow, and it is exactly what I needed to hear.

"Also." He pauses just outside the alpha house. "Do not ever threaten me with rejection again. Being Luna is not a game or a switch you can just turn off. You took on the responsibility, Kate. Time to grow up and face it."

I feel shame at his words. I keep telling him not to treat me like a child but then acted like one when he treated me like an adult. I swallow and nod.

He continues the conversation as if it isn't as heavy. "You will be able to speak to him tonight. The rogue, I mean." I see his apprehension, but I can also see his determination to satisfy this request.

Truth

I walk into the room that the rogue is being held in. His head is hanging low. I turn back to look at Gabriel. He gives me a shrug. I'm guessing he also doesn't understand the behavior. Gabriel shuts the door behind me.

I clear my throat. He slightly looks up. I catch his eye, and he raises his head. There is a kind of anger in his eyes. "Hello." I try. My voice is soft. "I wanted to come and say thank you."

"Don't." His tone is cut and dry, and I wonder for a moment if he's been beaten into regretting what he did. There are no visual bruises or open wounds, though.

"I'm sorry?"

"I betrayed my pack to help you." His voice holds anger as if it was my fault. "I will never be accepted back now."

Anger stirs in my belly now. How would they even know? It's not my fault I was attacked, and it's not my fault that he chose to help. "Then why intervene? Why not just let it happen? It was none of your business, so why help me?"

"Because!" He's breathing heavily. His eyes are wild with rage. "Above all else, I despise males who force themselves on women." I can hear the truth in his voice but also what he's not telling me.

"So what? I was about to be raped. Big deal. It happens to women every day. I am the mate of the alpha who imprisoned you. It should not have bothered you at all." The guard behind him straightened at my confession. I guess he'd forgotten.

"You must really be so childish to think my honor is measured by a grudge."

I laugh bitterly. "Your honor? Let me tell you what I think about your honor. A man with honor would never assist in the destruction of a pack. In the destruction of innocent men, women, and children. Don't grow a conscience now and talk about honor when you had every intention to sit idly by and watch us suffer the brutality of your pack leader!"

I don't know when it happened, but I am standing with my face inches from his. Every word was forced out in a rush, like a threat. Like a challenge to argue it. I want to shake the answers I need out of him.

I stand straight up. I'm so angry, I don't think I can speak to him without malice. I don't know why he can aggravate me so. I turn to leave the room.

"Thank you for your time," I whisper.

"Wait." I halt and look back at him. "I don't regret helping you. I need you to know that."

"Why? What good does knowing that do for me?" He doesn't answer. "What's your name?"

He hesitates but answers, "Samuel."

I don't sit back down. I stay standing and lean against the door. "What were you exiled for, Samuel?"

He looks down angrily. Seconds pass, and I can feel him refusing to answer. I take a step forward. My heart begins to pound in my chest like it's going to explode.

"What did they exile you for?" He shakes his head, looking away. Sweat beads against his forehead. I feel the perspiration too. "They exiled you because they believed you to be dangerous. What was your crime!"

"Rape!" he shouts. The guard behind him takes a step forward, preparing to restrain him. "I was accused of rape." His eyes look glassy, but I know that a tear would never fall. He was angry that he could do nothing to clear his name.

"You didn't do it," I say confidently. He looks at me, nearly falling apart. "I don't know how far gone my attacker was when Alpha killed him, but I remember the fury in your eyes. You were going to tear him apart yourself." He looks away and begins to dip his head again. "We're not finished. Lift your head," I demand. He does without hesitation. "You have two choices. You can continue to protect a bunch of angry criminals, or you can help us prepare to defend our land and our pack."

"I had no one but them for years. You really expect me to betray them?"

"Yes, I do. You want to restore your name and honor? Start by helping us." He goes quiet again. After a moment, he looks me in the eyes and nods. "My mate, the alpha, will question you."

"I'm sorry," he announces. I don't respond because I'm not sure what he's talking about. "Your parents," he answers my unasked question. "I never approved of his brutality. I made sure it never happened again."

My throat tightens. "You were there?"

"No. They boasted about it afterward."

Realization dawns on me, and I step back. "That's why you spoke only to me. That's why you came when I was attacked. You feel guilt." He looks down, and I know I guessed right. "And you're trying to make amends."

"I went to the site when I found out they left you alive. I wanted to make sure you were found and safe. When I got there—" I can see his struggle with telling me this. "I heard them talking about you. About how you ripped apart your own family. Then I realized what he wanted when he killed them." Tears go down my cheeks, and I don't try to stop them. I don't even care at this moment. "He's making rogues. He's building an army." All the air leaves my body.

"I was supposed to be exiled."

"But you were too young, so they kept you. I was sent when a new alpha took over this pack. I was sent to remind you of how they treated you."

"You were sent to collect me," I state. "Why? There is nothing specifically special about me. Why would he sacrifice two for me?"

"We weren't meant to get caught. It was supposed to be simply in, grab you, and then out."

"Through the tunnel," I finish.

"You found us as we arrived. I knew my task, but all I could think about was the image of you as a child, shaking as they questioned you. I needed to give you closure. You grew stronger than expected. You reminded me of—" He stops.

"Your daughter," I say. "I reminded you of the family that you were forced away from. I reminded you of the honorable man you once were."

"I was a good father. A good husband. When I was accused, they wanted to go with me. I forced them to stay. I knew that they would be exposed out there."

I wipe my face with the back of my hand. "Why were you accused? Was that the doing of your rogue alpha too?"

"No. It was the Luna of our pack." I gasp. "Her son. She was protecting her son. He was her youngest. He showed interest in one of my daughters. I allowed him to court her. I allowed him to take her out for a run alone. When she returned..." Tears choke him as he speaks. "Her clothes—were torn. Bruises covered her arms and thighs." He shakes his head. He sniffles before continuing. "I-I went after him, but before I could get to the alpha house, where he returned...the Luna had ordered my exile for attempting to rape my own daughter."

I shake my head. "Why didn't your daughter speak up?"

"She tried. The Luna made it perfectly clear that the whole family would be exiled if she did. She swore to me that if I left, her family would never come near mine again. I stayed close to the pack to make sure she kept her promise. When my daughters were old enough, my wife sent them to different packs so that she could return to my side in my exile. She passed before she could join me."

I never noticed his entrance, but I'm guessing Gabriel had been standing there for some time. "Your pack. Was it led by Alpha Sine?" he asks. Samuel nods. "Did you check to see what became of your daughters?"

He shakes his head. "They were better off without me."

"There is a nomad in my pack that my father took in years ago. As my mother put it, she never spoke to anyone. Refused all courtships. Then suddenly she asked to become a nomad. My mother was in charge of the travelers at the time. When my mother asked why someone so young would ask to travel, she thought she answered her own question. But the girl said she was looking for her father."

Samuel almost burst out of his seat. "Her name. What was her name?"

"Jane," Gabriel says simply.

"That's her. That's my oldest." Tears rain down his face.

"She belongs to this pack now. This is her home." Gabriel crosses his arms.

Samuel inhales deeply. Then he looks Gabriel in the eyes. "I will help you protect your home. I'll tell you what I know. All of it."

Need

Gabriel had finished the interrogation on his own after Samuel swore to help. It felt strange sleeping in Gabriel's bed, but then, I am his mate. He hadn't come to bed, though. Or rather I didn't feel him come to bed or leave the bed.

The following days, Leon had escorted me to meals. He wasn't ordered, but after the events, it didn't seem that anyone wanted to see me unprotected. It was a good thing that my training was to start today. I had a feeling everyone would feel better if they knew I could protect myself without having to turn.

"You really asked him why he killed Ronny? Kate, even if he never found out about Ronny's obsession with you..." Leon pauses. "I would have killed him. There was no way he would have gotten away with it, Kate."

"Yeah? What about four or five months ago?" His shoulders hunch uncomfortably. Gabriel asked me not to speak about Samuel's assistance because he had a suspicion that there was someone assisting the rogues. And he was ruling no one out. "Look, all I'm saying is that if no one cared about me, would he have still had an execution?"

Leon goes quiet in thought. I turn to look at everyone eating their first meal. Some laughing; some annoyed that they had to wake up early. We take everything we have for granted. Every breath. Every choice that we are given. Even sleeping soundly. We depend so much on the will of another—our wolves, the nomads, the perimeter guards, even Alpha. Still not one person gives thanks. We are more like the human race than we like to believe.

"I don't know," Leon answers, interrupting my thoughts. "I don't know if he would have gotten away with it, but I'd like to think that it would have been too much for Maddock and me to ignore."

I nod. I respect him so much more when he is honest with me. A piece of me knows that he would never ignore me in that situation. Another piece says he might have let me die a month ago.

After breakfast, I told him I was going to the training grounds. Of course, he wouldn't let me go alone. I could see a hint of pride in his eyes as he walks with me. His little sister finally learning the ways of her parent warriors. I understood. I believe that my parents would be proud that I'm following in their footsteps.

*****

"Again!" Joan, my training officer, yells at me. I rush her once more, and again, she easily dodges and pushes me past her.

"Again!" I'm sweating like crazy, and she is not going easy on me like I anticipated. Instead, she is pushing me much, much harder. I get into my stance again. My legs are shaking from soreness. "Don't you dare give up," she warns me. "You are Luna and must be able to fight even when your muscles protest." She circles me. "Ground yourself and take me down!" Pack members had gathered the moment I entered the training grounds earlier today. Some yell words of encouragement. Others look worried that I might get killed in here.

I ignore them and focus on the task in front of me. I plant my feet one more time and do my best to steady my breathing. I close my eyes and try to move past the nausea that I'm feeling. When I open my eyes, I'm ready. I feel Circe lending me a bit of her strength, and that's just the push I need. I charge at her and change direction twice. Her misstep gave me just enough time to sweep her off her feet. She falls hard on her back. I stand and refuse to celebrate. It took me hours to take her down, and even then, she, too, had been out here for hours and, I'm sure, is a tad bit winded.

Pack members holler in excitement. I huff and stretch my hand out to help her up. She takes my hand and gives a small smile. "Good, now we end for the day."

"Now?"

"Yes. You successfully took me down. Tomorrow you will perfect your craft, and then I will train you to counterattack."

I incline my head. "Sounds wonderful." I can't keep the sarcasm out of my voice.

Joan gives me a humorous look. "Don't worry, the first week is always the worst. Your body will adjust to the intense exercise. I will make you stronger."

"Then I will be your star pupil."

She grins. "Don't say it if you don't mean it."

"Oh, believe me, I mean it." I do. She's right; even if I never fight alongside my brothers, I should still need to be prepared for the worst. If all our defenses fail, I need to be able to fend for myself. Otherwise, I'll simply be deadweight to everyone around me. A liability.

I bid my farewells and head for the alpha house. I need a shower and food ASAP. Climbing the stairs to the room is like trying to conquer Mount Everest in seconds. Pack members gather around me when I nearly fall, without actually touching me. And I know it's out of respect.

"Thank you," I say to them. "But I'm okay. Just a little sore." Their faces show amused understanding, but they still watch me till I'm all the way up the stairs. When I finally make it to Gabriel's room, I strip out of the training gear that Gabriel said would help absorb most of the impact of a hit. It absorbed it all right, but it felt like fifteen pounds of lead on me. My movements were sluggish because of the gear. I'm in just my underwear and a bra when I turn to get a towel out of one of the drawers.

I scream loudly when I see Gabriel ogling me from the other side of the room. He has an amused and shocked look on his face.

"Please don't stop on my account."

I pull the towel to my front and huff. "What the hell are you doing just standing there?'

"I came in to get—"

"Never mind. Just get out!" He covers his mouth to hide his grin and leaves the room. Frustration makes me steam in anger.

"Kate?" he says from the other side of the door.

"What!"

"I wasn't done in there, so can you change or go into the shower?" I groan and rush into the bathroom, slamming the door behind me so he can hear it. I hear his deep chuckle on the other side. I turn the water on cold and step into the water. The temperature is a shock at first, but warm or hot water will only make me too comfortable, and then I'd want to nap the rest of the day away. So the cool water is a welcomed torture.

Lathering soap in my hands, I begin washing myself. I wash away the dirt and grime of the day. All my muscles are tense as my hand runs over them. I wonder how Gabriel did it. He had been raised training much harsher than that since he was just a child. Now I'm sure if I went into the training grounds with him today, he'd probably destroy me in endurance.

His muscles are so well-maintained and rock-hard. His biceps are larger than any other males in our community. His abs are incredibly defined, and his broad shoulders could probably carry a boulder on each of them. A small moan leaves my lips, and I then notice that my hand has stopped at my sex. I'm a little shell-shocked, but I don't pull my hand away. I have never had the urge till now to touch myself. I have done so before but only out of curiosity. Now I'm actually fantasizing about Gabriel.

About his hard abs and strong muscles. I slip a finger between my folds and rub my clitoris. An electric jolt runs up my spine, weakening my legs further, and I moan again. I rub faster, trying to get more traction between my thighs. I feel myself coming close to my climax when the bathroom door opens. I stop and see Gabriel over my shoulders. My lack of embarrassment surprises me. He has a heated look in his eyes, and I'm in no position to deny my need for him at this moment.

He moves slowly into the bathroom, never taking his eyes off me. He gets rid of his shirt and kicks off his boots. He only unbuttons his pants before stepping into the shower with me. He towers over me in the now-small shower. I don't try hiding myself. I need him. I need him badly.

"You are so beautiful," he whispers to me.

My eyes don't leave his when I say, "Your pants will get wet." His eyes light anew. I feel his need down within me. His gaze shifts down my body. The feeling is intense. I want his hands on me. I have never wanted a man's touch so much in my life before.

His forehead comes to rest on mine, and the feeling is so intense that I wrap my arms around his neck and pull him to me. I mesh my mouth to his. His hands still don't touch me, though, and it's killing me.

"Touch me," I beg.

"I don't want you to regret this decision."

"I promise, I won't. Please touch me. I need you." I can't help myself. I have never begged for anything before. Not even when I had been kicked in the dirt had I begged.

I run my fingers through his hair and then down his chest. I let my nails bite at his skin. He groans loudly. "You're driving me crazy, Kate."

"Then touch me."

"It is the tension from your training that's influencing your need."

"I don't care, Gabriel. I *need* you to touch me. Why are you making me beg?" My voice is whiny, and I have no shame in it.

He throws his head back and groans again. "I want you so bad, you have no idea."

"Then take me."

"Kate, if I take you now, I will lose all control, and I won't stop even if you beg."

The idea both frightens and excites me. I want this, though. I don't feel vulnerable or as if I'm being taken advantage of. I want all of him. I wrap my arms and hug him, my breasts squished against his chest. I can feel how much he's holding back.

"Lose control then." The moment the words leave my lips, Gabriel crushes me against the shower wall. I'm up in his arms with his mouth on mine. I wrap my legs around his core. His tongue finds mine in an exotic dance.

His pelvis grinds against mine deliciously. My thighs squeeze, trying to create more friction between us. I curse him for leaving his pants on. I move to his grinding, and a curse leaves his lips.

"Kate, fuck." He places me back down and then kneels. A wild moan leaves my throat when he begins suckling on my clit.

His expert tongue laps my sex, sending me over the edge. He grabs one of my knees and tosses my leg over his shoulder. It gives him more access. I'm close to climaxing when his fingers find their way to my breast. He pinches my nipple, making me scream out my orgasm. The waves of my orgasm die down, and my calf cramps up. No surprise there, all my weight is on my toes. Gabriel catches me, just as I begin to fall. He turns off the shower and walks us back into the bedroom.

Tossing me onto the bed, he strips off his soaking pants. Freedom comes to his large and erected penis. My body tenses slightly, but then it relaxes. My excitement begins to build again. It wasn't just needing to climax, I truly want him. He climbs onto the bed, leaving kisses as he goes. From my knees to my thighs, just above my sex, my navel, up my rib, on each breast, and the crook of my neck. I moan lowly. I love this feeling. I love it all. I love him.

The sudden confession to myself shocks me. Even if it is only in my head. I love him. I admit once more. His hand crawls under my thigh to my buttock. He holds me in place and lifts his head to gaze at me. "I won't stop, Kate," he whispers as the head of his cock rests just at the entrance of my sex.

"Don't," I whisper back.

He pushes slowly, never leaving my eyes. I begin to tense at the pain, but he grounds my hip from moving away. "It will pass," he says gently.

I nod but thrash my head back into the pillow as he pushes a bit further. He's a little less than halfway in when he stops moving completely. I know he's waiting for me to adjust to him. After a few moments of rushed breathing, I nod to him.

Instead of pushing all the way in again, he pulls all the way out instead. Then reenters. He repeats this a few times until I'm dripping and begging for more. Then he gives me everything. I gasp at the fullness, the intensity of him. My fingers grip his back. I hold on for dear life as he begins rocking furiously. Thrust after thrust makes me see stars.

"You are mine, Kate."

"Yes."

"All mine."

"Please," I moan.

"Come with me, my mate." Just as soon as he says so, a vicious orgasm rips through me, sending me to space.

He roars his climax and collapses beside me, pulling me into his arms in a possessive hold. My body is drenched, and I'm not sure if it's in sweat or the shower. Before I can think any more on it, I fall into a deep slumber.

Fool Me Once

"You never told me what you found in the tunnel," I say casually as I pick at the crumbs on my plate.

After our *intimate* moments, which I momentarily regretted out of embarrassment, Gabriel had woken me up to eat with everyone else. I was thankful for it. Had I slept past the meal, I'd be sick with hunger, especially after training. Our intimacy had also proven to be wake my hunger.

Strangely I didn't feel embarrassed afterward like I thought I would. In fact, I felt perfect. It was bound to happen. I just didn't think it would feel as natural and incredibly pleasing as it did. I remember how other girls would talk about how they'd lost their virginity to whoever while pretending I couldn't hear their conversations. They'd always talked about the pain and how big their partner was. None ever spoke about the insane pleasure or the intimacy that connected them to their partner. I'm happy that Gabriel and I could connect in such a way that seemed so perfectly sinful. Talking to Gabriel now, I can't help but feel joy that there is no awkwardness or distance between us. It's a wonderful secret between the two of us.

While eating, my mind has drifted to the conversation with Samuel. I begin to wonder what Samuel said about the tunnel. Gabriel hadn't once mentioned anything about the tunnel, and the curiosity has been eating at me.

Taking a swig from his cup, he looks at me from across the table. "It went deep. It was structured like a mine but..." He shakes his head and pops a piece of venison in his mouth.

"But we've been here for generations," I finish.

"The wood that was used has been treated and maintained. They've been working on it for a while. Right under our feet." He shakes his head again, disappointed.

"Well, we found it, that's what matters."

"You found it." He smirks. "I have a feeling that there are more."

"No, there can't be," I say unconsciously.

His eye dart to mine. "Don't be so sure."

"I'm not, but if there were more—okay, so this one was in a highly populated area, right? How is it that no one saw them before Circe sensed them? The area was dead. Not a soul was around. They can't always be sure where the next hole will open up to. So maybe luck kept them from being spotted, and maybe they just hid it really well, but how is it possible for them to cover their tracks so well that the ground looked completely undisturbed when Dylan fell into it? For them to have more, it's just not possible to be that lucky."

Gabriel ponders my words for a moment. His eyes scan the crowd that surrounds us. "I suspected a mole and hoped I was wrong. I hoped that if there was a mole, they'd only be toes deep. We have a rogue among us. Fabulous."

We immediately stop talking when Joan comes to speak to me. "Good hustle today, Luna. Think you'll be up for what's coming tomorrow?"

I smile up at her. "Well, it took me a few hours, but I took you down today."

She laughs loudly, and both Gabriel and I are surprised by it. We smile awkwardly. "Well, that's one small victory. Keep up the confidence, though." With that, she smiles and walks away.

Gabriel gives me a proud smile, as I roll my eyes. I stand and take the fruit I cut and wrapped earlier with me.

"I'm going to visit Dylan since everything happened, and I was sidetracked earlier."

"If I remember correctly, it was you who initiated it. But I'm not complaining." His grin spreads across his smug face.

I don't respond. I walk slowly to the Med Center, trying to wrap my mind around the recent events. I woke up from in a coma, then I took down a rogue, became Luna, found the tunnel, then I was nearly raped, and finally I was locked away for a day. On top of all that, Ronny's cremation will be tomorrow. Not that anyone will show after what he did. He had no living relatives. Even Leon had thought it a waste of time. This is too much in less than a month.

"Kate." I jump to the sound of my name. I turn to the soft voice and see the face of a woman who I once called my best friend. My mouth goes a bit dry, and I suddenly feel the tension in my shoulders. Emma opens her mouth to say something, but I shut her down quickly.

"Sorry, but I'm on my way to visit a friend. I'll have to talk to you later." I turn away.

"Please, just hear what I have to say. I promise it won't take long."

"No," I say flatly. "I really don't have time to listen to what you have to say." Her face drops.

"I'm sorry!" she blurts out. "I know it doesn't make up for any of the things I've said or done to you, but I was a stupid kid. I wanted to be popular, and I thought having a bunch of friends was important. I didn't want to be an outcast. I know I hurt you and left you alone. When Ruby gloated about pushing you into the river, my stomach dropped. I wanted to come see you, but I was afraid that you'd tell me to leave."

"You were afraid that I'd reject you, your concern, because of all the things you did to me? I smirk. "Pretty good guess." I shake my head. "You're right, your apology changes nothing. There is no going back for—"

"But you were so ready to forgive Ronny after he tries raping you!" she shouted with tears going down her face. Leon and Gabriel both come to my side.

"Something going on?" Leon asks. Emma looks away, wiping the tears from her face.

"No, just a friendly reunion," I say. When I look at Gabriel, I notice the amount of people looking our way.

My attention goes back to Emma when I hear her sniffle. "I'm sorry for bothering you, Luna." She's more composed as she turns away.

I exhale, annoyed at how right she was. I had defended Ronny to Gabriel after he forced himself on me. I had forgiven everyone else. A nagging sense of guilt tugged at me. I let out an annoyed sound.

"Wait!" Emma looks back at me. "I have to give this to a friend." I hold up my plate of fruit. "If you want to wait." She gives me a small and hopeful nod. I walk into the Med Center fuming. Why the hell did every little sad look fill me with guilt?

As Luna, it is only natural that you want your pack members to be happy.

It was rhetorical, Circe.

I understood. I shake my head at her dismissal.

"Well, it's about time!" Dylan snaps, interrupting my thoughts.

"Really! You're judging my timing? You sprained your ankle, yet you're still in the Med Center. Why?"

"Don't turn this around on me." He counters. "What did you bring me?"

"Fresh fruit. Delicious pineapple, kiwi, strawberries, and grapes."

"Ugh, you're a goddess." He takes the plate greedily.

"Okay, well, I'll be back tomorrow."

"What? You're leaving already!" He makes a pouty face.

"I have some unfinished business with..." I stop, not knowing what to call her. "Well, with an old acquaintance."

"An acquaintance? What the hell do you mean by that? Either they're friend or foe."

"I wouldn't call her a friend."

"Then she's a foe. What are you gonna do?"

"She wants to talk. Apologize, I guess."

"Are you gonna accept?"

"I don't know. I've forgiven everyone else, and she wasn't the worst of them."

"So what are you questioning?"

"It's just—she was my best friend growing up."

"And that spot is now filled, so categorize her elsewhere."

I laugh lightly. "Don't worry. Your spot is safe."

"Good, continue."

"I used to tell her everything. When things went sour, she used it all against me. I trusted her with so much. Even after she spread my secrets to everyone, I never let her secrets even slip from my lips. She was my last lifeline. I had hoped then that she would have had my back."

"But she didn't," he says, filling in the gap. "That's tough, Kate." His eyes then grow wide in realization. "But not as tough as nearly getting raped. You're worried about talking to some frenemy when you were almost raped a few days ago. Really!"

"Hey, focus on the problem at hand."

"Have you processed what happened to you?"

"Of course I have, and it's in the past. It's not like anything happened. Samuel came in just in time." Dylan gives me a sour look. He distrusts Samuel, and I can't blame him. He doesn't know all that I do. So I ignore his bitterness toward Samuel. "And then Gabriel came."

"And he tore him to pieces, then locked you up."

"How do you know all this?"

"Are you kidding? It's not like anything happened in secret. The whole damn pack has been talking about it."

"Oh, great."

"What do you expect, you guys do nothing in private, and you're Luna now. Of course, they're going to talk."

"Ugh, let me just get through today, then we can backtrack."

"Mm-hmm, sounds like a plan. Make sure you talk to someone, Kate."

"About?"

He shrugs his shoulders. "I just don't think you're processing this whole situation in a healthy way."

I head for the door. "I'll see you tomorrow."

"You know I'm just trying to help."

I nod. "I know. Thank you for caring." He dips his head. I walk out the door and prepare myself for the next hard conversation that I'm about to have.

I walk out of the small building and see Emma leaning against the building wall. I shove my hands into Gabriel's sweater pockets and step stiffly in front of her.

"What did you need to speak to me about?" I ask, guarded by my high walls. She could see them. She knew that it wouldn't be so easy to speak to me freely. Not after everything. There's something different about forgiving a friend after they've betrayed you.

Family is simpler because, somehow, that blood connection makes you want them in your life. At least until they do something unforgivable. With family, there's something inside that almost makes you trust them. With friends, you choose to trust them. You mold them into your heart. You love them as if they were family, and you confide in them as they will never hurt you. The family we choose. And if they hurt you, you have no one else to blame but yourself. It was your decision to allow them into your life and choose to trust them. So, in the end, it is your bad judgment that led you to get hurt.

Looking at Emma, memories of us laughing by the river come to mind. The way we'd choose a leaf each to race in the river with. We'd run along the river, encouraging our leaf to swim faster, as if they could hear us. Even though she is a year older than me, we had been as close as sisters. A deep ache settles in my chest, but I force it down.

She seems at a loss for words as her mouth opens and closes a few times. Gone are her tears from earlier. She is prepared to hold them back this time. I can see the determination in her eyes.

Finally, she swallows and opens her mouth. "I know that what I did is unforgivable." I don't respond. "I know there is nothing I can say to make you believe how sorry I am." I keep my expression blank. "I just wanted to tell you that I am sorry."

I suck in air through my teeth. What do I say to that? Nothing. There is nothing I can honestly say that that will appease either of us.

"I'll go now," she says quietly. I can see the disappointment in her hazel eyes. I can't stop her and tell her that I forgive her. She moves to walk around me. I stay unmoving.

I think back to those days when we'd swore we'd marry brothers so that we could become real sisters. She had been my rock then. The one I could turn to if I ever felt that I couldn't speak to my family. The friendship I once held onto is long gone; she had carved it out of my heart. It is sad, but thinking about it now, I have no feelings for her, one way or another.

I will always hold those memories close to me, but we can never be the friends that we once were. That being said, we don't have to be enemies either.

"Emma." Her shoulders hunch at the sound of her given name. She turns back. "Your secrets are still safe with me, but mine will never be safe with you again. Fool me once." Understanding passes through her eyes. She nods and continues walking.

I'm so on guard that I'm able to sense Gabriel somewhere behind me. His hand slides to my waist.

"Eavesdropping is rude."

"I just wanted to make sure you were okay, speaking with her." I look up at him with a small smile. "She was here the night we found you near the river. She asked if you'd be okay."

"And you're telling me this because…"

He shrugs. "I didn't know who she was then. She seemed sheepish that night. I guess nothing much has changed now that the sun is up.

I shrug this time. "She may have hurt me the most back then. I told her things I hadn't told another soul. I think that's why I can't reunite with her as if nothing happened."

"What do you mean?"

"When my brothers turned their backs on me, I was hurt, but I knew they had been filled with lies, and because of their grief, they chose to believe them. They needed someone to blame. Emma believed me when I said I hadn't done it. But when people became violent toward me, she didn't want to get dragged into the line of fire. So she left me behind and gave my secrets to others for ammunition."

His grip on my waist tightens. "You were too young to have to go through that alone. What secrets did she tell?"

I shake my head. "Nothing major, really. I was too young to have any real secrets, thank goodness. What I did tell her, she sold for companionship from others."

Gabriel takes my hand and brings it to his lips. "I will keep all our secrets from now on."

"And what about the ones about you?" I tease.

"You have secrets from me, about me?" His grin is arrogant. "Well, you didn't have Circe before. Now she can keep the ones you can't tell me, safe."

I will protect them till the end, Circe says, pulling a grateful smile from me.

*****

The next morning was pure hell. I thought I was sore yesterday. I was wrong. Every muscle that I needed to prepare for training pulsed in pain.

I stretch, doing my best to ignore the pain. Joan holds a knowing smile on her face. Everything inside me wants to slap it right off her.

She cackles, throwing her head back like she had yesterday. "Yes, be angry. You're gonna need that if you plan on getting through today.

She was right; I was knocked on my ass more times than I can count. I'm suddenly in denial that I ever took her down. She calls an end to the training when she nudges my leg from my stance, and I crumble under my own weight.

"Tomorrow, same time. Be prepared because I won't go easy on you like I did today." She walks off with a wide grin playing on her lips. She must be a sadist.

When I return to the alpha house from training, I inspect the entire room before underdressing. I'm in a towel when I scavenge through Gabriel's new clothes for something to wear. He had brought me some much more appropriate clothing, but I liked wearing his things. It felt as if I was showing off the fact that I was taken. Looking for a shirt, my hand hit something hard in the back of the drawer. It is sort of the drawer wall, and it slid when my hand hit it. I open the drawer all the way and find a book.

Training Games.

Call Me Luna

After my shower, I launch myself onto the bed with the bulky book. I have buried my head in it, telling myself that I'd only read a bit of it so that I have time to visit Dylan before the evening meal. I really don't understand why he's still in the Med Center. His leg was not as hurt as I initially thought. I make a mental note to ask him about it without letting him change the subject like he had yesterday.

Opening the book, I notice that the contents are handwritten. I skim through the book and find that not a single page is typed. I go back to the beginning to read the first page.

> Beware of the warrior who is consumed by these games. It is his soul which has left his body, and his rage to win is all that is left. Players, beware.

I flip the page eagerly. I had never heard of *Training Games*, but then again, I hadn't really been a part of this society for a while. Scrunching my nose at the thought, I read on.

"The Game of Bells," I read out loud.

I've heard of these games, Kate.

"You have? Where from?"

Waiting, in the black world. The warning in the beginning is not to be taken lightly.

"Why? What is it?"

These games are like exercises for warriors. The more they win, the stronger they get. But it comes at a price.

"What do you mean? What's the price?"

When a warrior is inducted into these games, they start small and simple. The first few will test their mentality when it comes to their victories. Then it tests your endurance…to see if you will continue to play, even when you are hurt. And lastly, it will test your morality.

"Your morality?" I ask, afraid of knowing what that meant.

Yes. The last will test the warrior in the most brutal way imaginable, that is almost unspeakable. Each time the warrior wins, a bit of their soul is ripped away from them.

"So when you heard of these games, it was from—"

Yes, because we are attached to your souls, the ones I heard from were ejected from their vessels. They had said that there was nothing left of the person they grew fond of.

"But why would someone willingly give up their wolf?"

"It is a last resort." I jump at the sound of Gabriel's voice. He is leaning against the doorframe, watching me with his arms folded over his chest. "Snooping?" he asks, and I pull my legs closer to my chest.

"I was looking for something to wear and found this." I hold up the book.

He smiles gently and comes in to sit beside me. He drapes an arm around me, and I snuggle into him. When had I become so comfortable around him?

"It was my father's and my grandfather's, all the way back to the first alpha of my bloodline."

"You said it was a last resort. For what?"

He takes a deep inhale before explaining. "In the past, there had been many battles for territory. Packs would fight to their last member to keep their land. The downside was that many of the women and children back then were too proud and angry to join another pack who'd slaughtered their husbands, brothers, and sons. They'd leave and settle elsewhere without protection or hunters. Many of these people died of starvation or sickness. Males kept their women safe, fed, and built a shelter for them. There was a proud alpha who had always feared that his pack may one day fall prey to another pack. He feared what might happen to his pregnant mate and the child if he wasn't around to protect them.

"So he pushed his warriors harder and harder every day to ensure that they'd always be ready for an invasion. He developed new training methods that he was sure would push them to their strongest suit. It wasn't until many of them had lost touch with their wolves that he realized the power of his methods because his warriors had been the strongest of them all. But the victory he felt was short-lived when he saw the distance his warriors put between themselves and their families. Then they became abusive to their women and children. Taking things they wanted from their families by force. Some took from others' families until the warriors were fighting and killing each other. Women and children were victims who had simply gotten in the way." I suck in a shaky breath.

"What happened to the pack?"

"When he realized the mistake he had made, he took the women and children that were left and started his pack again. His mate gave birth to a son. While his son was training, he gathered all the games he had and compiled them into a book. He told himself that it was a fail-safe. When his son became Alpha, he passed it down to him with the warning that it should not ever be used until he's down to his last few warriors. He told his son this same story and told him to make the right allies. He told his son that there will always be enemies, but with the right allies, his pack will never worry for their safety."

I swallow loudly. "That's so sad. He got so wrapped up in trying to keep everyone safe that he destroyed his own pack." Gabriel looks at me.

"He was not trying to keep his pack safe, Kate." I look at him, confused. "He was trying to keep his mate and child safe."

"But then—"

"Story never says that he lost his wolf. He hadn't lost his way and hurt his mate. He used his warriors, and they paid the price for his fears. He was not a wise alpha, he was a paranoid one."

I lick my lips and nod. "It's still sad. So many lives were ruined because of him. Didn't anyone blame him for it all?"

Gabriel nods. "Yes, two. Two had blamed him and told him that the blood of the fallen were on his hands."

"Who?"

"His mate and child. They were the only ones who really knew why the warriors lost their wolves and minds along with them. Out of their sorrow came their hatred toward him. For the unity of the pack, they acted as the perfect family. But there was no guessing as to why he only had one child."

"Do you think you'd ever need this?" He shakes his head, looking deeply at me.

"I would never ask any member of my pack to relinquish their souls and their wolves as well. It is suicide in its own way." I agree silently. "But if I had come down to the last of my warriors, I'd take you, our children, and whoever is left, to an allied pack. Where I'd know you'd all be safe." My heart rate jumps at his talk of children.

"So why do you have it, if you know you'll never use it?"

He shrugs slightly. "I guess I never found the urge to throw out the only gift from my father."

I scowl, and he chuckles. "He's really something."

Gabriel nods. "Something we don't have to talk about." He takes the book from my lap and places it on the end of the bed. "Now aren't you going to visit Dylan?"

I jump to my feet at the reminder. Jumping off the bed, I look out the window; they already started preparing for the evening meal. I'll only have an hour or so before we are called for it. I hear Gabriel's chuckle from the bed.

"As much as I love seeing you in my clothing, I think you look best out of them. Maybe you should change into—"

"Quiet! I'm not changing in front of you." He laughs again. I scrabble into my shoes and am out the door in the next few seconds.

I stop just outside the alpha house door when I see Dylan walking out of the Med Center from across the gathering area. He spots me and waves. I run up to him and pat him hard on the back.

"How ya doing? Hmm? Is your fake injury all healed up?"

He tries rubbing the spot I just smacked and smirks. "You have a mother's hand, you know that? Heavy and painful."

I smirk back. "Suck it up. So you never told me why you were in there so damn long." I cross my arms over my chest.

"Dylan," someone says from behind me. I turn and see Taylor. The one who Dylan said was his fated mate. My shoulders hunch, knowing how Dylan feels about the situation. Taylor gently pushes his hands into his pocket. "I tried visiting, but uh—"

"Yeah, the nurses didn't let any visitors in. They made an exception for Kate because she is Luna."

What? His ankle was only sprained; it's not like he was comatose.

Taylor nods awkwardly. "Well, uh, I'm glad to see your leg is healed up."

"Thanks, man, I really appreciated your help that day. But you didn't have to come down here to visit. You already helped out a lot. It was my fault that day I stepped and fell into a hole. It was a mistake." I feel sad for Taylor, hearing the message in Dylan's words. Taylor looks at me, and I give him a sad smile before his eyes go back to Dylan.

"I see. Since you're better, I won't bother you again." He looks back at me and dips his head. "Luna."

I cross my arms and turn to Dylan, furious, once Taylor walks away. "What the hell was that?"

"Shh." Dylan shushes, walking toward the alpha house. "I don't want to talk about it."

"Well, too bad." I pull his shoulder so that he has to look at me. "Look, Dylan, I can't begin to understand the pressure that is on your shoulders about keeping up an image for the sake of your sister. But take it from me, that was not the way to reject someone. You could have at least explained yourself to him. Explain why it can't be. Why he should move forward with his life."

"Kate."

"Call me Luna." Dylan straightens at my tone. "Go explain yourself to him. That's a command."

I see the anger in his eyes, but he doesn't say anything. Instead, his moves past me. I feel bad for meddling in his life, but I know that he will regret the way he rejected Taylor whenever he sees him around the community. It is large, but that doesn't mean they'll never run into each other. I hope that maybe he will decide to give Taylor a chance. They both deserve happiness.

I'm taking a seat at a table when Gabriel comes to join me. "I see you are reserving your seat early."

"Dylan is out of the Med Center. I figured I'll wait for everyone here." I don't know if Dylan told Gabriel, and I don't want to share his secret with anyone.

Gabriel nods, placing a hand around my waist. I wonder if all alphas are as possessive as him. It would make sense. While possessiveness may not be the greatest characteristic to some, alphas almost depend on it to protect what belongs to them. Whether that be territory, pack members, or their mates. Personally, I believe there is something primal about a possessive male. Primal and attractive.

"What are you thinking about?" I flush and shrug. It's almost like he knows.

"How is Samuel doing?" I change the subject.

"He's given us some good intel. So far, everything has checked out."

"Checked out? You've sent scouts to confirm his information?" I'm shocked.

"I didn't put them in any danger that they couldn't handle."

"Has he told you anything about the one who's been spying within the camp?"

Gabriel shakes his head. "No. I asked how he'd gotten out of the cell. I had assumed that he overthrew the guard since I'd taken the other to the tunnel with me." He pauses. "But he said that he'd awoken to a sound that night, and the guard was already unconscious and the cell unlocked. He was going to make a run for it, but he's noticed Ronny's interest in you before. When he saw Ronny heading for the alpha house, he went after him instead of escaping."

"How noble." I don't mean it sarcastically, but that's how it comes out. Gabriel nods slowly. "Do you believe him?"

"Unfortunately I do."

"Why is that unfortunate?"

"Because it means the mole is in deep with the rogues. They don't care at all who may get hurt."

"So what can we do?"

He smirks. "You can continue your training, grow strong, and then maybe I'll have you tell him that I've sent for our nomads to return home."

My heart is so full that it hurts in my chest. "You're bringing her back for him."

"Not just her. I've also sent word to the packs for his two other daughters. They will be here in a few weeks."

I want to cry. How did I get so lucky?

"Does that please my mate?" He smirks, holding me closer.

"You have no idea." He chuckles and kisses my cheek.

Habits

Hours had passed since I told Dylan to explain things to Taylor. He didn't show for the evening meal, and he hasn't shown up in the alpha house. The woods were darker than usual tonight because there was no moon. I sit, hunched up, hugging my legs, against a window that had a good view of the front of the house. I check my wristwatch, 10:06 p.m. I sigh and hope that maybe it's an hour ahead. Dread fills my belly when Gabriel comes to check on me.

"Are you coming to bed?" he asks gently. His fingers comb through my hair.

"I think I pushed him too far."

He presses his lips together. "I don't know what happened, but I'm sure he'll be fine."

"What if he doesn't come home tonight?"

Gabriel squats slowly to look me in the eye. "If he doesn't come home tonight, I'll go looking for him first thing tomorrow morning. Come to bed." His promise doesn't ease my guilt. I thought I was doing him a favor by sending him to speak with Taylor.

Thinking about it now, who am I to tell him what to do with his love life? I have had one relationship my entire life. Even then, I had my demands, and Gabriel had his. I had no right to tell him to speak to Taylor. It had probably been hard enough for him to have to reject Taylor.

"Kate," Gabriel calls me from my thoughts. His hand moves from my hair to my cheek. "If it gets too bad, I'll arrange for him to speak to his sister. She is a good friend of mine, and they are very close." I stare at him before nodding. I take his waiting hand and follow him to *our* bedroom.

I'm tossing and turning in bed, frustrated. Then I hear a door being shut downstairs. I rush off the bed, no doubt waking Gabriel, and swing the door open to try talking to Dylan. He's halfway up the stairs when he sees me. I give him a relieved smile, but it fades at his angry expression.

"How did it go?" I ask quietly, partially knowing the answer.

He scoffs and turns his head to me. "Fantastic." His tone is cold and short. Before I turn to go back into my room, he turns completely and says, "You know, the next time you want to intervene in someone's messy life, you should start with your own." With that, he's in his room with the door shut tightly behind him.

I feel my nose sting, and my throat grows tight. I turn to walk back into my room, but Gabriel's hard chest is in the way. I don't look up at him; I just wrap my arms around him and bury my face. His arms fold around me as he guides me back into the room.

*****

"Kate, you have to eat," Maddock says, trying to spoon-feed me.

"I am eating." I snap, slapping the spoon out of his hand. I have been poking around my plate for a few minutes and only have been able to take a couple of bites.

Gabriel had to leave early this morning to speak with other alphas about the rogues. He left with a supportive, "Don't worry about, Dylan. He'll be fine once he cools down a bit," thus leaving me to eat with my brothers.

"Kat," Leon starts before I shoot him a glare for using that old nickname. "Just finish the fruit, and then we'll leave."

"Well, lucky for me, I'm in no rush. You two, on the other hand, have your duties to attend to."

They look at each other and sigh in defeat. Then suddenly a strong hand slaps my shoulder painfully, though meant to be playful.
"

"Morning, Luna," Joan says with a wide grin as she puts her fists on her waist. "Ready for training?" I rub my shoulder, trying not to show the fact that it felt like she just punched me in the back.

I smile, and through gritted teeth, I say, "Just about."

She nods, her attention bouncing from Maddock and then to Leon. Her eyes linger a bit longer on Leon. A shock wave rolls through my belly suddenly.

Mates, Circe says loudly.

What? Leon stands abruptly.

"You okay?" Maddock asks, confused by Leon's behavior.

They are fated mates. I look at them in surprise.

That can't be. They've seen each other before, how could they suddenly be fated mates?

Yes, but Leon was not the same person as he is now. It is similar to a state of mind, only it is the state of heart. Leon must have accepted who he is completely. He accepted his mistakes and used them to grow stronger. Making him Joan's perfect match.

"Yeah, I'm fine," Leon replies, never taking his eyes off Joan. Joan, however, becomes a little breathless, and her eyes flicker to me, with a touch of regret in them. Her smile returns, but it doesn't quite reach her eyes.

"Luna, I'll be waiting for you in the training ring." Her eyes move to my untouched plate. "Make sure you eat. We may not have time for midmeal today." She turns away and walks toward the training area.

"Damn, I have training in an hour. There is no way I can digest that fast," I say, making Maddock laugh. Leon sits slowly, chasing after her with his eyes.

"That might not be a good idea," I say to him. Curse my non-existent filter.

Leon looks at me, a bit dewy-eyed. "What's not?"

"If she's your fated mate, then maybe you should use the time from now till I have to meet with her, to talk with her."

Maddock begins choking on whatever he's chewing. "Fated mate?" he says through gasps.

"You're right."

Oh, thank the goddess he didn't get upset. Once Maddock gets ahold of his breath, he stares at Leon in shock. Leon nearly falls over, trying to pull his leg over the bench we're sitting on.

"Keep her occupied so that I can eat," I yell as he jogs after her.

"What the hell is going on?" Maddock asks, taking a swig of water.

"None of your business," I say, forcing a spoonful of food into my mouth.

"They're fated mates?" he asks, astonished. I shrug. "Wait, how did you know?"

I look up at him and ask Circe the same question.

You are Luna. The more you care for your people, the more you know about them. Your love and understanding of them make you stronger.

I don't understand.

You forgave your old friend and accepted that you two would have to learn to live with each other, even after she betrayed you. You tried helping Dylan to be happy, even when he would rather ignore his own happiness. These actions are proof that you love the members of your pack and wish the best for them. The Luna is as strong as her pack is happy. Nothing you do is to gain anything. It is completely genuine.

There really is a lot to this Luna title.

No more than there is to an alpha's.

Gabriel has powers too?

Naturally. The difference is that his powers grow slowly. They grow along with the strength of his pack. If they are weak, physically or mentally, then his powers take the repercussion of it. Your powers do the same if the pack is emotionally struck.

Is there any exception?

None that I've ever known of.

I nod, taking another spoonful into my mouth, and then shrug to answer Maddock's question. "I have mate-dar," I joke with a mouthful.

"Why am I the only one without a mate? First you, then Leon. I'm gonna die alone."

"Maybe it's because you're a disgusting playboy." He looks at me wide-eyed. "Yep, I hear the talk from the girls whose hearts you've broken."

Maddock looks at his empty plate and lifts it. "I think I should give the cooks my plate, now that I'm done."

"Mm-hmm." I hum as he dodges the conversation.

I swallow and look at the alpha house. Dylan must be hungry by now. Getting up, I decided to take a plate of food to him. I haven't nearly finished my food, but I doubt it'd be a good idea anyways, especially when I hit the training pit with Joan in less than an hour.

My belly has butterflies as I approach his room door. I wipe my sweaty palm on my pants before closing my fist to knock.

"Dylan," I say lightly. My voice cracks in the process. I clear my throat to make my voice a bit stronger. "I brought you food." No answer. Bile fills my mouth, but I force it down. "I'm sorry I pushed you too far. I shouldn't have gotten involved." Still, no answer. I stay there for a moment, trying to hear inside. There is no noise, but I can somehow feel him closer. Maybe part of the whole Luna thing. "Look, you're my friend. I know you have your reasons for what you did, and I have no place to question them, but I just wanted you to be happy.

"I'm not sure when was the last time you did something for yourself, but I think you deserve to." I rest my head on the door. "Dylan, you don't have to come out, but please know how sorry I am. I didn't mean to cause you any more pain than I'm sure you felt having to say no." I gently lay the plate in front of the door. "I'll leave the plate here for you. I really am sorry."

Before I can turn, I'm embraced in a hug from behind.

"I'm sorry too," Dylan says. "I shouldn't have said that last night." I grip his arm that is wrapped around my front in an attempt to hug him back.

"It's okay," I whisper. "You were right."

He lets me go and spins me to look him in the eye. "No, I wasn't. You were just being a good friend, and I lashed out in anger. I'm sorry for what I said." We hug again, and I can hear him sniffle over my shoulder.

"Don't cry because then I'm gonna cry, and then Joan will beat the crybaby out of me."

He laughs through his sniffles. "Are you calling me a crybaby too?"

We both laugh and release each other. "Uh-oh, my mate and her enemy are at each other's throats again?" Gabriel asks from behind Dylan. We both turn and smile at him. "Hmm, hard to tell who won when you're both crying."

We both smile, and I shake my head. "We're not fighting."

"Too bad, I had my money on my beautiful mate," he says, grinning. "Shouldn't you be getting ready for training? Joan will be harder on you if you're late." I nod and look at Dylan.

"I'll meet you after," he says with a small smile. I maneuver around him and Gabriel to get past.

Gabriel stays and begins a conversation with Dylan. I can't make out the words from our room, but I'm sure it wasn't meant for my ears, so I let it go.

*****

"Are you all right?" I ask Joan. Twice I had nearly knocked her down. For so early in our training, it's a big deal. "You don't seem uh…"

"Are you still angry with your brothers?" she asks out of nowhere.

I drop my stance. "Is this a trick to catch me off guard?"

She looks down. "I just want to know if you've forgiven them?"

Realization hits me. "Joan, you don't need my permission to accept Leon."

Her face burns bright red. "I'm—" I can tell she is about to deny it, but I put up a hand to stop her.

"Save it. I already know."

"He told you?" More like I told him.

"No, but I could tell. He looked at you the way Alpha looks at me. Like there's only the two of you in the entire world."

She flushes again. I hadn't noticed before, but Joan is a very beautiful woman. Despite her outspoken attitude and painful playfulness, she has rather feminine physical features. Her pixie haircut makes her face seem sharper from her jawline to her chin. Her hazel eyes and dark-brown hair make her skin look fair and flawless despite her few scars. Looking at her now, she is a perfect combination of beauty and strength.

I give her a gentle smile. "Joan, if you want to say yes, then do it. But do it for yourself, no one else."

She smiles back, and for a moment, I think she's going to run off to tell Leon her answer, but then she gets into her stance with new determination in her eyes. "Well, come on then, future sister-in-law. Try taking me down." This will be a very long day.

I spotted Gabriel long before he got to the training pit that Joan and I were in. He approached hastily and watched me the entire time. It was distracting and unsettling. Joan threw me down harder each time for not paying attention. Even when I tried to ignore his presence, my gaze would find his like a magnet, and he would smirk. Suddenly I was filled with the determination to succeed in front of him. I am not one to willing make a fool of myself because of a guy.

I wasn't at Joan's level or even close, but one thing I had learned while training with her was that I could be slippery when I focused. I could almost sense where she was going to strike milliseconds before she did it. In those moments, I'd navigate in another direction. The only downside was that Joan recovered quickly and would adjust her strike so as to succeed in the following strike. I landed hard on my back in the dirt. Instead of getting up right away, I lay there for a bit, and Joan huffs her victory.

"You're getting better, Luna. Soon I won't be able to take you down at all." She gives me a hand to help me up, then looks over at Gabriel, who's resting his elbows on the fence that cages us. "You ready to hop into the pit, Alpha? I'll go easy on you?" She smiles, crossing her arms.

Gabriel put hands up in surrender and looks at me. "Just spectating."

Joan starts unwrapping her wrist from the protective tape. "Well, why don't you have a cool-down match with our Luna?"

I give him a death stare. His grin widens at the idea but then rejects politely. "As much as I'd love to, I'm afraid of my mate's power over me." You should be.

Joan laughs lightly and then calls it a day, and I thank the goddess for it. All my limbs feel strained, and my head is pounding from the repeated falls. Joan walks out of the pit, with me shortly behind. Gabriel catches me by the waist and presses his lips to mine.

"Why don't we go and have a shower?" he whispers into my ear. We hadn't engaged in that way since my first day of training. The idea of it makes me both embarrassed and ache for him. The embarrassment only came from the fact that he would say it in public. Though I have no shame in what we've done in private, I don't exactly care for other people knowing.

"Is that why you're suddenly done with all your work?" I whisper back.

He pecks the corner of my mouth. "I never said I was done with my work, but I do have time to spare. Time that I can't think of doing anything else other than spending it with you."

I grin but place a hand on his chest. "I can't. Dylan is gonna—"

"He is occupied right now. I let him know that I would come to get you while he sorts out his to-do list."

I give him a face. "Are you speaking in code? I have no idea what you are trying to say. What is he doing?"

"Doesn't matter. He's busy. He'll come around later." I see an unsaid comment in his eyes but choose to let it go.

"Then I guess I'm all yours." He grins and pulls me over his shoulder. I squeal in laughter when he begins to run through the community till we reach our room. I would have been embarrassed by it, but many looked at us in amusement instead of shame. Well, I'm positive they will all know what we are about to do.

Once inside, he tosses me on the bed and strips off my clothes easily. What would have taken me minutes to do only takes him seconds. In a few short moments, I am completely naked in front of him. His eyes roam over me as if inspecting his work. The heat in his eyes makes me want to shield myself but force my hands to stay at my sides. I stand slowly and walk to him.

"What about you?" I ask, placing a hand on his bare chest. He begins untying his pants. They fall to the floor, and his thick erection springs free. My cheeks warm at the sight.

I'm in his arms again in a second. He kisses me as if he is starved of my lips. His tongue invades my mouth, and his hands wander to my backside. We're in the shower moments later, under icy water, but the heat between us is enough to fog the glass doors of the shower.

"I think you like showering entirely too much," I say when his mouth falls to my shoulder. Just as I say it, though, his teeth graze my skin almost painfully. It is such a shock to me that my clit throbs in response. A strangled moan escapes me. He's marking me in such a primal way. Gabriel spins me so that I am facing away from him. One of his hands slips between my thighs, and the other comes to toy with my left taut nipple.

I gasp at the pleasure of the feeling and reach back to grip his hair. I pull gently, and Gabriel places his hand on the front of my neck, forcing me to look back at him. Our eyes meet.

"Do you know how badly I've wanted you these last few days? Each night was pure torture." I study his beautiful face. I had so much on my mind that I hadn't paid enough attention to our intimacy. I feel a bit sad by that. I have this beautiful man next to me every night, and I hadn't noticed his need. I must seem horrible to him.

"I—"

His mouth covers mine and then he cuts the shower off. "I need you now. I cannot wait any longer." In a moment, he spins and lifts me. Instinctively, my legs go around his waist. "You are so beautiful."

I smile but then wince. "I don't think I can stay like this for long. My legs are like jelly." My thighs shudder as I say it.

"Then I guess you'll have to trust that I won't drop you."

My eyes widen. "Gabriel—" I moan before finishing my sentence. He pushes inside me, deliciously. My whole body clenches in response. He thrusts a few times, and I'm on the edge of ecstasy.

"Mine." He growls in my ear. The primal instinct to claim me is plain on his face. His fingers dig into my thighs as if I'm going to disappear at any moment. My hips attempt to meet his thrusts, practically distracted from the strain of my arms and legs. My whole body wants to give out yet refuses to until I reach my orgasm.

His thrusts begin to speed up, driving me wild. My toes curl, and my head lolls downward. Gabriel presses his forehead to mine before I have a chance to rest it on his chest. My nails dig into his shoulders. "I'm—I'm…"

"Come for me, Kate." He thrusts harder, making my body tingle from the orgasm that rips through my body. I bite his shoulder to muzzle my scream. Gabriel groans his release. We sink to the floor of the shower. He holds me tightly.

Despite my enraged breathing, my eyes shutter sleepily. Gabriel chuckles, pulling me back to see my face.

"Just as I suspected. Sleepy?" I nod like a two-year-old. "Let's wash you up and get you in bed." I nod again.

*****

"Joan and I are mates," Leon announces with a wide grin as he approaches the table we chose for the evening meal. After my nap, we came outside right away to eat. I still haven't seen Dylan since the morning, but Gabriel assures me that he is fine, and he'd be out to join us soon. He has a possessive hand on my thigh the entire time, and when I'd try to wiggle free, his hand would drift upward as a warning. Maddock almost seemed uncomfortable with us. *Third wheel.* I smirk at his discomfort.

When Leon walks up with a hand on Joan's hip, we all had already guessed that she'd accepted.

"We know," Maddock says lazily. "Traitor."

Leon's wide grin falls a bit. "Right, well, she accepted me." His smile picks back up when he looks at her.

"I think they guessed as much, Leon." Joan takes his hand and guides them to sit next to Maddock and in front of us.

"Luna, Alpha." She inclines her head to us. Gabriel returns the gesture, and I smile.

"Happy?" I ask, grinning.

Joan laughs softly and tucks an invisible strand of hair behind her ear while glancing at Leon. "Yes, he's wonderful." I laugh. She must have already had a crush on him before.

Gabriel kisses my temple, pulling me closer to him. *Happy mate,* I think to myself.

"Kate," I hear Dylan shout from the alpha house. His hand is extended in the air, trying to wave us down. He jogs up and slams into me and Gabriel, sliding us over some. "Move over a bit, would ya?" I laugh and slide over to give him more room. "So what are we talking about?" He turns to look at me, and I see his face up close for the first time since this morning. A dark bruise is swollen around his right eye.

"Dylan, what happened to your eye!"

His eyes shift to Gabriel and then back to me. "Well, Mum—"

I grab his chin tightly. "Don't act stupid. What happened?"

"Geez, easy on the kung fu grip."

"Dylan!" I snap.

"I happened," Gabriel says from my left. I whip my head around to look at him. "After you two made up."

"Why!"

"Because I hurt you." Dylan chimes. "Really, Kate, it's fine. We have an understanding." They both grin as if there's an inside joke that I'm missing.

I worm out of Gabriel's grip, leaning close while pointing a finger in his chest. "Don't hit my friends." Gabriel pulls back a bit.

Gabriel nod noncommittally. "Okay." He pulls me back to him by the finger I poked him with and kisses me. I shoo him away, still angry that he hit Dylan.

"Kate, I'm fine. Gabriel and I were sparring partners in training. Believe me, I got off easy," Dylan says. I glare at him, and he clamps his mouth shut.

"Did you speak with her?" Gabriel asks Dylan, changing the subject.

"Who?" I interrupt.

"No," Dylan says.

"Speak to who?" I try again.

"She's busy. I don't want to pull her away from her duties."

Annoyed at the fact that they're ignoring me, I wave my hand in Gabriel's face. "Don't ignore me. Who are you talking about?" Gabriel gestures to Dylan.

"My sister is visiting."

I gasp. "Really! In the alpha house? I want to meet her!"

"No," they say in unison. I furrow my brows.

"I mean, not yet." Dylan chuckles awkwardly. "I should speak with her before anyone else. Besides Alpha, being that they have things to discuss."

"Yes, we speak tomorrow, and Dylan speaks with her after, then we'll introduce you to her."

"I'm sure she'll be happy to see that bruise on your eye. She'll probably think that we abuse you."

"Oh, I wish," Dylan jokes, wiggling his brows at me.

"Brave man to joke like that around her mate," Joan says with a glint in her eye. Uh-oh.

"He knows she's mine." Gabriel tries reassuring her.

Dylan nods with a wide grin on his face. "For now." Gabriel reaches around me to smack the back of his head.

"Do not disrespect them that way," Joan says, fuming.

"Joan, it's okay, he's like family to us." I try to calm her.

Leon wraps his hand around her middle in a soothing way. "Does he know that?" She snaps. Other members begin to catch on to the conversation.

Gabriel sits a bit straighter and places his free hand flat on the table gently. "I appreciate the fact that you are trying to defend my mate's honor, but I trust Dylan with my life. He likes to joke around, and I have no problem with that. Do not insult me by insinuating that there is something between my mate and my good friend right beneath my nose."

Her eyes widen a bit, and her eyes fall to her lap. "Forgive me, I didn't mean that you...," she trails off. "I'm sorry, I guess I'm not used to that kind of playfulness."

"Understandable, but do not question who I trust my mate with. He wouldn't be near her if I thought he was after something other than her companionship."

"Of course, Alpha," Joan responds without lifting her gaze.

Tension fills the table. "So when are you moving Joan in with you, Leon?" I ask, trying to liven up the atmosphere.

"Well, she's gonna stay with me tonight, and then we'll be moving her things tomorrow." So it really is that easy? Why did it have to be so complicated with me?

"Yes, so we will not be training tomorrow, Luna," Joan says shyly. I'm relieved that she is not staying quiet.

"That's good. You two are good for each other. She's beauty, brains, and strength. And you're none of those things. She completes you." I look at Leon, making them all laugh, cutting the tension to shreds.

Leon laughs. "That's true."

"Since we're done, I think we'll head off first," Gabriel says once the laughter dies down. "Good night."

"It's only—" I try to protest.

"It's time to go, Kate." Gabriel gives me a needful look. I lick my lips and agree silently.

"Good night, guys," I say without looking at them. How could they not catch our silent dialogue?

"Alpha," Dylan calls before we walk too far. He jogs up to us. "I left what you asked for in your private bathroom." Gabriel's expression becomes serious before he nods.

"So secretive recently." I raise a brow at them.

Gabriel smirks. "The same way you two have your secrets, he and I have our own."

"Mm-hmm," I hum.

"See you both tomorrow," Dylan says, wishing us good night.

Before we get to the alpha house, though, we pass Taylor. I catch a glimpse of his face, and my heart aches for him. His eyes are darkened, as if he hasn't slept. His hair looks like he's not bathed in a while. Gabriel follows my gaze and squeezes my hand.

"They'll be okay," he whispers. I look at him a bit shocked. He gives me a small smile. "He's my friend too, Kate. There's little he's able to hide from those who know him."

Of course, they've known each other much longer. Still, I'm saddened by it. Two mates not able to be with each other because of what people might think. Something twists inside me. It's not so different to my rejection. Gabriel was afraid of the pack's aversion to me. I exhale. I shouldn't intervene any more than I already have. I look back once more and notice that they've caught each other's eyes. There's longing in both of them before Dylan looks away. Another ping of pain enters my chest.

*****

I'm lying in Gabriel's arms as he runs his fingers up and down my naked back. I've never felt so at ease.

"The sun is still up," Gabriel says. I smile. The sun was setting, but I knew what he meant.

I nod. "Yeah, it is. I'm not tired. We should try to sleep."

He turns his head to me with a smile. "Or we could do something else."

"We already did that."

"I am a creature of habit. It's not a habit yet. Let's keep doing it till it becomes a habit." I can't stop laughing. I sit up and playfully smother him with my pillow.

"You haven't told me how things are going with Samuel."

He shoves the pillow away and runs his hands up and down my bare thighs. "What do you want to know? You got more information out of him than anyone ever could."

I cross my arms. "And what are you doing with that information?"

Gabriel exhales and sits up. "Okay." He pulls me to him so that I am seated between his thighs. "I had sent word to Dylan's sister and our other allied packs about the rogue alpha that decided to create an army of rogues. Samuel says that he made sure no one else was made a rogue after your parents. His only concern was that he has no idea how many were before you."

"Does he know how long the rogue alpha has been a rogue? If it wasn't long before what happened to my parents, then—"

"Yes. That was my first thought. Unfortunately, Samuel doesn't know. He did say that there were loyal rogue members long before he got tied in with them. His guess is that it had been years." Damn it.

"What about the rogue among us? Any news on that?"

"Samuel came up short there too. He says if there is a rouge with our pack, the rogue alpha never told him about it." Another dead end.

"Maybe we can bait the rogue."

"How do you suggest we do that?"

"We can spread a rumor that we have a powerful weapon that we can use against the rogues. Say that it's in the alpha house and that it's going to be moved soon. The rogue will come forward trying to steal it, and we'll be here to catch them."

Gabriel has a wide smile across his face when I look up at him. "You're adorable."

"Don't patronize me. What's wrong with my plan?"

"Kate, if we had such a weapon, why would we broadcast it?"

"So that the pack knows that they are protected."

"I love you, but it would seem too far-fetched. They would know it's a trap. They've been fooling us this entire time. If we had a weapon, why would we move it?" I face forward again, annoyed at how childish I must have seemed just now. Gabriel kisses the top of my head. "I love your creativity, though." Darkness has finally fallen, and I'm still wide awake.

"Can we go for a run? I'm not tired."

"Only if I can continue my favorite habits when we get back." I roll my eyes and pop off the bed to get ready. He does the same.

Perfect Days

"And another one bites the dust," a female's voice says from my left.

I had been reading "the apple book," as Dylan calls it, in front of the alpha house, when two males shift and begin fighting. I don't recognize either of them, but just as I come to my feet, others rush in to pull them apart. When I look at the woman to my left, I realize that I've never seen her before either.

Her eyes shift to me, and she smirks. "Luna." She inclines her head in a nod-like bow. "Didn't mean to disturb you," she says nonchalantly, taking the chair that is beside me to sit on.

I try being polite and smile, but it comes out awkward. I can't help but stare at her deep-blue eyes. They almost seem to be glowing, though I know it's not possible. Rays of light shine on her burgundy hair and pale skin. I back up into my seat and do my best not to make her feel uncomfortable, but I have never seen a more beautiful woman before. She crosses one leg over the other and folds her hand across her middle as she watches the males get pulled apart. Her figure is a damn near-perfect hourglass. Large bust, wide hips, and long legs. She's dressed in black homemade gear, similar to what Gabriel chooses to wear.

"Lost something?" she asks without looking at me.

"You are so damn beautiful. Are you real?" Filter gone. Embarrassment fuels my movement as I realize what I just said.

She turns to me and laughs genuinely. "You are the first female who has ever said anything like that to me."

"Sorry, I didn't mean to just blurt that out."

"No, please." She waves a dismissing hand at me. "I prefer blunt people to people who beat around the bush."

"Well, I'm nothing like that. But I'll pretend to be for the sake of this conversation." She laughs again.

"You're really funny." She leans in close. "So how did you get stuck with Gabriel as your mate?" I flinch at the use of his name.

My defense goes on high alert. "I'd like to think that he got stuck with me."

"Oh, please you're a sweet treat. Gabriel is somewhat of a dumbass when it comes to females."

"You know from experience?" I ask bitterly.

"I've known him my whole life. Might even say I know everything about him."

Jealousy stirs in my belly. I'm prepared to end the conversation when Gabriel steps out of the alpha house. His lips press a thin line when he sees me. "Kate, I see you've met Arura. Arura, this is my mate and Luna, Kate."

She nods. "Yep, and we were just talking about you in fact." A worried expression crosses his face, and it does nothing to ease my jealousy.

"Arura and I were in training together," he explains. "She's Dylan's sister."

My eyes widen. "What? Really?" The jealousy subsides for a moment. "Dylan's my best friend," I say, gaping at her.

"So Gabriel has said," she says, not as enthusiastic as me. My excitement dies. Was my sense of jealousy so apparent that she now sees me as less than?

"Have you spoken to Dylan?" I try.

"Of course, he *is* my brother," she says, rolling her eyes.

"I meant since you began your visit?" She doesn't answer. "I think he could really use some family time—"

"And what makes you the expert on family?" She looks at me with a sour smirk on her lips.

It hurts but not as much as it angers me. I look at Gabriel, and he looks away. I now know that he was the one to tell her of my life. I stand in front of her with my book under my arm. I lean over so that I am only inches from her face.

"I don't know what you think you know about me, but I can promise you that it's not much. Alpha or not, you will learn to respect me in our territory." My voice is low and even. I shove past Gabriel, angry that he would volunteer information about my family like that.

"Kate," Gabriel calls after me, but I keep walking. I hear someone shift, and dread fills my belly.

Release me, Circe says, and I do. But instead of turning to see who is chasing us, she runs into the forest. We run till we reach the cliff where Dylan and I stood on our first run. Finally, I see reddish fur and am annoyed that she came after me.

Circe sits and looks at her patiently. Soon Arura's wolf sits as well. A moment passes between us, and we are both calmer for it. Circe then releases me and shifts. Arura's wolf follows.

Arura stands with her hands in the pockets of her pants. She watches me as if I were something unusual. The blue of her eyes studies hard before she looks out over the cliff.

"You are strong," she says without looking at me. "My brother is lucky to have a friend like you. And Gabriel is lucky to have you as his mate." I stay quiet. "I'm very protective of my brother." I swallow. "Gabriel too." She finally looks in my direction. I grit my teeth, frustrated. "I see him as a brother." Her lips twitch, amused. "Dylan won't see me," she says, looking back to the scenery. My lips part slightly at her confession. "The whole time he's been here, he's written to me about the Luna with white fur, who packs a hell of a bite."

She smirks again. "He told me about how easily you get riled up. I wanted to test it for myself." One shoulder jumps in a shrug. "When I first got here, I expected him to introduce me to his new best friend and tell me of everything you two have done so far. Instead, he keeps himself busy so that he doesn't have to speak to me." Her eyes shift over to me. "I guess I was a bit jealous that he speaks to you and not me."

A bitter taste plays on my tongue. I know why he's avoiding her, but I have no right to tell. Telling her might solve things, though. At the same time, I had been so upset when he told Gabriel about my secrets. I'm so conflicted about what to do. Will telling her solve things or just make them worse? What if she agrees that he shouldn't accept a mate if it jeopardizes her title? Then he'll be hurt even more.

"You don't have to tell me," she says, interrupting my thoughts. "I can see it in your eyes. Whatever is wrong with him, I'm sure he'll tell me in his own time." I exhale and bite my lower lip. "I just wish he knew that I will always have his back."

Oh no, is this manipulation? Is she trying to get me to tell her? What was that term called, *reverse psychology*? It's working.

Like word vomit, I can't hold back. "He has a mate."

She stills, shell-shocked. "He what?"

"He found his fated mate." Slowly a smile presses her lips.

"Good." Her eyes hold a calmness at that moment. She is genuinely happy for him. "He'll introduce me when he's ready," she says confidently. I admire the faith she has in him.

"No, he won't." She looks at me almost angrily. "I don't mean because of you or anything, but he rejected his mate."

"Why?" Her voice is even and her expression impassive. I clench my jaw tightly. I think I've said too much. "Look, he is my brother. I have always looked out for him, and he has always looked out for me. I need to know why he would reject the gift of a fated mate."

My palms become sweaty. "He didn't want to disappoint anyone."

"Who?"

"Uh…He didn't want people to talk badly about…" I drift off.

"About me. He rejected his fated mate so that they wouldn't talk about me." Her fists close tightly; she shifts viciously and runs toward the community. Crap. Crap. Crap.

Circe!

Let's go!

We shift and chase after Arura. We're right on her tail, but she is determined. We reach the alpha house in record time, and she shifts back. I tackle her hard, and we both tumble to the ground through the doors of the alpha house. All eyes are on us in shock. I'm on top of her for half a second, when she flips me onto my belly, twisting one arm behind my back with her knee holding down my back. Gabriel rushes to us, panicked.

"Wait, please!" I yell at her, but Gabriel stops too. "I get it. I felt the same way when he told me. But this is his story to tell. You trust that he'll tell you in time, so give him that. I just wanted you to be prepared. He loves you this much." Her grip on my wrist loosens, but she doesn't let go immediately. My chin starts to hurt from the pressure of my head.

"Fine, but if he doesn't tell me before I have to leave—"

"Then have at him," I finish. She lets me go and sits back, resting on her hands. Gabriel grabs my elbow to help me up.

Arura huffs at the members who have stopped to stare. "I didn't think you'd tackle me." She seems annoyed, but I hear a bit of amusement in her voice. "You know I've trained for years to always win, and you decide to tackle me?"

I rub my wrist. "Yet I feel like I won." She smirks and shakes her head.

"What the hell is going on?" Dylan says, rushing through the doors. "Someone said you two were fighting?"

Arura jumps to her feet. "Just a little sparring practice. Her arms cross over her chest. "She's got a hell of a jump."

"Why are you sparring out in the open, without any gear on? And why Kate? She only just started her training and is nowhere near as advanced as you." His anger was genuine and for me. My heart flutters before I stand in front of her and put my hands up in surrender.

"It wasn't her fault, I tackled her. Then she showed me how my tackle could be used against me. She was just trying to help me so I wouldn't be caught off guard tomorrow with Joan." Dylan looks past me to Arura and back.

"Thanks, Kate, but I can fight my own battles." She gently ushers me back to Gabriel's protective arms. "Sorry for hurting your friend," she says it almost as if it pains her. "We were just horsing around."

He's calmed a little bit but is still red in the face. "Maybe this isn't the best place for your reunion." Gabriel looks at them and gestures for his office.

"No need. If my brother wanted to talk to me, he would have done so already," she retorts and walks to the front door and out. The crowd that had stopped their activities within the house disperses and carries on with their day.

Dylan runs his hand up his face and into his hair. It is so strange to see his cool-and-collected facade crumble to stressed and saddened. Gabriel pulls me away from Dylan and turns me to walk upstairs. I reluctantly walk away from my friend.

"He'll be okay, Kate. These things take time and even my head-strong Luna can't rush it." I swallow the lump in my throat as the image from Dylan's aggrieved face shows bright in my mind's eye.

An excruciating wolf cry brings me to my knees. I cup my ears and tears fall from the pain of the noise. I can't tell if it's in my head or out loud. I decide it's in my head when Gabriel wraps his arms tightly around me. His face is panicked. He is saying something, but I can't hear him.

No, Kate. This time, Alpha is wrong. Dylan needs you now. His wolf is in pain.

Wobbly, I elbow Gabriel's arms away while keeping my ears cuffed on instinct. Gabriel tries holding onto me, but I shake him off again. The whining doesn't stop. My head starts to pound painfully. My vision blurs, but I somehow make it downstairs. Dylan is no longer in the front area. I look around but don't see him. My eyes clamp shut as I begin to sweat. Gabriel holds me again, and members rush to our aid.

"Dylan." I whimper, though I can't hear my own voice.

Gabriel nods and points out the door. A few members nod and bolt out. What may have been seconds feels much longer when Dylan runs in anxiously. The whining finally dies down enough for me to uncuff my ears. Many members gasp when I do, but I pay them no mind.

"Dylan, you have to talk to her. You have to tell her. Please, you're in so much pain, and it's not going to get any better by pretending there is no problem. She needs to know." Gabriel is holding me tightly. If he lets me go, I know I'll crumble again. Dylan exhales hard but then nods and leaves. The whining is gone, and I feel completely drained by it.

"Get a doctor!" Gabriel says.

"No need. I'm already here." An elder man comes walking up to us.

"I'm fine." Even as I say it, I feel a splitting headache.

"Let's get her to bed." In the next few moments, I'm lying on our bed. Gabriel is kneeling beside me, wiping the side of my face with a warm towel.

"I'm fine," I say, guiding the towel away, and then I see it. Blood. "What's wrong with me?"

"Shh. It's okay, the doctor is making tea for you. It will help you sleep."

"I'm already sleepy." He doesn't respond, he only continues wiping.

Circe.

I am very tired as well, Kate. We need to rest.

Will we be okay?

Yes, but we need sleep.

I don't wait for the tea. I close my eyes and follow the darkness into a welcomed deep slumber.

*****

When I wake, it's with a jolt. My whole body is tense.

"Don't worry, Luna. You are safe. I gave you a small poke to ensure you are still with us."

I look over at the doctor from earlier. "Why wouldn't I be?"

"Kate." Gabriel is on the other side of me, gripping my hand tightly. He looks terrible. How long have I been asleep?

"What's wrong?" I ask him.

"Baby, you've been asleep for days." My belly flutters at the nickname.

"Days?" I sit up and notice that we aren't in the alpha house. We're in the Med Center. "What happened?"

We needed the rest, Circe answers sleepily. *You expended a lot of power wildly, and it drained our energy completely. But we are fine now.*

"I expended too much energy," I say to Gabriel. He looks relieved.

"You scared me, Kate." He places his forehead against mine. "Please don't do that again."

"I didn't know I was doing it," I whisper to him with a hand on his cheek. "But I'm sorry I scared you."

"She'll be fine." The doctor gives a worried look as he says it.

"What are you not saying?" Gabriel demands.

"Forgive me, Alpha. It's just, this is the first Luna in generations that have been gifted with powers. I'm not sure there is a doctor alive who will be able to accurately diagnose her should she ever fall ill."

"That's why we have wolves." Gabriel stands. "They give us their wisdom and knowledge where we fall short."

"I didn't mean to be so…incompetent, Alpha. What I mean to say is, we do not know where her power ends and her wolf's begins. We will not know if she should shift to give her strength or if that may just leave her vulnerable. There are times when shifting can endanger a person more." I can see Gabriel's frustration.

"Stop." I squeeze his hand. "He's only saying that there are a lot of missing variables. Even Circe told me that it's better for me to sleep this off instead of shifting. We had both exhausted our strength." I look at the doctor. "I guess we'll have to learn my limitation on a day-by-day basis."

The doctor looks at me with a gentle smile. "The only advice I can leave you with today, Luna, is that if your power were a muscle, it would be wise to exercise it. Learn how it works and learn to control it." I nod. "Well, I will be leaving now. I have given you some herbs that will help you sleep. My guess is that you will be needing it."

"Thank you, doctor." He leaves us to be alone with each other.

Gabriel sits back down and kisses my forehead. "I'm happy you're okay. I love you." My face gets hot. He's said it before, and I didn't get a chance to appreciate it.

"I love you too." I see something change in his eyes. Determination of sorts.

"You should eat. I'll bring you something."

"Wait, what happened with Dylan and—"

"Arura returned to her pack, and Dylan…" He drifts off, looking away from me. I think the worst. What happened to Dylan? Is he hurt? Worse?

"What! He's what!"

"He's outside, waiting on his turn to see you. Doctor thought it best that only one of us was in here at a time."

"I want to see him," I say hastily.

"What about me?" he asks.

"You're fine! I need to talk to Dylan. You can come in after." Gabriel pouts, but then gets up and calls Dylan in.

"Dylan! What happened with your sister?" Dylan rushes over to me and grips me in a tight hug.

"She's fine. How are you feeling."

"I'm fine, well-rested. Did you speak to her?"

He exhales and nods. "Yes, I spoke to her."

"And?" I ask after a grueling moment.

"And she wants me to accept my mate. She said she could handle her pack without me having to sacrifice my happiness."

"So have you?"

He hesitates for a moment. "We plan on moving in together in a few days."

"Ahh!" I scream in excitement. Gabriel and the doctor come rushing back in. I look at them happily. "My best friend has a fated mate!" I shout. The doctor chuckles and then walks back out. Gabriel simply smirks.

"No need to tell the whole world, Kate!"

"Alpha." A member comes in to speak to Gabriel. "It seems that you were correct. There is another hole." Gabriel shoots me a wary look.

"We'll talk about this in my office."

"No, wait." I call to the member. "What about a hole?"

He looks hesitantly at Gabriel, who is gritting his teeth. "I'm sorry, Luna. I didn't mean to cause you worry." With that, he walks back out faster than he came in.

"What hole? Is it the rogues?" I pull the thick blanket off my lap and try getting out of bed to confront but am held back by Dylan. I scowl at him, but he wavers.

"Give us a second," Gabriel says to Dylan. Dylan obeys with a hesitant glance at me. Once out of the room, Gabriel comes to sit beside me again. "I wanted to be sure that there were no other threats that could put anyone in danger. I had a team search the grounds for any other tunnels or holes that a person might be able to crawl through."

"Why didn't you tell me? Did you think I'd be so petty as to say I'm right?"

"That's not it, Kate."

"Then what?"

"I needed it to be discreet."

"You think I'd go around telling everyone?" I bite my lip out of anger.

"Kate, in the last month you…" He exhales and looks away.

"I what?"

"Everything that you've done or that has happened to you has been the topic of each day for the pack to talk about. I couldn't risk—" My anger subsides to hurt. How is it my fault that the pack talks? I only ever speak with Dylan, my brothers, or Joan. Somehow, though, I'm untrustworthy? My hands are in fists on my lap. I look away from Gabriel.

"Of course I'm to blame for gossip," I say.

"That's not what I'm saying, Kate."

"It's fine!" I snap. "It's not like I need to know anything. It's above my pay grade."

"Kate!" Gabriel snaps and grabs my chin, forcing me to look at him. His anger was clear on his face as mine. "Do not jump to conclusions without allowing me to speak. You are the new Luna. Whether you like it or not, you are physically the runt of the pack. You were hated for years because of something that was not your fault." Tears prick my eyes as he says it accusingly.

"Everyone's eyes are going to be on you because of those reasons alone. I know you wouldn't tell a soul if I had told you beforehand. I needed you to carry on with life as if nothing changed because all eyes are on you. In any pack, the members watch their Luna to see if there is something to be worried about. If you are jumpy, then they will be too." I blink my tears back. "I love you, Kate. Do you really think that I'd trust you with my family's book of terrible training games if I thought you'd go around telling everyone?" He sighs. "Do you believe me?" His eyes search mine.

"Yes," I say softly. "I'm sorry."

He shakes his head. "You are used to being attacked, that's why you become so defensive."

"Old habits die hard."

"Now that you know, I need you to do your best to let everyone know that there is nothing to worry about. If panic spreads, then there will be nothing left of us for the rogues to take."

I breathe slowly, trying to comprehend it all. How can there be another hole? It's not possible for someone to get that lucky twice. Unless—and I gasp at my realization. "Ruby," I say.

"What?"

"Ruby, she was there the day Dylan and I found the first tunnel. She was there alone, but why is it that the entire area was clear with the exception of her? She said she went there because she didn't want people to see her nose. If that was the case, then why leave her home at all?"

Gabriel's brow furrow. "You think she's a mole for the rogues?" He scratches the back of his neck. "I would have never guessed it would be her. She's not exactly organized. What would she have to gain from it?"

"Maybe she's not organized. But if they offered her something in return for helping them, then she'd probably follow their directions to the max." Gabriel nods, thinking it over.

"I'll have men watch her movements. I can't exactly blame her without proof."

"Pfft, she's done it to me for years."

"Kate, we're not sinking to her level...or my father's, for that matter." He stands. "I need to go talk to my advisers. I'll come back tonight." He kisses my forehead.

"Gabriel," I call before he reaches the door. He turns, and I can see the alpha in him. The protector of the pack. "Thank you for not brushing me off."

That triggers something in his expression. Suddenly he is back next to me and kissing me hard. I can barely get a breath in. When he pulls away, he responds with "I know better than to doubt my mate." I smile widely as he leaves the room.

Dylan, Leon, and Maddock come into the room a little while later, all wearing a smirk.

"What?" I ask.

"Don't you know how to stay out of harm's way?" Maddock asks.

"I didn't go looking for danger. That should count for something. And there isn't exactly a how-to-be-a-Luna manual." He comes up to me and hugs me gently. I return the gesture for his benefit.

"Excuses. Excuses," Leon says. I can see he wants to show his affection too, but he stays planted by the door. For once, I'm a little sad about it.

"So you ready to go?" Dylan asks.

"Go where?"

"Come on, you know the best way to heal is—"

"We brought you a change of clothes," Maddock says cutting off Dylan.

"We can make a distraction," Leon finishes.

I laugh. "You guys are crazy. The doctor will be angry, and so will Gabriel."

"All you needed was a bit of sleep. Come on, you're fine now," Dylan jokes.

Excitement fills my chest, and nervousness fills my belly. I really want to go just because I know I shouldn't. "What if we get caught?"

"Then we'll run, and you'll be on your own. We will deny knowing anything about it." The nonchalant tone in Maddock's voice makes me laugh again.

Why not? Circe intrudes. *Turning can help get our blood flowing through the legs.*

"Ugh, fine." I take a bag that Maddock hands me and change in the bathroom.

The next thing I know, I'm walking out of the room with Leon and Dylan in front of me and Maddock behind me. This is such a stupid idea. The doctor would have said yes if I asked. Even so, I'm excited by the thought of sneaking out.

Once we're outside, we run for the trees. Some look at us suspiciously, but I'm in a hoodie, and it's hard to see my face. Good thinking, guys. Except the fact that I'm the *smallest* person in this pack! Of course everyone is going to know it's me! Some even bow politely as I run by.

Finally we're far enough to shift. Dylan goes first, and we all follow suit. We run for a while before we end up at the alpha house.

I'm refreshed and happy. With the exception of the rogues and the possible threat of Ruby, everything seems perfect. My best friend has a mate that he will introduce me to tomorrow. My brother has a fierce mate that I will never argue with. And Gabriel isn't treating me like a child. Nothing could ruin this perfect day.

Just as this thought enters my mind, Gabriel storms out of the alpha house. For a moment, I think it's because of me. But he goes straight to Maddock.

"Find Ruby, now." He nods and quickly splits from the group.

They're here, Circe whispers.

A Precious Gift

Who's here?

Before she can answer, Gabriel has a hold of my arm. He puts both hands on either side of my face. "I need you to think. Is there anyone at all that you spoke to about the book?"

Dread pools in my stomach. "No, I honestly haven't had it on my mind at all. I swear."

He looks disappointed by my answer, but something tells me that it's not because of me. Gabriel turns to a warrior that had followed him out of the house. "Wake everyone. Have all the warriors searching the grounds."

"Gabriel, what's happened?"

He scrubs his hands over his face. "I went to grab some clothes for you to leave in. When I pulled open my drawer, I noticed the book was missing."

The rogues. I hear them. I still at Circe's words. Everyone looks at me, confused for a second. I don't respond. I just listen, trying to hear what Circe hears. No one tries speaking to me; they simply wait. I turn my face up toward the sky, and my eyes close. I can't even be sure if I caused this action through pure instinct or Circe did. Moments later, I can hear the footsteps so clearly it is as if I am there next to them.

My eyes snap open. I see the same dread on Gabriel's face. "They're here." My voice is barely a whisper.

Gabriel's eyes bulge. "Dylan, get everyone ready for an attack." Dylan nods and runs off. "Leon, go after Soro and tell him not to search the grounds. Keep everyone close. Go door-to-door with him. Wake all families. Get every warrior to the stronghold."

I understand the tactic. Because the stronghold is the only opening into our territory and also the only side guarded by fence, and the other sides are guarded by rocky mountain or cliffside. No one would be stupid enough to invade from anywhere besides the stronghold, lest they risk trapping themselves. But the rogues aren't stupid, they are cocky. Hearing them, I knew they weren't coming through the stronghold, and I knew why.

"No." I gasp. "They're not only coming through the stronghold. They're coming down the mountain too."

"The mountain, but why would they—" Dylan starts.

"They want to push us toward the cliff. So that we have no room to fight or flee," Gabriel says. "How far off are they, Kate?"

A mile, Circe answers quickly, and I relay it.

Gabriel runs a hand through his hair. "Okay, get half of the warriors to the stronghold and the other half to the mountain side" The pack member nods and disappears.

"I'm going to go help get everyone else to safety."

"No." He stops me before I can leave. "You need to keep yourself safe. Go to the forest and hide."

"Gabriel! These are my people too. They need us more than ever! I am not going to abandon them, and we don't have time to argue." His expression is grave, but he hugs me tightly and kisses me hard.

"I'll see you when it's over." I nod and dart away with Dylan.

My lungs burn with how hard I'm breathing. My legs feel as though they are moving in slow motion. Before I know it, Circe takes over.

Outside is complete chaos, understandably so. Families trying to keep ahold of each other as they follow Dylan to the forest. Some orphaned children are crying in fear as they try their best to keep up. Circe gives me full control. I stop in front of the children and kneel. They get the message and climb aboard. Many see and follow my example, carrying their young loved ones.

Soon every person with a wolf has shifted. As I run, I feel the children slide every now and then. I slow a tad for them to readjust themselves, then continue sprinting. We are more than a mile away when we hear the fighting begin. Whines, growls, the smell of our fallen fill the air. My chest tightens. I hang onto the hope that

Gabriel is not one of them. We all continue to run. Some run harder than before, desperate to keep their families safe.

The moon begins to rise, and my chest feels as if the moon is helping my heart pump. *Buh-dum. Buh-dum. Buh-dum.* I focus on the three small children on my back. We are near the downfall of the cliff, far right of the waterfall.

Goddess, let us make it to safety.

"Almost." I hear someone whisper. I stop dead in my tracks. Some, who were running beside me, stop as well. I raise my snout to the air and sniff. A dirty scent I don't recognize blows hard into my face. A trap!

It's too late. I hear someone in the front of our small herd get attacked. I kneel again, and the children jump off. The few that ran with me each take one of the children I carried. A silent message passes with a glance, and they run back toward the falls to find a place to hide for the time being. Goddess be with them. With one last look at them, I run to the front. At least ten rogues are there, ready and waiting. One pack member is limp and lifeless between the rogues and us. My heart breaks at the sight of Maddock.

Every emotion passes through me. Rage makes my hackles rise on end like a feline. A rogue stands above him with one paw on him. Every scent that passes by me, from the chilled air and the dirt my claws dig into, it all tells me that this is the rogue that killed my parents. He shifts to his human form, apathetic to the fact that the pack members and I are still in our wolf forms.

"Look at you, little wolf. All grown up now." His voice is a whisper, and his eyes rake over me, almost as if proud. I feel the fear radiating from the few members behind me. Dylan is by my side, showing all canines. The rogue turns his attention to him.

Did you really think that I'd attack the community where it is strongest? No, all the leverage I need is right here." He gestures to us with his arm stretched out wide. The other rogues surround us. "Now if you don't want your families hurt, shift."

The demand was unfathomable. We will be vulnerable and at his mercy completely. I want to resist, but one of the rogues to my left snaps at a child.

A bit of anger burns through me as I wonder why this one was not taken with the others. The child cries but is unharmed. They will have no mercy if we don't comply.

I shift first. The others follow my lead. The rogue alpha walks up to me. I'm much shorter than him. Dylan tenses at the shrinking proximity between the rogue and me.

"What do you want?" I demand as he stops right in front of me.

He smiles grimly. "What do I want?" He grabs my face with his palm over my mouth. "I just want you to understand. I want you all to understand. You were never safe." The gentleness in his voice churns my stomach. He pushes me away with a slight forcefulness. Dylan grabs me before I can fall.

"Stop!" Gabriel yells from somewhere behind us. The rogue yanks me back from Dylan's hold and puts a knife to my throat.

"No, no, no, little Alpha." Gabriel freezes. Some warriors stand behind him. "Now I heard that this little runt is your Luna. You don't really want to lose her tonight, do you?" No fear comes to my mind. Instead, I feel anger that this pathetic excuse of a man is using me against Gabriel. The knife presses harder against my neck, and I can feel a small trail of blood drip from the cut. I don't feel any pain, though.

"Just kill him." I grumble.

"Yes, Alpha, just kill him," the rogue alpha mocks quietly. My teeth clench hard when I hear a laugh but from Ruby. She creeps through the crowd and stands beside us. Fucking traitor.

"Ruby?" one of the pack members says in disbelief.

"Don't give me that look. Did you really think I'd stay on the losing side after you all turned your backs on me? Not one of you defended me when that little bitch hit me! And you, Gabriel." She smirks. "You would have been smart to choose me. 'Cause I know how to rule. But I found someone who is smarter."

"I should have drowned you," I say.

The rogue yanks my head back hard, by my hair. "Now, now, little wolf. Be nice, that's my future mate you're talking to." Gasps echo from all around. Disgusting.

"Let the innocent go. If it's my life you want, then take it!" Gabriel shouts.

I see his rage as palpable as mine. Joan is beside him, and for the first time, I catch her intense gaze on me. She wants me to fight. I had only practiced getting out of this hold once. *Once.*

The rogue whistles loud, and one of his followers shift and grabs the child from his mother's hold; everyone shouts and tries taking him back. The other rogues surrounding us keep them back. The mother shrieks in terror, holding her other child in tears. Her hand is reaching out, trying to ease her son back to her. The boy is no older than six.

"I just want you all to understand why. Understand how I've felt for the past ten years." The rogue nears the edge of the cliff with the boy. Everyone's eyes are on him. "Understand what you did to me." He whistles again, and the rogue tosses the boy from the cliff. Screams of horror fill the air. The boy's eyes are in tears as he tries grabbing for his captor. He disappears from sight, but his screams ring on—and then they are silenced.

Every fiber in my body trembles. Red blurs my vision. I feel my blood boil with wrath. I can see my powers like a weapon in my hand, and I wield it. The rogue followers whine viciously and crumble to their knees. All except the rogue leader. I grab the hand with the knife at my throat and twist hard. When it is hyperextended behind him, I slam my elbow down hard on it. There is a snap and a wicked cry of pain. He is in on one knee, in pain. Before he can react, I break his neck. At that moment, all other pack members shift and attack the rest of the rogues. I don't release them from the mental torture. I turn it up as the rogues try retreating. I look behind me to find Ruby screaming on the ground, cupping her ears. She looks at me in fear and tries running. I grab her by her hair and yank her to the ground effortlessly. She screams when I begin punching her.

I slam down fist after fist. She never thought she needed to know how to fight because she assumed someone would always fight for her. Her blood covers each of my hands. I pause for a moment and hold her bloody face up to mine.

"All that talk and all you are is a pretty face." My hands begin pounding again until she goes limp, but I don't stop. The noise in the background fades to silence when my hands finally come to a shaking stop. The bloodlust that fills my veins still isn't satisfied. A child. They killed an innocent child. When I look back, I notice the mother of the boy is ripping the rogue that threw her son off the cliff, to shreds. Not a lick of training needed be a grieving mother. All the rogues are dead, along with the noise and the sound of flesh ripping apart. Other than the grieving mother, many hold each other close in tight embraces.

"Mommy!" someone screams.

The woman shifts from her wolf form, and everyone looks around for the child we all heard. Coming from the decline of the cliff is Samuel, with the young boy that was thrown from the cliff, and a few other wolves that went to hide when I'd stopped earlier. The woman runs to her son and falls to her knees when she catches him in her arms as Samuel puts him down. Her other child comes running to hug him as well. Relief seems to settle around the crowd.

"How?" the woman asks, looking him over.

"Luna sent us to hide in another direction when we heard the first attack from the back. We stopped when we saw him. We thought he was a Rogue, but he helped us down the cliff safely. We declined near the waterfall and heard a scream when we looked up, we saw him falling. It was close, but he caught him," one of them says. "We were close enough to the top."

The three children that had been on my back run to hug me, holding on for dear life.

I huff, feeling the blood all over me. Yet they are not afraid to embrace me.

"Kate," Gabriel whispers from behind me. I turn with the children still holding on to me. Gabriel falls to his knees, looking up at me. The others fall to their knees as well. "Forgive me for ever doubting you in any way. You are the most precious gift the goddess has ever given to this pack. For all that we've done in doubt, we do not deserve you. I do not deserve you."

Tears finally fall at the scene of all the pack members on their knees for me. It's not happiness that I feel. I even see Gabriel's parents in the crowd but feel nothing but pain.

"Please get up." My voice is low. They rise to their feet. "We are one pack," I say.

Two warriors run to Maddock. One puts his ear to Maddock's wolf's chest. I feel a painful ache in my heart.

"He's…," the warrior starts. "He's still alive!" he shouts.

They both lift him carefully and rush him off. This time I fall to my knees. Tears fall like never before. Blood is everywhere. My brother is nearly killed. Pain and heartache are all I feel. I don't even know how many we lost back where the diversion took place. My head falls in my hands as I weep. The children are still holding me in a hugging embrace. Slowly I feel others coming nearer. When I look up, they are all wrapping their arms around us. I root myself in this moment. Never again will I allow a threat to come so close to killing us all. For the first time, I understand the desperation of Gabriel's great-grandfather to protect his family.

Slowly, we rise together and walk back to what is left of our home. I'm not sure how long it takes us to get back, but daybreak is now upon us. The sun peeks from just over the mountain. A new day is on us.

Every Tomorrow

The bloodshed from the night before had been evident when we arrived early morning. Many homes and buildings had been burned and ransacked. The Med Center was completely destroyed. Gabriel said that it was the first building hit. He told me that on the chance that we survived, the rogues didn't want us to recover. The bodies of our fallen were not in great numbers like I had thought they were. In fact, we had lost eleven warriors exactly. Our community is far from small and losing eleven warriors is a tragedy, but we are far from a vulnerable number.

After we have gathered our fallen, we give them a proper burial for the courage and sacrifice to save the rest of us. Two wooden rafts lay side by side. One has five warriors, and the other has six. The families and loved ones of the fallen gently push the rafts further into the lake. Even under their weight, the raft holds strong in the water. Once they are thirty meters in, flaming arrows are fired at the rafts, igniting them. Few of the fallen were single parents and left their heartbroken children behind.

A sharp pain enters my chest, understanding what they must be feeling. Grieving the loss of their parents so young. My heart twists, almost none of them were over ten.

"We will start reconstruction today," Gabriel announces. "I will need a team to hunt game for our meals. A team to gather lumber. A team to make blankets from the fabric that was left behind. And finally, a team to oversee the construction." One by one, members sort themselves out into those groups. Few are left standing without a job. "The rest of you will help care for the children and the wounded."

"Alpha, we believe the alpha house should be the first to rebuild," a member of the construction group says.

Gabriel and I turn our attention to the alpha house. We'd thought it wouldn't have survived the attack. It was ransacked, and there were some broken doors, but other than that, it was in pretty good shape.

"Few things need to be repaired on the packhouse. Luna and I will work on it ourselves. The Med Center should be first." He clears his throat and raises his voice to get everyone's attention. "If your home has been unaffected, please offer others shelter. Children of our fallen will stay in the alpha house until the packhouse is rebuilt." I agreed with the plan, though I didn't need to voice it.

*****

"I think you've got an admirer," Gabriel says, nodding at the orphan that had been following me around for the past week. Gabriel and I are helping with the packhouse since the alpha house needs near to nothing done to it. The boy's name is Mathew. It was the only thing he told me. All I knew was that he was one of the children that sat on my back the night of the attack. Others that helped with the orphaned children told me that his father had passed shortly after his mother had gotten pregnant. His mother hadn't made it past his birth.

The first night at the alpha house, he'd been awake when I went for some air late at night. He slept apart from the other children. I'd fallen asleep brushing my hand through his hair to try soothing him. It worked because I woke to Gabriel kissing my forehead and Mathew asleep on my lap.

"He's my little helper. Aren't you, Mathew?" Mathew blushes and hides behind me. I put a hand on his shoulder. Gabriel had made teasing remarks when he first noticed Mathew's interest in me.

Gabriel kneels in front of me and looks at Mathew. "Are you trying to steal my mate?" Mathew grips my trews and peeks at Gabriel. "Am I going to have to fight to get her back?" Mathew's forehead pushes into the back of my thigh as a goofy grin touches his lips. "I'm still really tired from my last fight, so you'll have to go easy on me. Okay?"

Gabriel smiles when Mathew nods his response. He stands and kisses me on the cheek. "Hey, none of that. We have work to do." Joan comes in carrying a box of supplies.

Gabriel smirks. "Kate's wishing me luck."

"Mm. Well, you do need a lot of that. But for what specifically?"

He shakes his head with a grin. "I have to fight this the pint size-warrior for my mate's attention."

Joan looks down at Mathew. "Is that true, little warrior?" Mathew smiles brightly and nods at Joan. "I don't know how you'll fair, Alpha. He looks determined. Goddess be with you." Gabriel smirks at Mathew when he makes a tiny fist and swings at the air gently.

"No, no, little warrior. If you want to strike, you must swing harder. Like this." Joan kneels behind Mathew and folds his fists in her hands and swings at Gabriel. Together they nick Gabriel's leg, and he crumbles dramatically.

"Mercy, please!" The members working around us laugh and cheer for Mathew's victory. Mathew shies from the attention, though, and hides back behind my legs. Everyone else gets back to work.

"Okay well, that was my good deed for the day," Joan says, helping Gabriel up off the floor. "I need to help Samuel with the training of the young warriors."

"Seems like you're coming around to him," I say, crossing my arms.

"I just keep telling myself that he saved you and that child. It helps me get through the day with him." Gabriel and I laugh.

Lunch rolls around, and Mathew clings to me as we find a place to sit. "Nomads!" someone yells. Gabriel and I stay seated as we watch Samuel bolt from somewhere behind us. Other members welcome the travelers back with hugs and kisses. Samuel waits not so patiently, trying to see over others' heads.

"Papa?" Jane says, and Samuel spots her disbelieving face in the crowd. I grab Gabriel's hand tightly. My heart pounds. They stand there, staring at each other, as if they can't believe the other is in front of them.

Then like lightning, they run to each other, hugging hard. Others watch in confusion. Leon sits in front of us but is turned away, watching as well.

"What is going on?" he asks.

"Samuel is reunited with his daughter," I say through tears. Recently, every little thing brings tear to my eyes.

Samuel pets her hair back and leaves kisses on her head and forehead. He holds her face in his hands. "Your mother would be so proud of the woman you've become." Sobs fill the air when everyone goes quiet, watching the exchange.

"Is this real?" she asks.

"Should I pinch you?" he asks. She giggles and wipes tears away from her face.

Gabriel holds my hand up and kisses it. "You did that," he whispers to me. When I look around, I notice that many have glassy eyes at the display of affection.

Soon the food is out, and Samuel is sitting with his daughter, talking. Some stare, not fully understanding the situation, while others go on about their business. Mathew tugs on my hand and points to his plate. He's eaten most of it. It's an achievement to the first day that real food was served. He'd barely touched it then.

"Good job." My praise earns a bashful smile. "I promise we'll go on a run in a little while, okay?" He nods and sits quietly beside me while everyone at the table resumes their conversations.

"But it's almost done, and that's what's important," Gabriel says to Leon.

"Yes, but if we focus resources on one building, then it takes longer for others to be built. I'm just saying that spreading attention equally will make finishing faster."

Gabriel turns to me. "See, even your brother agrees with me. You're neglecting me."

We all laugh at the random outburst. "I'm not neglecting you. You should learn to share attention."

"It wasn't a part of my training." He shrugs. I roll my eyes and look down at Mathew. He's not paying attention to the argument. Instead, his eyes are focused on other children, who've finished their meals and begun playing together.

"Do you want to go play with them?" I offer gently. For some reason, he's had a hard time connecting to other children. According to his caretakers, he speaks rarely, which makes it hard to make friends. He nods and slips off his seat to play.

I watch him run up to the other children without attempting to speak to them. He stands back and watches them try hitting an archery target with a rock. He picks one up and takes a single step forward before dropping it and walking back to me. He sits back down and hugs my waist. I pat his head and whisper, "You were so brave to walk up to them. Next time try talking, okay?" He nods without lifting his head.

"Alpha." One of Gabriel's advisers runs up to our table. "We have word from Alpha Arura."

Gabriel snatches the paper the adviser hands him. His eyes roam the parchment. "They were also attacked." His voice cuts the growing silence at our table. "Alpha Arura is sending word to all their allies as well about the growing rogue infestation. Apparently, there is more than one alpha." My throat tightens at the thought. More rogue alphas. Gabriel clenches his jaw and stands. "I need to send a response. I'll be back later." We all nod our understanding.

"Must be hard on him," Joan says. I nod, watching him disappear into the alpha house.

"Look who's back." Maddock walks to us slowly with a female under each arm. "Where'd Alpha go?"

"He saw you coming and decided not to deal with you," Dylan jokes, resting his head on his fist. Almost no one spoke about the fact that his mate happened to be Taylor. Though Taylor wasn't used to speaking as much as the rest of us, he still sat at our table, quietly observing.

"Up yours," Maddock responds, then laughs at his own joke. "Literally."

Dylan grabs a peach seed off his plate and throws it at Maddock. Unable to dodge, it hit him square between the eyes. I snorted at Maddock's expression. "Damn it."

"What are you gonna do, limp to me?" Dylan mocks.

"All right, sit down already," I say. One of the two girls offers to get him a plate of food while the other offers to get him a drink.

"This is the life. Two beautiful females coming to my every need." Maddock grins

"Don't worry, they'll wise up," Joan says through chews. Leon laughs next to her.

The rest of the day passes in a blur on working of the pack-house to checking on the wounded. Maddock had been lucky that he wasn't as severely injured as we all thought. There was no doubt that he was hurt, but his recovery was much more rapid than others.

Night falls quickly, and everyone has retired to their temporary or permanent sleeping arrangements. I lie in Gabriel's arms with my head tucked under his chin.

"Was there any news from our other allies?"

"No, I suspect they'll report around the same time that Samuel's other daughters arrive."

"It was nice seeing him reunite with Jane."

"Mm-hmm. You did good." I grin against his neck. "Go to sleep. We still have a lot to do tomorrow. The packhouse is almost done. I want it finished so that the kids don't have to share beds the way they do now."

"Yeah," I mumble sleepily.

A gentle knock at our door makes me snicker, and Gabriel groans quietly. "What are you gonna do when he goes back to the packhouse?" I ignore him, slipping off the bed.

I open the door to see Mathew standing in his makeshift night-gown. He looks at me with irresistible puppy dog eyes. I huff and walk him back to the room he's sharing. He lies in the bed with two other children and looks up at me. I sit beside the bed and grab the teddy bear he sleeps with.

Facing the bear to him, I sing him a lullaby that I had made up for him.

> Papa bear says,
> "It's time to go to sleep.
> It's time, it's time, it's time, it's time,
> It's time to go to sleep."
> Mama bear says,
> "It's time to go to sleep.
> It's time, it's time, it's time, it's time,

It's time you go to sleep."
Baby bear says,
"It's time to go to sleep.
It's time, it's time, it's time, it's time,
I think, I'll go to sleep."

Mathew closes his eyes halfway through the lullaby. I gently press my forehead to his, placing the bear under his arm, and then leave the room. I come back to a smirking Gabriel.

"He just has trouble sleeping." I defend.

"I understand that, but your enabling behavior isn't going to be any good for him when you two separate. Unless—" I hear the unspoken idea. Gabriel had hinted to it when he noticed just how much Mathew seems to need me.

"I already told you, I wouldn't be any good as his mother the way I am now." It's true. I'm too untrusting, and there is so much that I need to figure out about myself before I could raise a child.

"You would be a wonderful mother to him. You already make him feel loved and encourage him to be brave. You sing him a lullaby when he can't sleep and allow him to cling to you as if he were your child. You are as close to a mother than he has ever had." I sigh, look-ing down because I know that I am as much attached to Mathew as he is to me. "You wanna hear the clincher?" I meet his eyes. "You love him, and he loves you."

"And what about you?" I challenge.

"I love you both." My heart thumps hard.

"I don't want to mess him up…if that makes sense."

"I understand. But I think as long as you are there for him, you will succeed."

"I do love him."

Then what is really holding you back? Circe butts in.

"You really think I'll be a good mom to him?" Gabriel nods. His gentle eyes search for my yes. I can't hide my wide smile. "I have a son."

"We have a son," he corrects.

A Future

Three month later

It took a month for our buildings to be back to their living conditions. Some of the buildings were salvageable, saving us time and resources. The Med Center was the first major building completed in construction. Dr. Gene hadn't returned immediately, and Gabriel wondered if she had gotten the news about our village yet. He wondered, in the privacy of our own company, if her absence might have been too much of a coincidence. The thought had crossed my mind as well, but it felt wrong knowing how she had been there for me. When she had returned, she informed us that the village she was attending to had also been attacked. She returned only after ensuring that the worst was over with her patients there.

The peacefulness within the pack, the unity, made Gabriel's powers morph from within him like a bomb. They came rushing to him like a bull. Though his powers were much more physical than mental. His vision had seemed almost bionic, both in the daylight and the darkness. His physical strength had increased to impossible limits. Along with his vision, hearing, and brute strength, his endurance was unparalleled. Out of pride, many challenged their abilities to his new abilities. Over and over again, though, Gabriel was unbeatable. When Gabriel decided to build a border around the community, to give us a little extra protection, he built a quarter of it alone while others were still gathering the supplies for the rest of the fencing. He made quick work of it, telling me that it was for our defense. I didn't disagree.

The two orphans that were left without proper parents were adopted by Dylan and Taylor. The children love their fathers more than anything. Taylor became misty-eyed when he was first called daddy. We all teased him about it, but in the end, we were all happy that they had a great family together.

"Mommy?" Mathew calls timidly.

When the word had slipped from his lips the first time, he looked guilty at the fact. He explained that he just couldn't help that he felt like our real son. I explained to him that it was okay because he was, in fact, *our* son. It was no surprise that he quickly became comfortable calling us mommy and daddy, being that he never truly knew his biological parents. We reminded him, though, that his biological parents loved him.

"Yes, Mathew?"

"Are we going with Daddy to visit Alpha Arura's pack?"

I take his hand in mine as we walk to the gathering area to get our midday meals. "Yes, love. They were hurt like us, and we need to make sure our allies are still standing strong."

"Like us?"

"Yes, Mathew."

"But Daddy's the strongest. Is he gonna stay to make them strong?" He pouts a bit at the thought.

"No, Mathew. Daddy's not going to stay with them."

"Then how will we make them strong?"

We find a table to sit at before I answer. "We are visiting to make sure they are *still* strong because every pack has their own strengths, Mathew. We have our unity, love for one another, and our strength as warriors. Daddy says Alpha Arura's pack has technology." *But he doesn't exactly consider that a strength*, I think to myself.

"Like the tablet we have?"

"Yes, like the tablet, but they have much more." His eyes fill with wonder and excitement.

I know the feeling. When the nomad finally returned, along with Samuel's daughter, Gabriel collected the tablet before anything else and gave it to me. He was an expert at it, for someone who isn't fond of such things. Mathew and I had already watched a dozen movies that had been uploaded to the tablet before they had come back. The book I was reading, that Dylan had made fun of, had actually been turned into a five-movie saga. Dylan had stopped making fun of it, and from what I'm told by Taylor, they watch it a bit too often.

"Luna." Joan grips me in a headlock hug from behind. "Good afternoon!" She walks around and smiles widely at Mathew. "Good afternoon, little warrior."

He smiles back, revealing his adorable dimples. "Good afternoon, Auntie Joan." She always blushes whenever he calls her auntie.

"So how is the little warrior this morning?" she asks as Leon takes his seat beside her.

"Mommy took me to the cliff at the falls. It's scary, but Mommy showed me how pretty it can be. The world is big," he answers. Since adopting him, he'd begun to speak more and more each day. Gabriel had told me it was because I instilled confidence in Mathew.

"That's awesome, little warrior. How about you and I play in the river a little later? I found a cool spot where the current isn't so strong. I can teach you to swim there like I taught your mommy." Leon gleams at him.

Mathew looks at me pleadingly. "Mommy, can I?"

I sigh. I had forgiven Leon, but a tight pain enters my chest at the thought of my son going to the river with him. I feel guilt at it, but then I have every right to feel that way. Looking at Mathew, though, and his excitement, I can't say no. "Fine, but you have to wait an hour after eating. And you"—I point to Leon—"You will keep him safe."

Leon nods, and I sense that he knows what I'm thinking of. Lowly he says, "I swear."

"You swear what?" Gabriel says, sneaking up on us.

"Uncle Leon is going to teach me to swim in the river!" Mathew says, excited.

"Oh really. Well, that tops my news." He takes his seat on the other side of Mathew.

"What's your news, Daddy?"

We all look at him. "I just got word from the alpha training area, and they want to know when they will be expecting you." Silence falls on the table. Fear for my son enters my heart. Neither Gabriel nor Dylan had told me much about the training, but I could sense that it was brutal and dangerous for many.

"Isn't it a bit too soon for that?" I ask. "We only just adopted him."

Gabriel sees the worry in my eyes. "He at the right age, Kate. He is strong enough." His gaze goes to Mathew. "My son will be a good alpha."

"Mommy?" I look at Mathew. "If you believe in me, I think I can be strong enough." My heart shatters. Already I will be losing my son for the rest of his childhood life.

"Of course, I believe in you. I know you will be an amazing alpha one day."

At that moment, a wolf appears just behind him. Out of thin air. Before I can react, Circe calms me. *It is Mathew's wolf.*

What? His wolf! He's only seven!

Yes, but the wolf has already claimed him as his perfect vessel. Look around, Kate. You can see them now, right?

I look up and see wolves everywhere. All of them standing beside a person.

"I can see them." Everyone at the table looks at me.

"See what?" Leon asks.

"Wolves, I can see all your wolves. Their spirits are as real as you are sitting in front of me." And then they disappeared.

What happened?

Nothing, Kate. They are still there, but you only saw them because of your worry for Mathew. Knowing that he has a strong wolf with him will help to calm you. You needed to see them, so you did. When you have the need again, they will appear to you again.

Amazing.

"Your powers just keeping growing, don't they?" Gabriel teases.

"I can't help it. It happens on its own," I say. "Okay, I guess we better prepare you to go to your training."

"What about my little sister?" Mathew asks.

I hadn't even begun to show, but Dr. Gene had confirmed my pregnancy a few days ago. Morning sickness hadn't even hit me yet, but when my monthly hadn't come, I guessed it'd be best to make sure.

"Your sister?" Gabriel asks.

Mathew nods enthusiastically. "I had a dream that I and my little sister were playing together, but she was so small. Won't she go to the training too?"

"Only the firstborn goes to train, little warrior. And you were born first," Joan says ruffling his hair from across the table. "But don't worry, when you get back, you'll be able to protect her and the rest of us."

"But what if my sister wants to be alpha?" His question hangs in the air. In general, his questions have become increasingly hard to answer.

"Are you willing to share the alpha role?" Gabriel asks, knowing that there has never been such a thing.

Mathew shakes his head hard. We all laugh. "No, I won't share. If my sister wants to be alpha, then I'll give her my spot." Another tug at my heart makes fresh tears spring to my eyes. "So you should ask her when she's big like me. So that you can send her too, and we can train together."

"I promise we'll ask her," Gabriel says gleaming proudly at his son.

My heart flutters with the feeling of wholeness. Everything is perfect. Everything is as it should be. I am the first runt Luna to have such great powers. My feelings toward my brothers feel as if we didn't have so much time ripped away from us. Leon and Dylan both have fated mates. Maddock is entertaining the single young women who are dying for his proposal. Our pack has never been stronger. Still, peace is a luxury. One that we cannot afford to let us get too comfortable in.

Our allies were attacked the same day that we were. What was thought to have been a onetime incident by a mad rogue turned out to be much bigger than we could have ever imagined. Many packs have stopped allowing exile as punishment for fear that they will run to the rogue army. Most packs are now executing their pack offenders. Along with our fears that there were more rogues wanting to attack packs, we had never recovered the training book that was stolen. So even with this peacefulness, we are always preparing for another attack.

Epilogue

"Again, Mia!" Mathew yells at his younger sister.

"Ugh." The frustration of not being able to land a single punch has begun to dampen her enthusiasm. She pushes up from the spot where he'd thrown her.

"C'mon, no quit. Get it together." Mathew has tried every trick in the book, but she didn't seem to get the fighting skills of her alpha father or the determination to continue from her Luna mother.

She becomes dizzy as she stands. There is no way that she is going to successfully strike him with her weakened limbs. The gear her brother made for her to train in has begun to chafe her skin as her sweat dampens them. How can she be the daughter of the two strongest leaders in their history? Both have amazing abilities, contributing to the pack. Sure, the power had come from their titles, but it did not leave them when her brother became Alpha.

"What's the point, Matt?" She huffs as she places her hands on her knees. "I'm never going to be strong enough."

Mathew steps out of his stance and kneels in front of her. "You are strong enough, Mia. You need to find it within yourself to continue. Goddess forbid that we will ever have to defend ourselves from the rogues or humans. You need to be strong so that we will not worry about whether you will be okay on your own. Of course, I'm sure Aunt Joan would love to train you."

"No!" she snaps. Their aunt was the greatest fighter in their pack and trained the young warriors every day, but she seemed to make it harder on the ones she cared about. Tough love. "I can barely handle you. I won't last an hour with Aunt Joan."

"Don't be so sure." They both turn to see both their mother and father at the gate of the training enclosure, their father speaking up on the subject. "Your mother is, throughout history, the smallest wolf to have ever become Luna. She trained with your aunt nearly every day. And I guarantee that she can take Alpha down easily." They both look at their mother, who is a foot shorter than Mia. Their mother lifts a challenging brow.

"I'll take that bet," Mathew says, opening the gate for his mother to enter and his sister to walk out.

"Gabriel," their mother calls.

Their father, Gabriel, winks at his mate and starts the fight. Soon many members come to watch excitedly, many of them assuming that their alpha will take it easy on his mother.

"Remember, darling, I was your first teacher."

Without warning, Mathew swings first, but his mother, Kate, easily dodges. As he continues to strike and miss, on the sidelines, Mia is watching in awe. She had watched her mother spar with her aunt but only to stay fit. The sparring never went beyond what it was. Today it seemed that her mother was making an effort to win.

Her brother swings multiple times and misses every single time. Mia watches at her mother with pride.

"Do you know what it is that makes her better?" Gabriel whispers to his daughter.

She looks at him and tries to think but comes up empty. "She lived a large part of her life with everyone telling her she was weak because of her small physique. But when she had first begun to train with your aunt, she stopped trying to fight the way everyone wanted her to and found her own unique style. Can you see what it is?"

Again, Mia watches her mother. Each movement is quick and smooth, like a dance. No effort is wasted. Then it finally clicks. "She's sweating him."

Gabriel smiles. "It's her secret weapon. Because she's vastly shorter, she can maneuver her body around him before his strike is a half move. Her bite may not be the worst, but she can keep this up longer than he can continue to throw misses. Once his energy is drained, she will begin to strike."

Mia nods, understanding the strategy. "But I'm not small like Mom. I'm five eleven. There is no way I can fight like that," Mia argues.

"You're missing the point, little princess." Mia grins at her father's nickname for her. "Figure out what your strengths are instead of trying to live up to someone else's. I'll let you in on a secret. Your aunt Joan took it easy on your mom for a very long time before she realized that your mom no longer needed the safety of training. Practice on your own, if it helps figure out what your best skills are in fighting. Your brother will always be better at offense. He was professionally trained for years. You might have to take your mom's approach and use defense to your benefit."

She focuses on her mom and sees her brother striking in frustration. Mathew takes a breath and takes a single step back. It is an opening for Kate. She strikes easily, swinging her leg under him and then holding him in place on the ground, with her foot on his neck.

"I thought you loved me, Mother!" Mathew jokes as the members laugh at his defeat.

"Well, sometimes I have to remind you that you don't know everything." She lifts her foot and helps him up. Once up, he pecks her cheek and nods in respect.

"Once a Luna, always a Luna." He shrugs at the crowd.

Kate walks over to Mia. "How about me and you go for a nice long run each morning? It will relax your muscles, and Apollos will feel at ease." Mia's wolf, Apollos, is known, even in his realm, to only choose wolf pack members who will lead. When Kate told Mia this, she hardly believed it. Apollos hadn't spoken much to her. He had been a silent bystander within her. She turned when she was eleven, which clued everyone in that she had a wolf, but just as soon as she turned, her wolf went dormant.

Even to her mother, who could physically see Apollos next to Mia. He was very observant but never offered any encouragement of any kind to Mia. His name was all he gave her. She could turn if she wanted to, but it was always her in control. Apollos never took the wheel.

Mia nodded. "Sounds good." But she doubted that Apollos would ever show that he was pleased or angry or any emotion, for that matter.

"Alpha." A pack member runs up to them. "You are needed. Alpha Arura is asking for young warriors."

It has been a year since Alpha Arura's pack had been attacked by rogues for a second time. They had defeated them, but a single rogue had been able to sneak in during the attack and slaughtered many families single-handedly. He got away before help had arrived; they lost many members.

"Why don't I go?" Mia asks. The three of them look at her. "Maybe a change of scenery would help? Mom, I know I just agreed to run with you each morning, but I think this would help me. I think I should see more of the world, and Alpha Arura's pack is in the high mountains."

"Mia, listen to yourself. If you join another pack, there is no going back. You will become an official member of their pack with no ties to this one," Mathew says with care.

"That's not true. Look at Dylan. He is living happily here with his mate and children and still visits his parents and sister when he gets the chance," Mia argues.

"That was different. He left for different reasons."

"Not really. He was the child of an alpha, and so am I."

"Mia, you're not even a warrior."

"Enough you two," their mother scolds. "Mia, really think about this decision. Your brother is right that once you are a part of their pack, you can never be a part of this one again. It is your choice, and you can always visit, but really think about it. Don't simply decide to go because you feel the need to travel. I can make you a nomad if that is the case."

"I will think on it, and I know you will all worry for me if I go, but I promise to visit and write as often as possible if I do decide to go."

"I don't think that will be a problem. Alpha Arura is the queen of high-tech. She believes we are living in the Stone Age, so I'm sure she will have all sorts of gadgets to communicate with," Gabriel says, resting his elbows on the post of the training ring.

That night, Mia dreams of a new day with new and exciting things to come. And something else. She dreams of a man, with hazel eyes staring into the very pits of her soul.